THE SURROUNDED

The Woman Who Owned the Shadows
by Paula Gunn Allen

The Way of the Priests/
The Dark Way/
The White Path
by Robert J. Conley

Waterlily
by Ella Cara Deloria

The Surrounded
by D'Arcy McNickle

House Made of Dawn
by N. Scott Momaday

Ceremony
by Leslie Marmon Silko

The Heirs of Columbus
by Gerald Vizenor

Fools Crow
by James Welch

Black Eagle Child:
The Facepaint Narratives
by Ray A. Young Bear

**FIRE
KEEPERS**

THE SURROUNDED

D'ARCY McNICKLE

FIRE
KEEPERS

Quality Paperback Book Club
New York

To

JORAN

Note

In this story of the Salish people are elements which will be recognized as belonging to the story of tribes from Hudson Bay southward. The particular facts may be found in the journals of Ross Cox, David Thompson, Alexander Henry the younger, John Work, Major John Owen; in the journals and other writings of Pierre J. De Smet, S.J., and Lawrence B. Palladino, S.J., and in later writers. Marius Barbeau has collected some fine stories of the Mountain Indians ("Indian Days in the Canadian Rockies"), and to him I am indebted for Big Raven's story of the wistful search for "The Thing That Was to Make Life Easy." The "Story of Flint" was told by Chief Charlot, the last of the Flatheads to leave the ancestral homeland when the Government gave the order to move on. It was collected by Mrs. Helen Fitzgerald Sanders in her "Trails Through Western Woods," an excellent book.

D'ARCY MCNICKLE

THE SURROUNDED

—THEY CALLED THAT PLACE *Sniél-emen*
(MOUNTAINS OF THE SURROUNDED) BE-
CAUSE THERE THEY HAD BEEN SET UPON
AND DESTROYED

Chapter One

ARCHILDE LEON had been away from his father's ranch for nearly a year, yet when he left the stage road and began the half-mile walk to the house he did not hurry. When he emerged from behind a clump of thornbush and cottonwood and caught his first glimpse of the cluster of buildings before him, he looked once, and that was all.

He avoided the front of the big house, where his father would most likely be sitting, and made for the dirt-roofed log cabin which occupied lower ground, down toward the creek. Two dogs, one yellow and one black and white, leaped and howled, but they were the only ones to meet him.

He walked past the big house, which was his father's, and went to the cabin, his mother's. There she was, as he knew she would be, sitting in the shade. If she heard him she did not look up at once. But she was a little deaf and a little blind—perhaps she had not sensed his approach. He let the heavy suitcase slip from his sweating hand.

Then she looked up. A sigh escaped her and a quick smile multiplied the many fine lines in her wrinkled brown face.

Here he was, the best of her sons, and the youngest,

1

home again after a year—but would he stay? She had only a faint idea of where he had been; the world out that way was so unlike Sniél-emen; she had even less of an idea of what he did when he went away. But never mind. Here he was again. She smiled quickly, a little at a distance; she did not wish to embarrass him with her attention.

"So you have come back," she said.

"Yes, I am here." He turned his suitcase over on its side for a seat.

"Where have you been this time?"

"To Portland. That's where the stinking water is."

She let the word echo in her ears, saying nothing herself, but it had no meaning. If he had said he had been down toward the mouth of the Snpoilshi (Columbia) River, she would have known what he meant. But Portland! Her red-rimmed eyes gazed toward the timber which came down to the far bank of the creek. Two boys were splashing in the water down there.

"You have been gone a long time."

"I had a job. I played my fiddle in a show house. I can always get a job now any time I go away."

She looked at him quickly, taking him in. He wore a blue suit and a white shirt and his tan shoes were new and polished. So he could go away any time now? He did not have to be fed at home?

"They paid me this money. Look!" She barely glanced at the offered money. It was all strange, she could not make it into a picture. An Indian boy, she thought, belonged with his people.

They sat in silence for some time. It was useless to speak of fiddle-playing, and for a while Archilde could think of nothing that was not equally useless. When you came home to your Indian mother you had to remember that it was a different world. Anyhow you had not come to show your money and talk about yourself. There would be fishing, riding, climbing a mountainside—those things you wanted to do one more time. Why talk of fiddle-playing?

The heat of the afternoon lingered. The three horses in the pasture below the house were bothered by the flies. They had been in the timber across the creek since midday and had come out only a short while before. As they ate, they moved along, stopping now and then to rub their muzzles on their forelegs or to kick themselves under the belly.

His gaze returned to his mother. How did she look after a year? No different. He had not expected her to look any different. Her eyes, which were getting weaker each year, were watery slits in the brown skin. She wore a handkerchief around her head and her calico dress was long and full and held in at the waist by a beaded belt. Her buckskin moccasins gave off a pungent odor of smoke. Nothing was any different. He knew it without looking. He had not come all the way from Portland to these mountains in Montana to satisfy himself on that score.

"No one fishes when you are away. My bones groan so loud when I walk the fish stay under their rocks."

It seemed impossible that no one cared to fish. The

creek was full of swift, cunning trout. He got excited just thinking about it. Tomorrow he would cut himself a pole and try it.

The old lady was saying something else. "I will have some people here. We will make a feast and my friends will see you again."

That was something he had forgotten to include in his visit—the old lady and her feasts! You gorged yourself on meat until you felt sick, and a lot of old people told tiresome stories. He frowned. He ought to refuse. He had not come for a feast. She ought to be told that. But it was a small matter. His mother was old. It was a small matter.

"How is everybody?" He had begun to smoke a cigarette which he took ready rolled out of a package.

The question made the old lady sigh. Eheu! It was bad!

"Louis stole some horses last week. I think no one knows it yet. He's in the mountains."

"He'll go to pen if they find him."

"He'll go to hell!"

Already he was hearing the old stories—quarreling, stealing, fighting. His brothers knew nothing else. And his mother knew nothing but the fear of hell, for herself and for her sons.

A small girl, his niece, came to the corner of the cabin. Her hair was braided, with white strings tied to the end of each braid. She was bashful and kept her chin on her breast.

"Gran'pa wants to see you," she announced when

she was still a dozen paces away.

"Come and shake hands, Annie!"

She looked at him but hugged the cabin wall.

Archilde got to his feet and stretched himself. He looked toward the mountains in the east, and then upward to the fleckless sky. Nowhere in the world, he imagined, was there a sky of such depth and freshness. He wanted never to forget it, wherever he might be in times to come. Yes, wherever he might be!

Down by the creek his two nephews were standing uncertainly and watching the house. They had just seen Archilde. Their shouts died away and they went behind the brush to dress.

As Archilde picked up his suitcase and walked toward the house he realized of a sudden that he dreaded meeting his father, Max Leon, the Spaniard. That dread was something which went back a long time, and Archilde, who was growing into a man now, was disturbed by it. It ought not to be.

His father had just awakened from his afternoon nap and was sitting on the front porch, his gray hair tousled and matted. Every afternoon on awakening he drank a whisky eggnog. A half-empty glass stood on the table at his elbow. He stretched out his hand.

It was a thin, bony hand. Archilde looked down at it with some surprise. This was his father's hand.

"Sit down, my *son!*" With what sarcasm he could utter that word! "Agnes said you were here. Where have you been this time?" His voice was deep and its least variation gave strong emphasis to his words. He handled his voice like a whip.

"In Portland."

"Portland, I suppose, is a busy city. They make you work to live. And what did you do? I see you have good clothes."

"I played in an orchestra."

"Yes? What do you play—the accordion, or mouth-harp?"

"The fiddle."

"Really? I've never heard you. You never play for your people at home."

Archilde sat down then and looked at his Spanish father. He was of middle size and build, of stocky limbs. His face sagged into pouches and under the stubble of gray whiskers the skin looked oily. He had a high forehead and a long nose. It was not a weak face, and not a commonplace one. What was it in that face that could so dominate one who was no longer a child? Archilde gazed steadily at his father and tried not to show his irritation.

"Some day you must play for me," his father was saying.

"I have no fiddle now. I gave it to a friend."

"In a card game, perhaps?" There was a slight smile.

"No, it was a present."

"But don't you play cards?"

"No."

"What kind of Indian are you, then?"

Archilde shrugged his shoulders. His confidence

was failing him. It was just as it had always been in recent years; after a few more thrusts from Max he would be helpless before him. He had thought it would never happen again.

"You haven't many answers. But tell me this, have you any money after working, as you say?"

Archilde showed his money. He wanted to refuse, out of defiance, but he showed the money.

"You better let me put it in the bank for you."

"No. I'll keep it."

"So! You have learned nothing! You will blow your money on a good time and then go on living off me!"

It was more than Archilde could stand. He had to speak out in anger and so confess his helplessness.

"I didn't come to live off you, God damn it! I came to see my mother, not you, and in a few days I'm going again. Keep your stinking money!" He knew it was the answer of a child.

Old Leon laughed. "I see you're getting a good opinion of yourself." He said it insultingly, and yet his eyes looked closely at the boy. At least he had not slunk away like a whipped dog.

A horseman appeared in the lane, riding swiftly, a cloud of dust hanging like a plume in the still air. The rider, a rancher from the flatlands of the valley, tied his horse and entered the front gate.

"You're riding fast on a hot day," Max called out. "Come up in the shade!"

"That's fine grain you got down by the road. On the flat we're burned out."

"So I've heard. No doubt you're thirsty. Here, Agnes! Bring water to Emile Pariseau!"

Agnes, his daughter, kept his house. Her full-blood husband had had his head kicked in by a horse, and Max, though he spoke profanely of her husband, brought her and her three children to live with him. She appeared on the porch with a pail of water and a long-handled dipper.

Max scowled. "Where's the pitcher? You're not bringing water to an Indian!"

The rancher was good-natured. "I never drink out of a pitcher—this is all right." Seeing Archilde standing off to one side Pariseau spoke to him.

"How long you been away, Arsheel?"

When the question was answered another was asked. "Have you seen your brother Louis?" The rancher avoided Max's eyes.

"No. I've just come."

"Are you looking for Louis?" Max asked. "God knows where he is, Pariseau. I probably know less about my family than you do."

"That's what I come to see you about."

Archilde went inside. He had waited to be dismissed but Max appeared to ignore him.

Pariseau stopped to roll a cigarette, saying nothing meanwhile. When he had finished he looked up.

"What I come to tell you is this. Louis stole some horses from me. We got the goods on him. Somebody seen him with the horses."

Max's face went cold. "What's that got to do with me?"

"Well, we used to be neighbors—I wanted to tell you. If we catch him it'll have to go hard. There's too damn much horse stealing by these young fellows—"

"Good!" Max cut in on him. "Send 'em up to pen, hang 'em—but what's it got to do with me?"

"Well, I dunno. I just thought I'd tell you. Then you could tell him to lay low—or you could maybe tell me where to find him." The rancher grinned.

"I see none of these sons-of-bitches unless they come here to eat—and they never stay long. I don't know where you'll find him. His mother's relations are everywhere. Don't ask me."

In a little while the rancher rode away, having heard Max Leon curse his sons up one side and down the other, as they say.

He sat motionless for several minutes, watching the rider disappear behind a cloud of dust. His eyes had been alert before the rancher came; now they looked dull. He was slow and heavy in getting to his feet. His legs were slightly bowed from many years of riding. He walked toward his wife's cabin.

She was sitting as Archilde had left her an hour before. The shadow of the cabin had lengthened. Max stopped and looked down at his Indian wife. When he talked to her he had to use her tongue, since if he tried to use English, which she knew perfectly, she would pretend not to understand. He had tried to overcome her obstinacy by never talking to her. That was some years ago. He had not been able to keep it up, there were occasions when he had to speak, and in the end he had decided that it was better to get an answer than to fight an endless battle. So he spoke her Salish.

"Where's Louis?"

"How should I know!"

"Have you heard about him?"

"I hear nothing. My sons are scattered."

"He stole some horses."

She was silent, gesturing slightly with her hand.

"A friend has come to warn me. He said the police would hang him. If you know where he is tell me."

"I know nothing. My sons are afraid to come here."

"I'll send a rider to warn him."

A silence.

He had been married for forty years to this woman, she had borne him eleven children, and he had come no closer to her than that. She would not tell him what he knew she knew. She did not trust him. That was something to make a man reflect on the meaning and purpose of his life.

He spat and walked away. He entered his house through the kitchen. It was as well furnished as any white man's house. A stove with nickel trimmings, a linoleum covering on the floor, a white enameled kitchen cabinet against the wall, a well-stocked pantry

—no white man with a white woman for wife had more.

Agnes sat on the floor by the window peeling potatoes. Max took a drink from the water bucket.

"Where's Louis?" he asked as he stood drinking.

"Perhaps in town. I don't know."

He stood there for a moment on the point of asking another question, but scowled and walked away. To Archilde, who was drinking coffee at the kitchen table, he motioned to follow him to the porch.

"What does your mother say about Louis?"

Archilde appeared to reflect. "His name wasn't mentioned. Did Pariseau want him?"

"He's been stealing horses. You didn't know about that, eh?"

Archilde didn't know.

Max was wrathful, his face deeply colored. "So! You're going to be like the rest! Lying to me already and you're not home an hour! I'm telling you this for Louis' good. If they catch him they'll hang him! Tell the old lady yourself, if you won't take my word. I'll save his damn neck; I'll do that much. Understand?"

Archilde started to walk away.

"Don't let her know I talked to you about this."

That was how matters always stood in Max Leon's family. There was always this distrust, this warfare.

He was a tall youth, just short of six feet, and built with a slim waist and swinging limbs. He had a long head, much like his father's, and his face was distinguished by thinness of lips, fineness of nostrils and alert eyes.

He had not walked far when he observed through the tail of his eye someone moving in a clump of willows near the creek. He kept his eyes lowered as he walked along and appeared to take no notice. He waited until he had gone a little way past, then he whirled quickly in his tracks.

His two small nephews, taken unawares, were caught in the act of running to cover. They had been following him down the creek, too bashful to come out in the open. They started to run but stopped when he called.

"Hey, there! Mike and Narcisse! Wait a minute! I've got a cigarette here!"

They kept their heads lowered as he came up to them. When he gave them cigarettes their eyes sparkled.

"Now tell me, why do you run like rabbits?"

Neither answered at once; then the older, a boy of twelve, the one who was called Narcisse, found his nerve.

"Let's see your money!"

Archilde laughed. "Just look!"

"Where you steal that?" asked Mike, younger by three years.

"I didn't steal it! I worked for it!" He scowled. "Who tells you about stealing?"

Such a question pained Mike. He did not have to

be told such things.

The boys flopped down in the grass beside their uncle. They were no longer shy.

"Where's Louis?" he asked. They looked at each other and did not answer.

"Don't look stupid like a calf. The old lady told me already. Don't tell Max anything if he asks."

"That's what the old lady said," Narcisse remarked.

"How many horses did he steal?"

"About fifty, I guess," Mike said proudly.

"Big liar!" Narcisse pushed him over in the grass. "The old lady said six big mares. He came last week and got meat. I guess he's in the mountains."

"Last week I shot a grouse," Mike bragged.

"You shot him on the ground! I shot him out of the tree!" Narcisse was scornful.

"Pouf! Your shot just tickled him. Me, I killed him!"

"Neither of you catch fish, the old lady tells me."

"We got no hooks," Narcisse explained.

"Make a spear then."

"You talk crazy!" Mike said. "You got to have a hook to make a spear!"

"That shows what empty heads you got. All you need is a piece of wire."

"Buy us hooks! Who wants to fish with wire?"

"All right. But tell me, how was it in school?"

"Huh. Those Fathers don't know much!" Mike would not explain further what he meant but he was positive about meaning what he said. Narcisse had to explain.

"They called him Little Lord Jesus in school because he won't cut his hair. He thinks he'll be a chief if he don't cut it off."

"No sir!" Mike kicked out at his brother and they rolled over together in the grass. Archilde stopped the fight.

"I'll take you to the barber, Mike. He'll put nice smell in your hair."

"Then I'll smell like a skunk cabbage."

"No, like a horse's poop!" Again the boys tangled.

"Stop fighting! It's supper time." They were on their feet in an instant and were racing across the meadow.

Archilde followed more slowly. He had been home just these few hours and he was wishing to God that he had stayed away. But perhaps he would know enough next time. Tomorrow he would go fishing. He would look at the sky some more. He would ride his horse. Then wherever he might go, he would always keep the memory of these things.

Chapter Two

AFTER supper Archilde sat in the kitchen doorway. Narcisse and Mike were playing in the yard with their sister Annie, who came between them in age. They made her the butt of their games, but she was good-natured.

"Maybe you'll stay here now?" Agnes asked. She was older by more than fifteen years and so she had the privilege of speaking her mind. This she did timidly. Just the same Archilde resented the questions she put to him. What good was it to try to answer her? Out of boredom he replied.

"I have seen enough already. Tell me what you think a fellow can do here—steal horses like Louis? Drink and run around? No. The world's big. I'll find something to do."

For a moment he had subdued her. She was afraid of her young brother, the first in the family to educate himself (through high school), who was not afraid of the world beyond the mountains. She scarcely expected to be heard and yet she ventured a suggestion which no doubt she had kept in mind for a long time.

"Max will die. Somebody should keep this land and have cattle, like in old times."

That spurred him. He turned scornful. "He treats

us like dogs—and still you want his land. How's that?"

Agnes' voice became even fainter but she persisted. "Max is a good fellow, if you're good to him. But bite and he bites back. I've seen. He's an old man now."

Archilde would hear no more about the Spaniard. He stood up and saw that evening had spread over the land. There were crickets in the damp grass and farm lights gleamed at a distance. Bats flew around his head. This, too, was something he would take away with him—these evening sounds and smells, this softness in the air.

"How's my horse?" he asked.

"Fat and mean. No one rides him."

"Tomorrow I'll ride him."

"Max has a big blue car. He just bought it."

"He can keep it!" He swore and then walked away.

At the creek's edge he sat on an old log and listened to the water which, though night had come, was still awake, swirling in eddies, slapping upon stones. Owls talked back and forth. There were odors of the thimbleberry, of wet gravel, and, he thought, of fish, but that was imagination. It was a peculiar thing how images of such things entwined themselves into one's life; they were nothing that could be touched and yet they had strength and substance. He had come a thousand miles because of their pull upon him; someday they might pull him from across half the world.

He heard the brush crackle. Involuntarily he held

his breath and searched the gloom. A figure stepped out of the shadow across the creek. It was his brother Louis.

Archilde stood up and whistled softly. Louis crossed the creek on a bridging log.

There was still light enough to see him rather clearly when he had come near. He was strongly built. He had a stern mouth and shifting eyes, and in general a disposition of unruliness. He had spent a few years in school but little had come of it. Whether that was the fault of the school or of Louis no one had ever inquired. He looked sharply at Archilde.

"So *you* are home again?"

"So I am." Archilde smiled at the gruffness which his brother put on. Louis had a slow mind and the only way he could hold his own was by growling. Archilde knew him. A stranger would not have taken them for brothers, and they too knew how dissimilar they were. Archilde had a sly laugh that enraged his brother.

"Better look out for Max." Archilde tried to be friendly. "A white man came to see him today."

"What white man?"

"Pariseau from out on the flat."

"Oh, him!" Louis shrugged his shoulders. He was carrying a rifle. He too assumed a friendly tone.

"Come in the mountains with me. My partner's run off. I got some horses up there, see! We'll take 'em to the other side and sell 'em. That's big money. "

"They'll hang you by the neck first."

"For Christ's sake!"

"They're looking for you."

"For Christ's sake! Let 'em catch me! Well, will you come?"

Archilde laughed at him. "Do I look like I was born yesterday? I want none of your big money."

"Chicken!"

"You don't bother me."

"Get out! You make me sick! I'm going to the old lady and you stay away."

"I've told you—they're looking for you. They probably got Dave Quigley on your trail."

For a moment Louis stared at Archilde, questioning him with his eyes. That name, Dave Quigley—Sheriff Quigley that was—was enough to sober most young bucks in high spirits! The sheriff had a reputation for getting what he went after. He was a tough one.

Louis decided to shrug at the name. "If he wants me I'll be waiting with my gun!"

"You're a bag of wind!" Archilde gave it up. "I'm going to the pasture to see my horse."

"What horse?"

"My Nigger."

Louis looked sly. "So that's your horse? Well, I'm riding him now."

"Are you lying? Agnes said he's in the pasture."

"What does she know? She don't go to the pasture. I got him for a month now. But he's no good! You can have him again."

"You bastard!" Archilde called him a string of

names. "When you get through a horse is no good! You break his wind, you cripple him—I ought to break your neck!"

Louis began to bounce around and hold his hands up in position to fight, but Archilde walked past him, almost brushing him to one side, and Louis did not touch him.

Up at the cabin Louis found his mother getting ready for bed. She was sitting in the doorway braiding her hair. She made a growling sound.

"When did that fool Arsheel come?" He kept his voice low and he looked carefully about before squatting in the shadow of the cabin. "What's he want here? He's no good!"

"He's a good boy."

"He's a chicken! Just now I asked him to fight and he ran."

"Wind bag! What man is afraid of you!"

"Listen." Louis switched to another subject. "My partner, Steve, he ran away. You get Arsheel to come with me."

"Go your way and leave him alone! But talk to him yourself, and see if he won't laugh at you."

"I didn't come for your preaching! I want some meat."

"The mountains have meat and fish. Are you so lazy?"

"What an old fool! Am I going to shoot my gun in the mountains when they're looking for me?"

"You took all my dry meat last week. I have none."

"That's a lie! You had two sacks left."

"What will I eat when it's winter? You think it is all right if I starve, eh? You turn those horses loose. They'll find their way home. Then live in peace and you'll have enough to eat."

"Save your words for Arsheel and just give me some meat."

"I have none."

"Then I'll take some!"

"If you can find it. I'm no fool!"

Louis scowled but made no attempt to carry out his threat. After he had considered a moment he tried a new way.

"I will do as you say. I will loose the horses. I will even drive them back on the flat. Then the white men will have nothing to say."

"Good! Only do it."

"I said I would. Now let me have some meat. I have eaten nothing today."

The old lady turned her bleary eyes on his dim outline. In her heart she was sure he was lying but she had no defence. She got to her feet with infinite labor and waddled into the darkness of her low cabin. In a moment she returned with a small bundle.

"This is the last time, unless you do as you say." She gave him the sack. "If you are hungry I have some supper."

"I'll eat this. Tell Arsheel the next time I see him I'll kick his behind!" He walked away.

"Dear Jesus! Save him from hell!"

She rocked back and forth in the gloom, frightened and uncomfortable in the knowledge the priests had given her. She had been obedient to the fathers always. Her memory did not go beyond them, it began with them. It began with that day at the end of summer when the missionaries came through the twisting defile which led from the Jocko River into the valley of Sniél-émen and planted their Cross. It went with her father to meet them and spread the blanket for them. It heard her father speak. His words were unnamed birds to her; she heard them fly about but did not know them, yet this is what they said: "Now Kolinzuten * has answered us, he has fulfilled us. We have long asked for black-robed teachers, they who have no wives, and who carry the cross. Thrice we have sent runners to St. Louis as all men know. Now, Father, speak, and we will do as you tell us."

Her memory began on that day when she was but four years of age and when her father, who was the chief of his branch of the Salish people, went out to meet the black-gowned priests. And from that day to this she had been obedient to the fathers. She had been baptized as Catharine Le Loup, after her father, who was known as Running Wolf (baptized Grégoire). The Fathers called her "Faithful Catharine" and by that name she was known to her people.

"Friend!" they told her father, "we shall teach your child great happiness. She will be among the precious on earth."

* This was God, the Maker.

Those, too, were words which no longer lived in her ears, but she saw her father's solemn face and felt his hand rest lightly on her shoulder as he turned her about and sent her to her mother. That night he gave a feast by way of expressing his gratitude.

From that day to this she had been "Faithful Catharine," and now in old age she looked upon a chaotic world—so many things dead, so many words for which she knew no meaning; her sons developing into creatures such as had never lived in her childhood (a son might steal horses but a mother was respected); the fires of hell slashing the gloom of a summer evening. She had borne eleven children, seven sons, to this man who now lived alone in the big house and held her in contempt, and she could not understand the ruin that had overtaken her. What had come about since that day of the planting of the cross? How was it that when one day was like another there should be, at the end of many days, a world of confusion and dread and emptiness?

Chapter Three

ARCHILDE was drawing pictures on his hat, making pictures out of his head, or maybe remembering pictures he had seen somewhere. In front he drew a lean buffalo bull. On the left side he made a picture of an old cow and her calf with their butts turned to a blizzard. On the right side a mare was running with her colt. The back of the hat was still blank and Mike and Narcisse were advising him on a subject.

"You gotta have a bucking horse," was Mike's idea.

"I said no, three times," Archilde pointed out. "I want no buckaroos on my hat."

"A bucking steer then."

"He don't want no kind of bucking," Narcisse had to explain. "Make a grizzly."

"That's no good! Make a coyote stealing a chicken."

"Always something about stealing!" Archilde looked up at Mike. "How about geese flying in spring?"

"How can it look like spring?" Narcisse looked puzzled.

"Ah! Make a—make a—" Mike was stuck.

"I'll make an elk with big horns!"

"That's bum!" Mike shouted. "Make a fence post! That's all you can do!"

"Sure! I'll make a fence post with a chicken hawk on it."

"Aw! I'll come along and shoot it!" Mike shouted.

"Ho! You couldn't shoot a haystack!"

"You liar!" Mike tried to push his brother off the doorstep and that started a fight.

Archilde set to his drawing. He spat on the end of his indelible pencil before each stroke. His fingers had lightning; just a few lines here and there, then another spit, and the picture was finished. There was a chicken hawk coming to rest on a post, with its wings still spread and its tail dipped. It was wonderful to see him do it. Although the boys stopped their brawling to watch, they tried not to show their admiration. When the picture was finished Mike made a face at it.

"Who wants to look at a hawk!"

"Then don't look."

"Now give us our hooks and come fishing. I'll show you where there's some big ones."

Archilde put on his new big hat, all decorated, and tipped it at an angle. In place of his city clothes he wore waist-length overalls, a broad bucking belt studded with nickel spots, and a blue cotton shirt. His shoes were half-length riding boots with high heels, and he had leather cuffs on his arms. This was the old way of dressing, and this morning it pleased him. He swaggered a little.

Max watched him cross the yard.

"So you've joined the tribe again, eh?"

Archilde looked back. "We're going fishing."

"Yeh, next week you'll be back to the blanket!"

"Well, what about it?" He matched his father's contempt with a tone of challenge, but the tone was weaker than he intended. He could not quite equal his father's contempt.

"You'll make a good Indian!" Max heaped it on and ended by scowling.

As he walked into the cool timber Archilde had little to say to his nephews. His father's words would not lie down. He answered them angrily, to himself, and still they came back and danced in his mind. The pleasure he had been feeling in his gaudy clothes and his swagger turned thin. It was not what he wanted.

To Max Leon, the years had brought change and they had brought anger. It was well enough to possess money and land and to have sold off his cattle just before the range was thrown open to settlement; all that was his gain, but his was not a temperament to rejoice and sing praises over mere gain. He thought of his losses and he thought most of all of his humiliation. But no! That was a lie! He was not humbled! It was only that men thought so. "That proud Spanish bastard!" their eyes said when he was near. "Sure, he's got a few stinking dollars, but would you trade places? Not me!" Men's eyes exchanged these confidences when he passed. It would have been some satisfaction if these thoughts had been expressed aloud and so given him an excuse for putting his muscular brown hands around a windpipe, but that was denied him. He got nothing but smiles and hailing words.

He had seven sons—damn them to hell!—and in order to get a small crop of wheat cut he had to apply for hired hands! There was the sore spot. Seven sons, they might have been seven dogs!

He drove to town, to the holy Mission town of St. Xavier, and if he had been astride a horse he would have used the quirt. As it was his big blue automobile, nickel trimmed, the gaudiest of the machines which had just opened a new age in the valley, roared and threw up dust like an angry bull.

One of the men whom Max most despised, because in his own peculiar way he managed to express disdain more pointedly than others, was the former Indian trader, now merchant George Moser. Everybody was in debt to him; he was in everyone's affairs, and he had a way of exerting his importance for all it was worth. He wore glasses pinched on his nose, and, more than that, he had a bulging stomach, thin legs, and soft white hands which somehow or other managed to stow away more money than any dozen grimed, gnarled, hard-fisted hands. He was smiling at Max from behind his desk, talking "in confidence." This was one of the ways he took to drive Max into a rage.

"I hear Louis is up to something again."

Max was all for blurting out that Louis was none of Moser's business, but he decided to wait. He would let him put his whole foot into the trap before he sprang it. He only stared.

"I'd like to talk about it, in a friendly way." There he was, pretending that there was no trap and that he was only saying what any friend would say. "There was a meeting last night—some men here in town. I was there too, since they asked me. They put up a reward for him—five hundred dollars! They want to make it tough for horse thieves around here. Folks'll scratch the hills with a hay rake till they find him."

"Well—what do you want of me?" A little more and Max would explode. He was wondering why in all these years he had not cut Moser's throat, just up and slipped a knife through the fat pink skin and let him slide gently to the floor. Instead of doing that he had gone on year after year, letting Moser find a buyer for his cattle, giving him a fee for it, buying supplies from him, keeping him alive—and all the time wondering why he didn't let him feel the point of a knife.

Moser was explaining. "I wanted to warn you. Perhaps you can get word to him to lay low. I know how you feel. Boys have too much of the devil in them, but in time they always straighten out. I know from my own case."

The silky, insinuating voice never hesitated. It seemed to know exactly how far it could go, and it always went the limit. When Max did not reply, only growled under his breath, the voice went on as smoothly as ever.

"I hear your youngest boy has just come home. Now, there's a promising youngster. I like the way he carries himself. You can see he's made of good stuff—"

It was too much. It was more than he could bear. Max rose to his feet, the flame of his blood showing on his brow. But he didn't explode. That was the peculiar thing. There was enough bitterness in his tongue and enough strength in his brown hands to have damned the man's soul and broken his soft body. But nothing happened. When Max spoke he was cold and incisive.

"I came to get four harvest hands. Have them wait here till I come back."

He walked out of the office without saying anything more and without wishing he had said more. It was always that way. He remembered always, and just in time, that the man was a louse; and a man did not waste breath on a louse.

From Moser's office he emerged into the store and walked through groups of ranchers come to buy harvest supplies. He answered spoken greetings with a quick nod and never paused. Men let their eyes follow his square-set, belligerent figure until it reached the front door and passed into the sunshine.

"Looks like he's out to get somebody's hide." There was an admiring tone in the voice.

"Yeh, old Max. He'll hang Moser's up to dry one o' these days."

That was how they talked behind his back, only Max did not understand. He distrusted them. Their smiles, he misinterpreted.

George Moser sat where Max had left him. There were no papers on his desk, he had nothing in his hands, he simply sat and stared. He had tried to be friendly with Max Leon, not just now but for years, and he had never succeeded. He could not understand it. He thought he had detected a change in the old Spaniard recently; his greeting had been a little warmer, so it seemed, and Moser had tried to nurse along the good feeling. He thought over what he had just said and for the life of him he could discover nothing that could have given offense. He had gone so far as to violate a confidence in giving out the news about the reward for Louis before notices were posted. A sour look was all he got for his pains.

Moser sighed, shifted a little in his chair, and continued his vacant-eyed staring. He was really in difficulties, but no one would have believed him if he had admitted the facts. He was everybody's meat. He knew what was said about his business sharpness and his gouging, and he knew that as an Indian trader he was reported to have taken everything but the Indians' breech-cloths. He wished there had been a little truth in it. The fact was that he had turned to Indian trading because he had heard that fortunes were being made at it, but he had come too late. The fur trade was gone when he arrived and the Salish Indians were a starving lot, once their game was killed off. The only money they had was what the Government advanced them, and somebody else got that. The Indians saw little of it and he, trading to them, scraped up only a few crumbs, a bare living. The greater disappointment came later.

Everybody had expected that great benefits would result from throwing open the Reservation to white settlement. Even the Indians would gain by it, people said. At bottom, if you looked closely, there was a question of justice to the Indians. Years before, in the middle of last century, as Mr. Moser understood it, the Indians had agreed to give up their hereditary claims to all of western Montana and northern Idaho in return for a fixed reserve—which was to be set apart for their exclusive use—and additional compensation of money. The money disappeared into quicksand— there was lots of quicksand in the government service —and the reserve proved of little value to them as soon as the game vanished. That didn't take long. And finally, at the opening of the new century, each Indian was given a separate piece of land, a "garden plot," of eighty acres, and the remaining area was opened for white settlement. There was a theory behind all that; he had heard it expounded but he couldn't have repeated it now. It had something to do with civilizing the Indians.

The justice of the procedure was, he admitted, a question, if you looked closely. But at the time the step was taken he believed with everybody else that the benefits which the Indians would secure would offset the wrong done them. If some white man also benefited, the Indians ought not to object; it was a fifty-fifty proposition. That was the talk.

There was great activity, much coming and going, forming of land companies, distributing of handbooks with photographs of oats-six-feet-tall-without-irrigation and baskets of melon-size potatoes, and much talk, just before the Reservation was thrown open. Everybody went slightly crazy. Mr. Moser now knew this and rued his own touch of insanity. Land prices shot skyward, and he bought up a good deal all the way up, some at the top. He lent money on the basis of those fabulous valuations, and few such loans were repaid; the land fell upon him. He extended credit right and left on no more than a man's word and the wonderful promise of the future, and he had the wind for his pains (for his faith in human nature, he termed it).

A decade had passed since then and the bottom had fallen out of everything, including faith in human nature. Moser was up to his neck in land, "heavy black loam which needs only to be scratched to bring forth wealth," as the handbooks used to put it. His business had expanded of course. Where he used to sell supplies, on credit, to a score of ranchers, he now helped to keep about two hundred going—on credit. In good years they came in "to settle," which meant reducing the balance owed anywhere from one percent to fifty percent, never entirely; and on bad years they just came in and told jokes. If he stopped giving credit somebody else would come in and take away the business. He had already several competitors who

were cutting in on him all the time. They gave
away fifty-pound sacks of flour and flitches of bacon
as if they were things that just popped up out of that
black loam he owned.

His difficulties were not all black loam and easy
credit. His wife wanted to go away. He had married
her just about the time the Reservation opened, in the
midst of his crazy spell, and there were moments when
this seemed the least sane of all the steps he had taken.
She was a girl from his own little village in Pennsyl-
vania and she was good and sick of the Noble Red
Man as a neighbor. She liked him in a Wild West
show, but his smell invaded her parlor and caused her
to keep linen covers on her horsehair furniture the
year round; even with that precaution she was not
sure she would dare return to civilization with such
contaminated belongings. Her temper was growing
sharper recently and she was complaining of losing
weight and feeling dizzy. The ailment, he surmised
secretly (he had not yet come to the point of accusing
her of it), was imaginary and would disappear as soon
as she had won her way. Just the same it was serious.
She wept and made scenes. Only last night when he
returned late from that meeting of business men who
wanted to catch and hang the horse thief, Louis Leon,
she was waiting for him in the unlighted parlor. He
almost tripped over her chair.

"Don't turn on the light!" she yelled. A sob caught
her voice. "Your dinner's on the table—cold."

As a matter of fact, he remembered, he had had

dinner. It was nothing new. Business took him to every corner of the valley, which was fifty miles long —almost a hundred if you included the lake at the upper end—and he was used to stopping where night overtook him. But tonight he realized that he was being accused of not eating with her.

"What's the matter, Sara?" What a useless question, he thought.

And then he had it all over again. She was sick and tired of the filthy place. He had been promising for five years to go away. Maybe *he* enjoyed associating with Indians (she made it sound like a nasty word) but *she* didn't. She wouldn't wait any longer. At least he had enough money to send her back to her parents. If he didn't send her soon she'd go mad. Her brain felt numb already.

He had been up until midnight trying to soothe her. He had got himself all mixed up in philosophical reasoning that went something like this: "The way I look at it is, we're here on earth to make the best of what we've got. If we don't like the way things go, why I guess they'll be different later on. But when that time comes around we'll be wanting something else. So why not be satisfied with what you got? This talk about going mad is all humbug. Take things the way they come is the way I look at it."

There were fresh outbursts, nose-blowings, deep sighs, and finally Sara had agreed to try it for a while longer. How long that would last he didn't know, but he would have it all to go through again, and yet again, if he didn't sell out. As a matter of fact, he would have sold some time ago. He had seen what was coming, once he had come out of his dizzy spell. The difficulty was—a purchaser. Ah, yes, a purchaser, with money.

Once more he fell to thinking about Max Leon. Why was it that he could not make friends with that man? What was it just now that had sent him off on his high horse? He was a proud man, but he had not been too proud to marry an Indian squaw. That was how Mr. Moser looked at it.

Chapter Four

THE mission town of St. Xavier belonged to two ages. A brief sixty years separated its primitive from its modern, but the division was deeper than years.

The opening up of the Indian reserve brought new townsmen and new houses. The newcomers, after one look at what was there before them—sway-backed cabins, rag-stuffed windows, refuse strewn about—moved on and erected their neat clapboard bungalows on the opposite side of Buffalo Creek. Over there they laid a few cement sidewalks, hid their outhouses in woodsheds, planted round flower beds (which were soon neglected), and ran fences around their lots. That was the "Townsite," the up-to-date quarter.

The old town, which was usually called Indiantown, was left to itself, but not out of mercy. Its lack of plan and of sanitation saved it.

The center of life was the mission church, a tall structure of red brick, with steep roof, lanced windows, a vestigial transept and an abrupt bell tower. Plain as it was, the hovels which were set against it gave it an air of grandeur. The newcomers thought Indiantown had been built without a plan, but they were wrong. There had been a plan, even if it didn't lend itself to street construction and regularity. Each cabin faced the church. Each door—there were no windows—gave a full view of God's tall house and the cropped poplar trees around it. The newcomers saw only the confusion.

Max Leon left his automobile in the narrow lane which penetrated the maze of Indian cabins and led to the Mission grounds. He opened a white gate in a thorn hedge and an iron weight hung on a rope shut the gate behind him. As he walked through a lane of poplars he could just see the roof of the church above the Mission buildings. Birds chittered in the branches above him. The graveled path was bordered on one side by the wall of the school play yard and on the other by a garden. The air was sweet with damp loam and vegetable growth.

The path ended in a paved court around three sides of which were buildings, strange buildings with mansard roofs and galleries. He walked to the front which faced upon an open yard. The bell, rung by the turn of a handle, sounded rusty.

Father Grepilloux no longer held the title of Superior. He was simply an old man come home to die. The Mission was his creation. He had reared it up in the wilderness and then, years ago, had gone on to other duties like a soldier whose course is plotted for him by his superiors. A year ago, after he had passed his eightieth birthday and could no longer keep up with younger workers, he had come back to write a history of his work and to sink peacefully into oblivion. His mind was still remarkably clear and the liveliness of his talk was in contrast with the frailty of his body. A close friendship had grown up between Max Leon and the priest in the old days when Max had come to live with the Indians, and now that Grepilloux had returned they were often together. Because he would occasionally supply a forgotten fact or stray recollection for the little book of memoirs, the old priest called him his *vade mecum*.

The room had a high window but because of the large trees just outside the light was subdued. The walls were hidden behind bookshelves and the two tables in the center of the room were heavily burdened. A small space had been cleared on the table before which the priest sat, giving him room to work.

Father Grepilloux was just complaining of his memory. "There are days when I am very dull. Only this morning I spent an hour looking for my favorite pen and, can you believe it, I had it in my hand all the time! I gave myself a good lecture. There are some things I want to ask you, about your early days in the valley—but later on. First I want to hear about you. I understand your youngest boy has returned."

It seemed that everyone insisted on reminding Max of a fact in which, he told himself, he was not interested.

"I suppose he is glad to be back. Boys like to come home."

Max could not see it so prettily. What did such boys as these know about home, even if someone had made one for them? Old and venerable ideas were

meaningless when you dealt with these people. Max
had come to speak of these things. One of his great
difficulties was that he could not unburden himself
readily. If he had been less proud, life would have
been easier for him. He could have gone from neighbor to neighbor complaining of his troubles and been
solaced by their amused tolerance. Pride kept him
from that, a pride which seemed to be lacking in most
men.

The one person before whom he could unburden
himself was this priest, and he did not come often to
him for that purpose.

"I have come to see you about my boys. No doubt
you have heard that Louis stole some horses and they
are hunting him. For my older boys I don't care a
straw, as you know. It is a long time since they've been
in my house, and even before that I ceased calling
them my sons. Louis, I thought, would make a good
man. When he was young he rode with me and was
useful around stock. But for five years he has been
drinking and going with bad Indians. Now he's as bad
as any. I know you think well of this Archilde; so do
others. But consider this: at home my fields are standing with ripe grain, and he goes fishing! He tells me
he makes money as a fiddler. How has he learned so
suddenly to be a fiddler?"

After a moment's pause Max continued in a more
subdued voice. To him it was a hopeless subject to
discuss and that was what his voice expressed. "A man
at my age begins to think of what he will leave be-

hind. This boy is the only one I haven't yet kicked out of my house. He has made his home with me since he returned from the Government school. It's true he hasn't been home much these last few years, but I haven't tried to hold him. My luck with the others cured me of trying to act a father's part. So far as I know the boy hasn't been in trouble, and so long as he stays honest he can share my house. But—" A pause. "What is he going to do? How are my affairs to be settled?" Again he took thought. "Understand me, Father. If this boy showed promise, if he was willing to be useful, I'd turn everything over to him. If I can't do that, it goes to your Mission. That's my decision."

Father Grepilloux did not speak at once. Many times before he had heard Max's story of his sons; each year it grew more confused, more hopeless. He was not one to utter unctuous beatitudes. He was prone to think practically of human problems.

"I didn't know he played the violin. When did he learn?" he asked quietly.

Max didn't know anything about it.

"We have been trying to build up a choir, but we have no instruments. Maybe we can get him to play for us. What do you think?"

The question didn't interest Max. "He's a fiddler! He plays for dances. That stuff."

"If he's gifted he can be taught." When Max shrugged his shoulders the priest laughed gently, "Well, if you won't let me turn your boy into a musician maybe you'll help me write some history." He knew that the Spaniard had a generous nature, and that also he had a kind of hardness that could not be softened by picking at it.

Of Father Grepilloux's history, personal as it was intended to be, there was very little about the man and everything about what the man represented. It was a record of days, but it was first of all a testament of faith. He wrote in his book: "My part in making a garden in the wilderness was not much. I do not deprecate, I speak with conviction. I was a witness of the building of the Temple of God which is in every man. The Indians needed few explanations and they needed little help, once they were shown how to use tools and once they were given faith, the greatest tool of all."

He was not the actual founder of the Mission, inasmuch as he was not in charge of the party sent out by the Missouri Province of the Jesuit Order; he was very young at the time, just past his majority. No one, however, had spent a longer time there, or been more devoted, or succeeded so well in winning the affection and loyalty of the Salish people. Of all the white men they knew, they used to say in the early days, he was the only one who did not speak "with a forked tongue." And on his part the feeling he bore them was simple, undivided and unfailing devotion. He might bewail their ignorance, but he never cast doubt on their native ability. He might denounce their occasional lapses into paganism, as when the men made too free use of each other's wives, but he never thought them depraved.

"What were the Indians like? How did they seem to you?" This was what he wanted Max to answer. The Spaniard was perplexed and seemed to have no clear recollection of his first impressions. He remembered vividly the occasion of his first view of the Sniél-emen valley, but of the Indians he had only a vague image.

The view really was impressive. No man who ever stood where Max had stood that first day failed to be astonished and to write or speak eloquently. The letters of the early missionaries, and even of brisk, hardheaded fur traders, bear frequent reference to that particular corner of the wide wilderness.

"You stood there," Max said, "and what you saw made you over. You were born again. What you had done before that moment was of no consequence. I had seen a good bit of the West by then but I knew at once that I would never care to move from that spot. Perhaps that was my mistake." His mind had skipped forward to later events and he lost his enthusiasm for the memory he had called up.

Why he had gone to live with the Indians Max could not explain, except to say that he wanted a free life and they had it. He knew that wasn't enough of an explanation. A free life might mean much to an Old World man, but hardly enough by itself to win him from his loyalty to the past and what it had made of him. Some men went to the Indians because they

were lazy, physically and morally, and saw in these
simple people a chance to satisfy all their appetites
with a minimum of effort. But Max hardly belonged
in that class. He tired quickly of their footloose and
improvident existence, and as soon as he married
Catharine, the daughter of the only Indian he ever
really admired, old Running Wolf, he settled down
and began to build up his ranch. And on that he labored strenuously. He cut logs for his houses and
barns, put up wild hay for winter feeding and, with
rails of his own splitting, snake-fenced a large home
lot. In the work of those early years he rarely had
anyone to help.

It was not laziness, and it was not romanticism. He
never thought the Indians were "noble" or children
of a lost paradise. While it was true that the old life
was much cleaner than the present existence, it was
still hard for a white man to stomach. They were like
any other people in this respect—that individuals
varied exceedingly; some you admired and some you
detested on sight. People were always asking him what
he thought of the Indians, what were their chief char-
acteristics, and it was nonsense. He didn't know. You
could say that jack-rabbits had long legs and were
swift runners, hoppers rather, but there was no single
trait he knew of to describe all Indians. Even the first
thing you thought of, color, had almost as many varia-
tions as there were single Indians. The one thing he
had never seen was a red Indian. There were all
shades of brown, some almost black ones, and a good

many were as olive-skinned as a Spaniard.

No, as far as he could make out, the thing that had attracted him was the land. He came of Spanish peasant stock and he had an instinctive attachment to the land. It was all right to turn trapper and roam at will, more or less. He had had two years of that before stumbling upon Sniél-emen. That was enough. He was so disgusted with wandering, half-starved, through gameless country, with the risks one took in meeting unfriendly Indians, and most of all with the loneliness of those nameless rivers and mountains, that he was ready to give up. If he had been nearer to Spain he would have gone back to the ancestral home and settled into the life for which he was intended. But western Montana, especially in 1870, was a long journey from the homeland. He had mounted that treeless, grass-blown, unnamed hill on a day in early June, having no notion what he would find on the other side—and at the summit he literally fell on his knees and prayed. There was the end of his wandering. He knew it at once.

The hill he climbed that day was the high barrier which closed off the southern end of the valley. Northward, the eye traveled up a pleasant valley for fifty miles before haze and a gradually ascending tableland blurred on the horizon. A stranger would not have suspected that just beyond lay a great lake, a mirror to the sky for forty miles. But the most startling vision were the mountains. Without foothills, though with curving approaches which spread some distance out upon the valley floor, the mountains raised a magnificent barricade against the eastern sky, the highest jagged crests floating in morning mist 8ooo feet above the valley. One felt humbled and contrite.

"The most welcome sight, Father," Max paused slightly for his climax, or rather anticlimax, "was the Cross. When I looked down from the hill, there was the Mission, almost under my feet. I thought I had come to the end of the world, the moon lay beyond—and there you were. If I had shouted I suppose you might have heard me."

The priest laughed. "We had been there sixteen years then. We were old settlers."

"I thought I was an explorer. But if I had just used my eyes a little I could have followed your wagon road instead of dragging my pony over loose rocks and washed out gulleys. I was never any good as a woodsman. When I went out with others they spent most of their time looking for me."

Up to that point he could understand everything that had happened to him. But there was no explaining what came afterward, not at once, but gradually. Every one of his sons had shown promise at the start. They were strong, quick, willing; they learned readily what he taught them; but long before they had become men he had lost all influence over them. When he tried to assert his authority they simply left him flat. They felt no loyalty to him and, as far as he could see, their respect for their mother was no greater, though she kept a certain hold on them by demanding nothing and giving everything.

He had not answered the priest's question. He had not answered anything. He was back where he started.

"No, you haven't told me what you first thought of the Indians, but never mind." Father Grepilloux was thoughtfully gazing at some pages of manuscript before him. "My book will have to state your problem. As for solving it, my friend, I am as baffled as you. For the truth is, a change has come over these children. I have been away this last time almost twenty years, and there is a difference.

"When I asked you that question I hoped you might have remembered something which I could compare with my old journal. I kept a daybook during those years. It makes strange reading today. If it had been kept by a stranger and I were reading it for the first time I might have questioned whether such things had ever happened. Somehow or other the bad Indians you were just speaking of have come upon the scene. Who turned them loose I don't know. They spoiled your boys for you. I'm afraid they have also taken many children from the Church. Did you know those children, Max? Let me show you what they were like."

Chapter Five

THE first excerpt read by Father Grepilloux was dated
in the fall of 1854 at the time the company of Jesuits
appeared in the valley of Sniél-emen. When the entry
was written Max Leon was a twelve-year-old schoolboy
in Spain. On reflection it seemed impossible that that
schoolboy, whom he remembered so vaguely, could
have come so far and got himself so thoroughly lost in
the wilds. He had been born into a static world, in
which nothing had happened to his family for genera-
tions, beyond the events of birth and death. Yet here
he was. . . . These thoughts played through his head
as he listened.

As we had been invited by these Indians to come
here and instruct them, we counted on some sort of
welcome, yet nothing like what we received. A large
Company was there, with their tents pitched on the
Plain. Behind them, were Great Mountains, which we
had no notion of finding as we climbed a steep, dry hill
in the last hour. They are most solemn Mountains.
We were led at once to the Great Chief, a Patriarchal
man, with a most open and friendly face. In his hand
he carried the Wing of an Eagle, and afterward I
learned that this Symbol of his Office was never absent
from his hand. I looked about me at the waiting men,
at the women who kept off some distance, and at the

46

solemn children, and I was struck by the air of expectancy. I thought they understood perfectly what this moment meant to them, and that in their hearts, they were praising the Author of their Beings. This impression was heightened, later, when Chief Running Wolf spoke to Father Lamberti. His words were translated by the faithful Ignace, who had met us at the Green River Rendezvous, and conducted us to this place. In effect, the Chief said: "We have been worshiping False Gods, and we want you to teach us the True God." Then he would have given over his Badge of Office, his Eagle Wing. When Ignace explained this offer, Father Lamberti simply bestowed his blessing on the Symbol of Power, and returned it to the Chief, explaining at the time that we would not interfere in temporal matters, and wished nothing of them but to be allowed to minister to their Spiritual Health. I thought the people looked disappointed, and I have no doubt they would willingly have delivered themselves to us. They have the hearts of children. . . .

Another entry in the same year added this note on the character of the Salish people:

We had heard reports of the mildness of these Indians, and also that they had tried for several years to be instructed in the True Faith. In this matter, they were truly heroic. Some years before our arrival, hearing that a "Black Robe" was passing through the Country, they sent messengers to intercept Him. Now, it seems that this was a Protestant Minister, who was traveling to the Oregon Country with his wife and a Company of fur traders; and according to the practice among Protestants, he wore no Robes or other dress to distinguish him from his fellows. This our Faithful

Children knew was not right, and they said to him:
"You are not the Teacher we seek. You are not of those
Black Robes who take no wives, who say the Mass, and
who carry the Cross." They had heard of these things
from some Iroquois Indians, who had gone to live
with them, and they heard from these same Faithful
Children that they should send Deputies to St. Louis,
to the Father Superior. The story touched me deeply,
how they sent four young men through the country
of their hereditary enemies, the Sioux, how they arrived in St. Louis, after many weeks of weary marching, and then could find no one who knew their
strange Language. They had attained their Goal, but
could not make known their wishes. And greater
misfortune befell them. Two of the party became
mortally ill in St. Louis, and as they had spent many
hours in the protection of the Cathedral, which appeared to delight them, they were Baptized and buried
in the Parish Churchyard. The other two began the
journey home, but only one got back alive. A year
later they sent a second party, and some time later a
third party, of which every member was massacred by
the Sioux Indians. Here are brave souls for the Calendar of Saints . . .

To Max, who had never heard them, these stories
were surprising. He knew in a vague way that the
Salish people had a reputation for having met the
white men with open friendliness; but now to say that
they had stood ready to be Christianized, and even
sought out the priests—that was bewildering. It made
him feel all at once that he was ignorant of these
people, which was somewhat like being told that he
knew nothing about the back of his neck, after he had

lived with it all his life. It could be true. So far as his knowledge of the Indians was concerned, he had never pretended to any. He had lived with them, had married one of their women, but he had kept apart always. And they had learned not to hang around his ranch. When he tried to recall his impressions of them nothing clear-cut came to mind. He saw silent, straight-walking figures; he saw them at the hunt, which they went at efficiently but with an unnecessary amount of ceremonial before and after; he saw them in many emergencies and saw them become frightened and lose their heads; but what was under the skin, in the mind and heart, he had not the vaguest notion. He had taken them as they were and learned to get used to them without trying to find out what made them go. He hated people who were always prying into their neighbors. But he was interested in these stories.

"Then you think they understood your ideas?"

Such doubts had never lived in the old priest's head.

"They understood because they believed. Really it was not difficult to teach them. They wanted to know the right Faith, their hearts were inclined. Let me read something more."

Entry made in 1865: These People have a saying, "The Whip has covered the Fault." Back of that expression is a custom which seems to be very old. A story has gone abroad, that the Fathers have instituted flogging among the Indians, but it is a lie. They who say it overlook the important fact that the Creator has instilled in these Wilderness Children, as in us all, a sense of his Moral Law. It is true that they understood it imperfectly, and we have had to teach them a number of refinements, but essentially they knew, that to transgress was to Sin, and that Sin must be Expiated. So it was that, from time immemorial, these people have punished Sinful Action. It was part of the Custom, also, that a man or woman should confess wrong-doing. A man might be accused, if he did not speak up of his own accord; but more often than not, the Sin was openly confessed. The occasion for this scrutinizing of the heart fell on the eve of their Native Feasts. There were several means by which a man might make amends. If he had wronged another in a small matter, he might simply sit down with him and smoke the Pipe. In a larger transgression, he might go to the aggrieved in his lodge, and give him some equivalent for what injury he had inflicted. In that case, they said, "The wound is covered." The more formal expiation was made in the presence of the Chief, his Principal Advisers, and all the tribe. If a man were accused of wrongdoing and the accusation were false, the accused one could speak for himself. The Chiefs judged the case. Most usually, though, a man or woman came forward alone, and confessed and asked to be whipped. In that case, the Chief decided how many lashes the Sinner should be given; he was then led to a blanket spread upon the ground, in presence of the assembled Tribe. He lay down on this, and the lash was applied. When we came to these People, we explained that they might discontinue their practice of whipping, since the Sacrament of Confession provided for Absolution. But they have been reluctant to comply. So it happens now, that before an important

Church Festival, the Tribe gathers with the Chief and his assistants in the Church Square. Their faults are first "covered by the whip" and then they come to be confessed by the Priest.

Father Grepilloux was smiling as he read the end of the passage. "Blessed children!" he murmured to himself. To Max he said: "Before you decide that they did not rely on our power to absolve them, let me read you some more. This note was written about the same time":

The opportunity of confessing their Sins is of vital importance to these people. They seemed to know, by some Divine instinct, that their spiritual health depended upon the cleansing of their souls, and they are anxious to do this. Some of them, if it were possible, would confess several times a day; and as it is, the Confessionals, when attended, are continuously engaged. I have gone out with the annual hunting parties and, in the middle of night, have had my toes pulled by some earnest soul who wished Asolution before another day should dawn. I write this entry following a characteristic happening. As I sat here in my chamber the door suddenly opened, without a warning knock. I ought to add this observation that, while we have a bell on our front door, it is never sounded; and the doors to our private chambers, which we never lock, are liable to swing open at any hour of the day or night. Just now, the door opened, and my visitor was my dear friend Kai-Kai-She. I had not seen him for several months, and had understood that he had been off with a small raiding party, in the Blackfeet Country. According to the habit of these People, he said nothing for several minutes, but simply sat on the floor. Then he explained his wish to confess. At that, he moved toward me and sat down again, just in front of my chair. Then he brought forth a small bundle from under his blanket. When he had undone the bundle, I saw that it contained many dry twigs, all straight and carefully trimmed. These he laid before me and sorted out according to size. The biggest ones were off to one side, and carefully separated, so none should be lost sight of. The others were ranged in order. These were his Sins. He had begun collecting the sticks as soon as he left home two months before, and for each act for which he would have to do Penance, he had added a stick. In that way, he had forgotten nothing. I was glad my door was never locked. . . .

The twinkle in Father Grepilloux's eyes was extinguished in a look of soberness which spread from his tightening smile.

"There are many little stories like these. Somewhere here I have written the history of a very different affair. This event took place some years after the incidents I have been describing. I went away early in the seventies and was at Colville for a while, then at Santa Clara. I returned in eighty-four, as you know, and that was when I learned all the details in Big Paul's story. There are many versions, some of which I suppose you've heard. The account I have written I believe is accurate. Let me read it.

"I had known Big Paul since his birth. I also knew his brothers, of whom there were four, his three sisters, and his parents. His father was Nine-Pipe, who was called the Judge, because for many years he had acted as peacemaker in the tribe. When a quarrel could not be settled, it was taken to Nine-Pipe, and he showed them who was at fault and how it should be made up. There was something distinguished about that family. The girls were unusually fine featured, and the boys were tall and strong, and, like their father, of a peaceful nature. Big Paul was the youngest but one of the boys, and he was the ablest. It is my belief that he was the brightest boy I ever taught in any Indian tribe. It was more than sharpness. His quick mind was only one side of a superior nature.

"The trouble began when the father was killed by a white man, Here is how that happened. The Indians were on their fall hunt and one of the tepees was occupied by white men. There was nothing especially wrong with these white men, except that they drank, and they never took the trouble to observe ordinary courtesy in their treatment of their Indian hosts. On this night, the Judge was telling a story to a company of friends. Among the guests in his tepee were two of the white men, one of whom was named Jeff Irving. The other man was either his brother or his brother-in-law.

"Evidently, the men had been drinking, and Jeff Irving became insulting. When the Judge made a statement, Irving would say it was a lie. The old man ignored him and talked to the others, but Irving would raise his voice and make himself heard. The Judge finished his story and sat silent, neither rebuking the man, nor in any way showing displeasure. It

was for such forbearance that he had come to be
called the Judge. The old man's friends were enraged.
They left the tepee, one at a time, until there were
only the Judge and the two white men. But if his
friends expected him to revenge himself, they were
disappointed. He sat without speaking, and finally
the white men went away. Later that night, when
Irving was in his own tepee, and the fire threw his
shadow against the skin covering, someone who
watched from outside aimed a gun at that shadow
and fired. The man had one side of his head shot
away. That was how the trouble started. Before the
night had passed, Irving's friends had gone to the
tepee of the Judge, and had driven a knife through
his heart. Then they left the camp. In their stupidity,
they never asked themselves whether the old man
could have committed that murder. If they had questioned him before they took his life, he would have
been shocked by what had taken place, and I have no
doubt that he would have impoverished himself, in
order to make amends.

"According to the ancient custom, it was now up
to his family to avenge the murder. There was a division of opinion at once. The older boys were far from
dull, but they lacked Big Paul's clear head. The primitive law still swayed them, and it did no good to have
Big Paul remind them that times were changed.
When he saw that it was useless to reason, he refused
to take part in the affair. 'I tell you this,' he said.
'If you are killed, I will not carry on this foolishness.

You will just have to die by your own stubbornness. I will help you catch these men and give them to the Indian Agent, but I will not put my own neck in a rope.' The brothers cursed him and made their plans without him. There was much excitement and talk among the Indians. Some were on the side of the older brothers, and others, mostly young men, defended Big Paul. 'It is different now,' they said. 'If you shoot a man they hang you by a rope, But if you give a man to the police, the police will hang him and it is all right. That is what they tell us.' So they argued.

"Then word came one day that the oldest brother, Jerome, had gone fearlessly into the mining camp, where the Irving family was then living, and he had shot the brother of Jeff Irving. Of course, he did not get away. He was shot down on the spot, and his body was dragged out of camp. The next brother, Martin, was not so reckless. He hid in the mountains near the camp and waited until he had located the Irving mining claim. The Irvings went there to dig every day, always heavily armed. Martin lay in ambush, and when the opportunity came, he killed two men and wounded a third. He got away before anyone had seen him. The miners got up a pursuit party, which overrode a village of Kootenay Indians, who had nothing whatever to do with the affair. They slashed up some tepees and used a whip on an old woman, who had scolded them, but no one was killed. When this story came to the Salish people, it agitated them greatly. 'You see,' Big Paul's friends said, 'These miners will murder the first Indian they find. If this goes on, they will make war against us and we will be killed like dogs.' The hotbloods became angry at that. They called Big Paul and his friends cowards, and declared their willingness to die fighting.

"Big Paul was no coward, as even his enemies should have known. He went to the mining camp, unarmed, alone, and offered himself as a hostage. If his brother were not found and brought to trial, then they could try him instead. I have been told this by a man who was living in the mining camp at the time.

"An unfortunate thing happened then. Members of the Irving family found Martin. How this happened, I can't explain. The white men had very little knowledge of the mountains and Martin could have eluded them easily. It was sheer coincidence, aided no doubt by Martin's own carelessness. At any rate, they murdered him, and left his battered body just outside the Indian village. When that happened, Big Paul's friends deserted him. He was accused of betraying his brother and his friends were afraid to defend him any longer. They had no way of knowing what Big Paul had told the miners; it wasn't even clear why he had gone to the camp, if not to play the traitor. A party was organized to go after him, and this party was led by the youngest of the Judge's sons, the eighteen-year-old Slem-Hak-Kah (Little Claw of the Grizzly Bear). It was then midwinter and the snow was piled deeply in the pass of the Bitter Root mountains, but that was no obstacle to a party of hotbloods.

"The Irvings reached the mining camp ahead of Slem-Hak-Kah's party, and when they learned that Big Paul was there, no doubt they were pleased. They were desperate men. When Government officials finally got around to investigate the affair, it was discovered that not only Jeff Irving but several of his brothers were wanted for murders they had committed around Virginia City and elsewhere.

"Big Paul was invited to a saloon as soon as the Irvings returned. My informant tells me that the original purpose of the miners had been to hold a mock trial, with someone counterfeiting the part of a judge, at which Big Paul was to be sentenced to hang, and, of course, to be hanged in all earnestness. The Irvings must have decided on a different ruse. They wanted quicker action. As Big Paul stood near the bar, several men who stood next to him appeared to become involved in a dispute. Hot words suddenly gave way to flying fists, and one of the belligerents was knocked against him. In an instant, he had turned upon Big Paul and accused him of interfering. Others began to press forward. They began to shout at Big Paul. Someone had closed and bolted the front door. He must have understood by then what they were about; perhaps he glanced around and calculated his chances against that mob.

"Suddenly the fight was on in earnest. Big Paul had a hatchet in his hand. No one knew where it came from, whether he had been carrying it all the time, or whether he found it behind the bar. He had jumped behind the bar at the beginning of the fight; later he plunged in among them and fought like a madman. Heads were split open, blood flowed. Men were afraid to shoot because they might kill their friends. They used their revolvers like clubs. He dodged the blows and for a while held a man in a grip of iron, making a shield of him. My witness tells me that Big Paul enjoyed the fight. He was smiling through it. He began to taunt them because they could not overpower him. He cleared a path through the mob and sang his war song as he went swinging. He was bleeding from many wounds but he stayed on his feet.

"Somehow, he got hold of a revolver. With a hatchet and a revolver he was a demon. He dropped one man with a shot and the others fell back. They had a taste of his temper. With the hatchet he broke a window out and jumped to the ground. The first man to appear at the window, in pursuit, was shot down, and the others hesitated. He turned and ran.

"At that very minute, Slem-Hak-Kah's party rode into the mining camp. Big Paul staggered toward them through the snow, and without stopping to ask a single question, they fell upon him and stabbed him to death. It is said that every man in the party drove a knife into his wounded body.

"Without molesting the miners, the Indians turned about and rode home over the mountains. The feud ended at that."

That was the story of Big Paul.

Father Grepilloux closed the battered daybook but his thoughts continued to move through the yellow pages in which he had recorded the lost life of a primitive world. The entries were written some in Latin and some in French, and the chirography was clear, small and unadorned. Then he said something which Max never forgot.

"You have least to complain of. You lose your sons, but these people have lost a way of life, and with it their pride, their dignity, their strength. Men like Jeff Irving have murdered their fathers and their sons with impunity. Gross-natured officials have despoiled them, they are insulted when they present grievances. Of course"—since Grepilloux was a priest, and a faithful one, he added what in his heart seemed to balance all that he had set against it—"they have God."

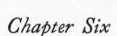

Chapter Six

ON the same day that Max Leon visited Father
Grepilloux at the Mission, Archilde's mother invited
her relatives and friends to a feast in honor of her
returned son. She killed one of her own steers—of
which she had more than a few head, as she had horses
also—and before sundown the fires were burning. Five
tepees had been set up in the low ground by the creek,
where they were hidden from the big house. After
nightfall the flames would light up the black encircling
pines and the reflection would fall upon the windows
of the house and cast a soft glow in Max's bedroom.
There would be voices rising up to him, too. He
would lie in bed, swearing at the noise and wondering
what it signified, whether the voices were sad or
happy.

Archilde sat near the entrance of the principal
tepee, that of old Modeste, the blind chief, who was
either the uncle or the brother-in-law of his mother.
Indian relationships, in the old style, were always a
bit vague to him. Modeste he knew as a gentle old
man who had appeared at intervals during his life in
some act of generosity, either giving him, as a child,
a finely wrought bow and bone-tipped arrows, such
as had not been made in many years, and teaching him

to shoot it; or sending him, when he was going away to school, a "safe-keeper" which the old man had carried since his own boyhood (Archilde still possessed two such amulets from Modeste's hand, one an eagle-bone whistle and the other the polished claw of a grizzly); and then, when Archilde had quite grown, giving him a horse, saddle and bridle. That was old Modeste. There he sat, smoking and waiting for the women to serve the meat, his sightless eyes blinking to his thought.

Archilde's mother occupied a place of distinction in the tribe. She was the daughter of the chief Running Wolf who had welcomed the Fathers, and since the title was hereditary she was still of the chief's family. More than that, she was a woman whose opinions were valued, and they were given only when sought. Just now she was directing the several women who were preparing the meal and drawing laughter from the women with her sharp comments. "Rose has such big buttocks now she can't bend to stir the fire. Look! Mine? Aih, you see I keep them out of sight. I sit on them."

This was true of his mother, but Archilde had never thought of it as a matter of any importance. It did not count in his scale of values. Old Modeste, more than his mother, made what he was seem important. If he had commanded an action, you would have to do it; while if his mother commanded you might do it, but you would be amused, you would smile and tease her a little by pretending that you weren't going to do it.

Actually, in the way he was learning the world, neither Modeste nor his mother was important. They were not real people. Buffaloes were not real to him either, yet he could go and look at buffaloes every day if he wished, behind the wire enclosure of the Biological Survey reserve. He knew that buffaloes had been real things to his mother, and to the old people who had come to eat with her tonight. To him they were just fenced up animals that couldn't be shot, though you could take photographs of them.

Amusing was what it was. After living in Portland, playing the violin, living in a boarding house, reading baseball scores—it was funny to come home and sit at his mother's feast. His eyes saw the old faces, faces he had forgotten about, never thought to see again; and now to be sitting in the circle of firelight and looking at them—but it wasn't really funny, not deeply funny. The deeper feeling was impatience, irritation, an uneasy feeling in the stomach. Why could he not endure them for just these few hours? Why did they make him feel sick? It was not to be reasoned with. It did no good to remind himself that the old faces were not at fault; that his mother, who had never struck him, scarcely even spoken angrily to him, was in no way to blame for what he felt; and neither were the buffalo to blame for being no longer free. Reason wouldn't quite do the trick, but he would try it. He would sit quietly and try not to see or hear or smell too much. He would try not to speak, lest he say more than was necessary. And in a few hours, days— He had come home this time because it would be the last time. When he went away again—this he knew—he would not return.

He tried to eat, the way one had to at a feast. He tried to play the part. But when he had devoured about a pound of roasted meat he began to feel sick. The old people joked him.

"Here is a lump of hot fat the size of your head. That will do you good!"

His stomach turned. He felt the blood drain out of his face.

"That would kill a dog." His voice sounded weak.

"A pleasant death. A dog wouldn't mind dying with a full belly."

"Asilde"—the native Salish had no r's and the old people could not pronounce his name the way it was written—"in the old days your mother would have been ashamed of you." An ancient aunt, Mrs. Beaverfoot, made this observation. She never had got over the fact that Catharine was *Pu-Soiapi;* that is, she had married a white man.

"If I had been born in the old days"—Archilde tried to be unconcerned in his tone, though the remark made him angry—"then I would not be as I am now. You people talk about the old days as if they were here. But they're gone, dead. So don't tell me what I ought to do to be like that."

"Aih! The boy is right." This was Modeste. "You old women forget that what our children are like they cannot help. It began before their time." At that they all shook their heads and looked mournful. All conversations among the old people ended in this way. No matter what they talked about, before they had finished they were shaking their heads and thinking about what was gone.

Now that they were started, they would go on digging up their troubles and telling stories of the old days. Archilde with his impertinent new ways of thinking would be forgotten. He could sink back, glad not to be noticed and let them talk. Time would pass that way.

The first story was told by an old woman. Her scarcity of teeth gave an odd sound to some of her words but the story was an old one and nothing was lost.

"In the long ago the animals had tribes just like men. Coyote had his own tribe and this was one of the mightiest. Now he was hungry and all his people were hungry. They had nothing to eat. He sat in his tepee and pulled his blanket close.

" 'If I just had something to put on my arrow,' he said.

"It was like this. He had nothing to put on his arrow. He had just bark and you can see that would not go through a buffalo. When he shot something with the bark it just bounced off and the buffalo said 'Now I will eat that fly if he doesn't go away.'

"And Coyote had nothing to eat.

"Next day he went to see Fox, and Fox was cooking a piece of meat on a stick. He was holding it to the fire. Coyote sat down and watched the meat getting cooked. And he smelled the hot fat. And he got very hungry. Then when it was all cooked Coyote jumped and grabbed the meat and put it in his mouth all at once. But when he bit there was something hard in it. And it was the Flint.

" 'Now why didn't you tell me you had the Flint?' Coyote asked. 'When did the Flint go along here?'

"Fox said it was three days now since the Flint went by.

"Then Coyote took his blanket and his things and started after the Flint. When he had walked all day he said, 'Here is where the Flint camped.' Then he slept. Another day he traveled and then he said, 'The Flint made his bed here.' And he slept in that place. Then he walked the next day and at night he said, 'The Flint started from here this morning,' and so he slept again. Next morning he got up early and walked fast and there he saw the Flint going along the road. Coyote went out that way and then went faster and got ahead of the Flint and waited. And when the Flint came Coyote said:

" 'So here you are. Come here now and I will fight you.'

And the Flint said, 'All right. We will fight.'

"Then they were fighting and going this way and that way and Coyote took what he had in his hand— it was a war club—and he hit the Flint very hard and the Flint broke all to pieces.

" 'Hoh!' said Coyote. 'It is done.' And he put the

pieces in his blanket and put it on his shoulder and started back. And he said to his people 'Just put some flint on the point of your arrows and we will kill buffalo.' Then he went to all the tribes and gave them flint and after that they did not have to starve.

"That is the story of Flint."

When the story was told everybody laughed. It was a very old story, the kind grandmothers told to grandchildren, and it always made people laugh. Archilde had not intended to listen, yet he had heard every word. The story had amused him in spite of himself. It left a spark of gay remembrance in his mind.

The next story was told by Whitey, an old man who had been born, they said, with a streak of white hair running through the black. His story was about "The Thing that was to make life easy." It went like this:

"There was an old man who had a dream and in this dream it said that something was coming that would make life easy. They would not have to hunt or dig for roots or do any kind of work. But they had to watch out and not let this thing that was to make life easy escape their notice.

"When the old man had this dream he was astonished and he went about telling people 'Something is coming that will make life easy.' Then he sat down to watch for it. He would not go on the hunt and he would not dig for roots or do any kind of work. He did not want to miss it. His people laughed at him. They said 'He was always a lazy man. Now he will never work.' So they went off to hunt and get food and left him sitting. And it went that way for many years. He sat in front of his lodge and waited. Sometimes he got very hungry because the hunters brought him nothing. Only his little grandchild kept him from starving. She took a piece of meat from her mother and brought it to Old Man. She did this every day.

"One day Old Man went away. They did not see him go but when they came by his lodge he was not sitting there. 'Where did Old Man go?' they asked. Nobody knew. Even the grandchild did not know. 'He just found a softer seat some place,' they said. And then they went hunting. All the men went out from the village and left only the women and children and the very old ones. They were gone a long time, as they had to cross the mountains in the east and go to the plains where they hunted buffalo. So there were no men in the village when Old Man came back. Yes, he came back finally, that old man. He carried something under his blanket. They looked at him but they were afraid to ask what it was. He sent out a call that all were to come to his lodge, and when they came there he said, 'Make me a meal and then I will show you the thing that is to make life easy.'

"When he had eaten he said, 'Come with me to the woods and I will show you this thing.' He went first carrying a bundle in his arms, and all those women and children and the very old ones followed. Their eyes were big and they said, 'Is it true or is Old Man a fool now?' And the old ones grumbled because everybody was walking so fast.

He stopped when he came to a young cottonwood by the water. He put his bundle on the ground, then he spoke to the people who had crowded near. 'Oh, you foolish ones!' that was how he spoke to them. 'You did not believe it would come, but it is here. The thing that will make life easy is here now.' So he opened his bundle, and there it was. The people looked at the shiny thing and they were full of wonder.

" 'I will strike that tree five times and it will fall.' That was what he told them. It was not a very large tree but even so in the old days it would take a man maybe half a day to make it fall because in those times their axes were made of stone. And this thing that was to make life easy was an iron axe.

"Now the people could not believe what he said. They laughed. 'Hoh! Old Man! You can hit that tree ten times—twenty times—and it will not fall.' But some were not so sure. They looked at that shiny thing and it seemed to wink at them. And these said, 'Yes, it will fall. It will fall.'

"Old Man was angry at those who would not believe even now, and he went to that tree and struck it a mighty blow. A big chip flew out. Then he hit it a mighty blow on the other side. Again a big chip flew out. Once more on each side, four blows in all, and the tree died. It fell on some old people who had come too close and did not expect it to fall.

"The old man wrapped the axe in his bundle again and did not wait for their cries of astonishment. He went quickly to the trail which led away from the village. That way the hunters would come when they returned from across the mountains. And there he began to chop down the trees. He chopped every tree that stood near the trail and made a pile of the big chips right in the trail. Then he went home.

"When the hunters came from across the mountains they just stopped and cried in astonishment. Then they sat down around that pile of big chips and stared at it. 'It has come!' they said. 'The thing that is to make life easy has come and we were not here to meet it.'

"When the men entered the village Old Man was waiting for them. He began to laugh when he saw them and then everybody began to laugh. It made them happy. Now they had the thing that was going to make life easy.

"That is the story."

Archilde heard that story also. He wondered at it. And the more he reflected on it the more wonderful it grew. A story like that, he realized, was full of meaning.

Others told their stories, then they turned at last to Modeste, the blind chief. He would have to tell a story. They urged him. His sightless eyes blinked rapidly as he gathered his thought before speaking. He was going far back into the past.

"These stories make the heart light," he said in his high voice. "My story will have to be a different one. I will tell it for this boy who has just come home after traveling out to the world. You have just heard him say that those old days are dead and won't come again. And it's true. But let me tell this story so he will see better just what it was like back in those times.

"I will tell you first that in old times, before any white men came, his people were a mighty race and their land went from the plains east of the mountains to the Snpoilshi * River. This is no boast about something that never was. When we made a treaty with the Government they saw how it was, and that was the country we owned. We had a strong nation and those who later became our greatest enemies, the Blackfeet and their kinsmen, and the Crows too, they respected us. We went twice a year to hunt on the Missouri and there were few who dared invade our hunting ground. It had been that way for longer than any man can say. And then it happened. How it was I cannot say. Up there at Fort-des-Prairies they began to give guns to the Blackfeet. No other Indians got these guns, only the Blackfeet. That was when our trouble began.

"The years that followed were bad. When we went to hunt on the Missouri the Blackfeet were there ahead of us with their guns. We had bows and arrows and our war clubs. Our people were frightened out of their senses. They had never seen that kind of fighting. A man dropped dead before he came near the enemy. Every year when we came back from the hunt there were lodges of women and children with no men. There were lodges of old people too with no

* Columbia.

young sons. At our councils there were some who said we should stay away from the buffalo country and that we could live just as well on mountain game. But those weak ones were not listened to. That land belonged to us and we had always hunted the buffalo. If we did not fight they would treat us like dogs and in a little while they would take the mountains away too. No, we would not listen to those weak ones.

"It went on that way a long time, and then the white men came to us in the mountains. There were foolish ones in our councils who said that we ought to just kill every white man that came along because they had given the guns to the Blackfeet. These foolish ones were not listened to either. We made peace with the first ones that came and helped them to find their way through the mountains, and we kept that peace with all of them. Today we can say that we never had the blood of any white man on our hands. It was not that we feared them, but we had to have their guns. And we could not stop being friendly once we had got some guns, as the foolish ones wished, because we had to have more guns. It was a different world from that time. In the old days of our wars a few men would be killed and fighting was a thing you could enjoy, like hunting. But now it became a bitter thing. Old scores of blood revenge could never be settled because too many were killed. Maybe this year it was your son, next year it would be your father, then your brother, then your wife, and each time your heart grew heavier. You cut off your hair so many times that men forgot how they had lived before all this happened. The old ones could say it had not always been thus, but the young ones thought they talked in dreams. For them the world had always been bitter.

"When we got our guns we had a great battle with the Piegans, the kinsmen of the Blackfeet. They did not know we had these guns and they rode foolishly at us. We were lying down on a ridge. They rode quite close and then we fired all at once. Their confusion was so great that some just fell off their horses. Their war chiefs tried to get them to come at us again but instead they ran the other way and left their wounded behind. That was a great battle."

At that point he paused and once more addressed himself to Archilde, for whom this story was intended. "Perhaps this talk of fighting and men dying means little to you. It is a little thing now, but when it was happening it seemed big. You will die easily, but if you had lived then you might have died fighting to live."

Modeste continued his story. "We thought guns would save our hunting grounds and make the old times return. But that was a mistake. This new kind of fighting just meant that more men were killed. It was bitter fighting. And we gained nothing. The Piegans made a peace but it was not to be trusted. Men said: 'We used to sleep all night, but now that we have peace with our enemies we sleep in the day and watch all night.' It was this way, that a man feared to go hunting alone or in a small company, for the Piegans were always waiting. We dared not leave our villages unprotected, for our enemies would shoot our women and children and carry off everything. That was what it had come to.

"Our wise ones said we had to try something else. They began to look about. Many went off alone on praying-fasts. It was clear that something had gone wrong, the people had lost their power. We had so few fighting men left we were afraid to count. It might be a bad thing to count men. So our wise ones began to say that we must find something new. Our voices, they said, no longer reach Amotkan.* Maybe he has gone too far away or maybe our voices have become weak, but when we speak in the old ways we are not heard.

"Now some Indians came to us from the East. Perhaps you know about them. They were from the Iroquois nation. They came here to trap, but when they had been here a while we made them our brothers and asked them to live with us. They were the ones who told us about the black-robe Fathers. We must send for them. The Fathers would help us to be strong. They had a power, a Somesh, and it was like this: it was two sticks, one stick across the other like this. The black-robe Fathers called it the crucifix. If they brought it to us we would be strong again. That was what they told us and it was what our own wise

* The old word for God. It could be rendered the Old Man, or the Venerable One.

ones were looking for. This was the new thing.

"So we sent for the black-robe Fathers. Four different times we sent our people all the way to St. Louis. And finally the Fathers came to us here. They built a church. They baptized us. . . ."

Here Modeste paused. No one looked up. No one stirred. In their thoughts they dwelt on that time in the past to which the old man had carried them. Then they heard him sigh.

"We thought they would bring back the power we had lost—but today we have less. This boy tells us the truth." Then his lips mumbled "Ies choopminzin" (I stop talking to you).

Archilde, listening closely, felt something die within him. Some stiffness, some pride, went weak before the old man's bitter simple words.

For the first time he had really seen it happen. First the great numbers and the power, then the falling away, the battles and starvation in the snow, the new hopes and the slow facing of disappointment, and then no hope at all, just this living in the past. He had heard the story many times, but he had not listened. It had tired him. Now he saw that it had happened and it left him feeling weak. It destroyed his stiffness toward the old people. He sat and thought about it and the flames shot upward and made light on the circle of black pines.

In the big house Max tried to sleep but his eyes would open and there would be the glow of light on the walls of his bedroom. Voices would come up to him. He would frown and turn his face away. He tried to be angry at them for the noise they made, but pity was there ahead of his anger. Why was it that after forty years he did not know these people and was not trusted by them? He had never interfered in their affairs, and he had never cheated them. They had lost a way of life, as Father Grepilloux said, but—damn it! why couldn't just one of his sons have the sense and the courage to make himself a new way of life! He rolled away from the glow of light, but still the voices reached him. What were they saying? Why didn't they talk to him?

Chapter Seven

THE grain was being cut on Max Leon's ranch. In the morning he put on his riding boots and followed the men with their two binders into the field. He rode a white mare with a well-shaped head. After an oiling and a last tightening up the first binder was set to work. As the white arms revolved they tossed the tall grain stalks against the flying sickle and on to the moving aprons. A bundle collected at the side, was tied with twine and kicked into the carriage. A second bundle followed, then a third. The wheat was heavy and the bundles came through quickly. The second binder started into action.

Max sat astride his mare and watched, then he trotted up to the machines and rode alongside for a while. The mare disliked the noise and the motion of the whirling arms and had to be coaxed and scolded by turns. This had not continued for long before the leading machine stopped with a banging noise.

"God damn!" Max exploded. "I never knew one of these damn things to run yet. What's the matter?"

It was a broken drive chain, a small matter. "That's all right, Max," the driver said calmly. "I got some extra links."

"In a few days that grain'll be too ripe, so you got

to keep moving." Then he rode back to the house. At the kitchen door he called for Agnes.

"Send your boys to the field with a jug of water. Tell 'em to stay till the water's drunk up, then fetch more. They got to tend to that while the men are working or I'll give 'em my whip."

Agnes looked around the yard. "They're not here," she said.

"Then where are they?"

"Fishing, maybe. I don't know."

"Well, damn it all! Find 'em! They got to bring water to the men!"

He scowled. It was no good telling her to look for the boys. He started up the creek himself. He looked back and saw that Agnes had already gone into the house. It was none of her affair. He swore out loud.

In the timber there was quiet. While the mare drank at the creek he dismounted and drank too, lying on his stomach. He followed a trail through the brush.

It was some time before he found the boys. They were lying quietly on a pile of driftwood in the center of the stream, waiting for a shy trout to get into position to be speared. They had already brought up several in that way. Archilde handled the spear and the boys watched closely. They would have to try it later and they didn't want to blunder and be laughed at. They were too engrossed in this occupation to see or hear anything.

Max rode up close before he shouted. The boys

were on their feet in a second and ready to run.

"Why don't you stay home?" Max called. "You got to carry water to the field! Men are working."

"We want to fish."

"You fish and run in the woods all summer. Now come and work like men for a few days. It won't hurt you."

The boys stood looking at each other. Max had not spoken to Archilde.

"Come on, now! You can get behind me on the mare."

"That old whitey will buck us off!" Narcisse protested.

"You're not afraid of that! You're buckaroos!"

"We don't want to go back!" Mike cried. "Arsheel's got to come too," he added.

"Archilde can stay and be a buck Indian! You two, come and learn something. You'll get good pay. Jump up behind me, now!"

The offer attracted them—there was pay, and they could ride the white mare. If they had tried that without permission they'd have had their necks broken. They stood there debating. Then Archilde spoke.

"Yes, you two. Go and help. The fish will stay in the creek."

He did not look up to see how his words would be received, but Max gave him a quick, inquiring glance. Mike and Narcisse needed no further urging and crawled up behind Max. The white mare switched her tail and tried to walk sideways, but when she had been coaxed enough she went all right.

"Make her run!" Mike cried and at the same time kicked her with his heels. The mare turned back her ears and started through the woods at a gallop.

"You little devils! Keep your feet still!"

When they had disappeared among the trees Archilde got to his feet. For a moment he looked indecisive, then he started down the trail. He expected contempt from Max; he was accustomed to it. But since he had come home this time it bit into him as it never had before. Max was stupid if he could not see better, if he did not understand.

That afternoon one of the binders broke down again and Max had to go for repairs. He was in a rage.

"Pshaw, that's all right." George Moser tried to calm him. "You always have a few stops when you start harvesting. Things will run smooth now, you see."

In his own household things were going smoothly enough and the storekeeper was inclined to see the world in a cheery mood. For two days now Mrs. Moser had not said a word about going home to her parents and it had begun to seem as if she were ready to act on his advice of taking things as they came. If he had felt any resentment toward Max Leon the other day he had forgotten it. He still had hopes of winning the Spaniard's friendship.

"Won't you step into my office and have a drink?" He had met Max out in the store with people all around and this invitation was whispered. Max either did not hear or pretended not to hear. He was grumbling.

"God damn farm machinery! They make it out of paper. They rob you when you buy it—but that's not enough. They go on robbing you to keep it repaired! A bunch of robbers! When you run cattle all you need is a horse, only you must also have as much sense as the horse!"

"Pshaw, that's all right! Things will run smooth now." Mr. Moser repeated his consoling observation, but the invitation to have a drink he did not repeat. After all, a man had to have some pride.

The second binder was making its round of the field. Sometimes as it started up a slight rise in the ground the whirring of its sickle could be heard plainly, and then as it dipped down the sound faded away. Max stopped his car in the lane and walked across the field with his repair parts. He glanced shrewdly at the width of the cut and estimated how long the second binder had been idle while the men talked.

"You're sure lucky they had the spare part. We was layin' five to one they'd have to tellygraph for it," the driver said.

The afternoon was slipping away and the heat grew less intense. Over against the timber the shadows lay long and cool. The machine was repaired and started up.

The men who were bunching the sheaves had made

a circle of the field and now they were approaching Max as he stood watching the flying arms of the reaper. He turned toward the men and something made him blink—Archilde was working with them! Max's mouth dropped open in amazement.

He walked over and watched Archilde pick up a bundle under each arm and place the two on end, leaning against each other for support. When he had brought others and completed a bunch Max spoke.

"Why didn't you say you'd help? Now I got an extra man."

"You didn't ask me."

That made Max snort. "You got eyes! You saw this field ready to be cut! You saw the men start!"

"But you didn't ask me."

Max let his mouth hang open without saying a word. Then he let the scorn go out of his voice. He was curious.

"Where'd you learn to shock wheat?"

"It's nothing to learn. I just watched a few times. Is it all right?"

Sure! Hell, yes! It was all right!

"Well, if you're going to help I can let a man go. There's no use having an extra man to feed." He had become businesslike.

"Where's those kids? They been carrying water?"

They had gone for a fresh jug. Archilde resumed his work and Max walked away. He did not mean to make too much of this. It might not last. He went to his car standing in the lane. Suddenly he began to laugh. "Hell! I didn't ask him! What do you know about that!"

"Have you got a good supper?" he asked Agnes. "The men are working hard and you want to feed them good." He looked into her pots on the stove to see what was cooking. "You must keep it clean around here," he ended.

Agnes went about noiselessly in her moccasined feet and paid no attention to Max. Little Annie sat in the doorway nursing a stick of wood wrapped in an old shawl.

From the house Max walked to the creek, and he seemed full of thought. There was a fall of three or four feet over a ledge of rock. He had often planned to lay a dam there and build a small grist mill. The stream ran more than enough water for the power needed. Economies had not bothered him when he raised cattle, but as old age came upon him and he began to look backward, he realized some of the opportunities that had been missed. Much had been wasted, much destroyed, and men would have been richer if they had been satisfied with less. Here was this water, unused. An old time cattle grower would have snorted at the idea of such prudent husbandry, but a change was coming over the world. Such things would be thought of in future. New management was necessary. Perhaps he had a mental picture of a young man going about and changing things according to the new order. New ideas and fresh strength were necessary. It was too bad that these acres lay idle, that this water was unused.

When he returned to the house the men were coming in from the field. They had separated the horses from the two binders and each man rode a horse. Even Mike and Narcisse had a horse apiece. The tug chains jangled softly and someone was whistling a tune.

The sun had set in its usual brilliance. That too was something unused, rarely seen.

Chapter Eight

THE threshing machine was a long time in getting
to Max Leon's ranch. There was rain and the usual
breakdowns and delays. The wheat shocks in the field
were no longer golden but had become bleached. At
last the thresher, drawn by its belching steam engine,
squared off in the middle of the field and the last stage
of the harvesting began. And Archilde was there,
working like a man brought up to it.

Max went around often to get a look at him. There
was a quality in the way a man worked that told a lot
—but in this case Max was in the dark. What he saw
looked all right, but could he trust what he saw?

The season had changed. The sun was always seen
through a mist. There were forest fires lingering in
the surrounding mountains, and on some days when
the wind was right the world seemed to wander all at
sea in a warm fog. The nights sparkled with a promise
of frost, and mist rose from the earth until the middle of the forenoon. Sounds hung in the air so that
sometimes men talking in a distant field sounded near
at hand. The world had become enchanted.

For a week Max had been watching the men plow-
ing his fields. He wore a jacket now when he went to
the porch. The shade had a chill touch. His face

84

looked thinner and there were heavier pouches under his eyes. He would sit there and with the aid of a pair of binoculars watch the progress of the work.

On this morning, an hour after breakfast, he went to his accustomed chair. The stillness of mid-morning brought relaxation. He let the glasses lie idle in his lap and rested. Half smilingly, he reflected that he was getting old. At every opportunity he rested, like an old tomcat.

Then he came awake. There were sounds from an upstairs room which suddenly took on meaning. It was Archilde's room, and the sound he heard was of his son walking. The steps went one-two-three-four, then pause; one-two-three-four, pause; one-two-three-four, pause. He had heard this for perhaps ten minutes before he understood what it meant. The boy was walking from his bed to the chest in which he kept his clothes. Then he saw, as clearly as if he had been in the room, that there was an open suitcase on the bed.

Max got to his feet, feeling a little shaken. What was to be done? He had meant to speak to him before this, and now—was it too late?

The suitcase was on the bed just as Max had imagined it. It was almost packed. Archilde's working clothes of overalls, blue shirt and heavy shoes were thrown into a corner. He was wearing the blue suit in which he had come back from Portland. His shoes were new and polished. He stood before the suitcase and wondered where to put the last articles.

Then he heard heavy steps on the stairway. They came up slowly. He knew it was Max and wondered what it meant.

Max waited in the doorway, saying nothing. It was an extraordinary thing for him to do, almost like paying a social visit. It had never happened before. Archilde had never received a visit from Max.

"Well—" Max let his voice trail off. He didn't know how to begin. "I guess you're going away then?" he managed to ask.

This too was surprising. It had not occurred to Archilde that Max would be interested in his going away. There had been an end to hard words while he had worked in the field; sometimes, when he happened to look at his father at the supper table, there had even been a nod, perhaps a half smile. Nothing more. He had not attached any meaning to it.

"Well—what will you do? You have plans?"

"I'll go away. I'll find something." Archilde too was cautious. He could not feel sure that this interest was friendly. It might end with a remark about his going back to the blanket. That was how it used to be.

Max let his eyes gaze through the window. "I never wanted much from my boys. Just for them to take a man's place, know how to work and do things. Not to have them work for me. Hell, no! That's not what I wanted. But a man ought to know how to work for his own good. That's what I wanted." He said this without looking at the boy and might have been talking to himself.

Archilde did not answer him. There was nothing to answer. Work was a small matter. One knew about it. It seemed useless to talk about so ordinary a subject.

Max was kind of mumbling, still gazing at the window. "When you go away from here the only thing anybody will be interested in is: What can you do? Can you work? That's what they'll want to know. If you know how to do something, why, that's all there's to it. You don't have to worry."

The pause was intended as a question. Archilde felt it.

"There's lots of things a fellow can do. I never have trouble. Sometimes I work washing dishes, or I press clothes in a tailor shop. It doesn't take much. When my luck is good I get a job playing the fiddle. I can do that pretty good now."

The resulting silence was a long one. Max had moved away from the doorway and made a quick examination of the opened suitcase. At the window he turned back.

"Maybe you need more clothes? It costs money to keep yourself in clothes."

"I have enough until I get to making money."

"You have money coming from me for your work. We'll have to settle."

Archilde protested quickly. "That's nothing. I didn't do that for money. No, you don't owe me anything for that."

He was determined about it. Max was on the point of shouting him down in the old style, then he caught

himself. He laughed suddenly. There was less spar-
ring now; now they were talking to each other.

"Well, if you won't take the damn money then I'll
make a bargain with you. You know Father Grepilloux, eh? You like him?"

When he had been answered, Max continued:
"Then I want you to go and have a talk with him. I
don't know what it's about exactly but he asked me.
So, will you do that?"

Archilde would. He remembered Father Grepilloux
from long ago, and the recollection was pleasant. The
priest knew how to talk to boys; after they had not
seen him for years they still remembered that he had
been all right.

That was how it happened. He had promised, and
so he went to see Father Grepilloux. He left his suitcase still open, lying on the bed.

He remembered the large room, with its books and
its subdued light. He had been there once, it seemed
to be many years ago. The priest, beaming at him
through his spectacles, lost no time in preliminaries.
There were no useless questions.

"You're grown up, I see. You're ready to do things
for yourself. Do you know why I sent for you?"

Archilde didn't know. The question rather startled
him since he did not understand that he had been
sent for for a purpose. He had thought it was simply
to say hello.

"You want to play the violin and I can help you.

That's all. But first I should know how much instruction you've had. Have you been playing long?"

He stared at the priest while he thought over what
had happened. He had talked only to his family about
violin playing, and therefore Max had brought the
information to Father Grepilloux. They had been discussing the subject between them. This was surprising.

His violin playing, now—well, he had begun that
some years ago. He was at the Indian school in Oregon
when he began it. It was a long time since he had
thought of those days.

Chapter Nine

THE school was a large institution attended by Indians gathered from the various Western Reservations and from Alaska. Some had come as infants and grew to manhood there, never going home, never knowing any other life. Archilde was there from his tenth to his fourteenth year, and of that period the only days he remembered with any happiness were those he had spent with Mr. Duffield.

Mr. Duffield was the man in charge of the printing shop, but it seemed that he wasn't especially interested in printing. At that time the Government paid a salary to a bandmaster, a ladylike old man with a white mustache who got pleasure out of marching his corps about; and there was no provision for teaching music as a pure study. If the Indian boys wished to make a big horn bellow, the Government would pay for it, but that was as far as it would go. That was where Mr. Duffield found his opportunity. He was a musician by nature and a printer by accident. If he took an interest in a boy and if the boy showed any musical ability, he had the protégé enrolled in the printing department and gave him music lessons. He wasn't paid for this—a small matter.

When Archilde first met Mr. Duffield he was working as an orderly in the administration building, a three-story building smelling of mucilage and varnished furniture and the oil-soaked sawdust which was spread on the floors at sweeping time. The superintendent's office occupied the first two floors, and the top story was given over to the printing department.

Up there every morning the printing press made a sound like galloping horses, but in afternoon quiet there was music; sometimes a piano, but more often a violin. Nothing charming was ever played. It was always ladder climbing, going up and coming down again. Simple as it was, it fascinated Archilde. His blood froze and thawed again just listening to a violin go from a growl to a scream.

He soon got into the habit of climbing to the top floor to listen to the music. The upper hall was dark and he could sit in the shadows without being observed. When Mr. Snodgrass, the superintendent, rang —as he would do if he had not gone to sleep—Archilde would slide down the banister and not be heard on the steps.

Late one afternoon, as the sun drove through autumn mist, Mr. Duffield opened his door to dismiss a student and had the startling experience of seeing a small boy fall in on him, then bound for the stairway.

"Here! Here!" His voice was arresting but not stern.

Archilde came into the lamplight to explain, after prodding, that he had fallen asleep while the music played.

The teacher looked amused as he scanned his visitor with a downward side glance.

"How did you get here? Where do you belong?"

"Downstairs."

"Downstairs? Ah, yes, the orderly. Mr. Snodgrass must be looking for you. He'll probably skin you for letting him oversleep. Better run! But what were you doing up here? Looking for some sleep yourself?"

"I didn't mean to go to sleep! I came to hear the music! Honest, that's all!"

Mr. Duffield laughed and bent a little downward, barely touching Archilde's shoulder with his dismissing hand.

"I'll speak to Mr. Snodgrass. Now run down to him."

He did not mention what he meant to say to the superintendent and Archilde went away with the simple but joyous feeling that the printer meant to keep him from a skinning.

He got the skinning, then and there, for he ran into Mr. Snodgrass in the act of putting on his hat, in the mood of a thunder storm undischarged of its fire. Archilde's coming in on tiptoe was the necessary spark.

"You little sneak! You lazybones! You numbskull! Damme! Where've you been? What d'you mean turning up at this hour? I've broken my damned bell thumping for you! The office has been turned inside out! And here you come, pussyfooting!"

He pulled his left ear, then his right ear, rapped

his head with his knuckles, jerked him from place to place, slapped his hands down when he lifted them as a shield, pinched his arms—and continued his vociferation.

Mr. Duffield did not interfere. Evidently he had closed his door and heard nothing. Archilde realized that he had been too eager to accept words without questioning their meaning. He had been betrayed by his own simplicity. The tears began to flow, and Mr. Snodgrass, feeling that he had accomplished his purpose, left off pummeling and began to adjust his starched cuffs and his cravat.

"You may go. But mind that you're on time in the morning, or I'll give you a real thrashing!"

Archilde went away, oblivious of the superintendent, thinking only of how foolish he had been.

Two days later, on Saturday, he was playing on the lawn in front of the office. The grass had just been cut and he had rigged up a miniature haystacker out of bent wire and string, and with this device had made a haystack several feet long.

The orderly bell rang, and in his eagerness to present himself he stumbled into his handiwork, wrecking the effort of several hours.

Mr. Snodgrass was surprisingly temperate in his speech. Instead of thumping out an order, he began to offer advice.

"Always take an interest in your work. No matter how much you dislike a job, or how unimportant it seems to you, if it is your job, do it with a will and to

the best of your ability. That is the way to make yourself valuable and to win success. I wasn't as fortunate
as you. I was twenty years old before an old teacher
gave me the advice I'm giving you now. But I took it
to heart and it's been my motto ever since—work with
a will. That's how I might put it."

This continued for fifteen minutes. Archilde took
it first on one foot and then on the other, feeling all
the time that he would surely catch hell after such a
long-winded start. Finally, when he had had his fill
of words, Mr. Snodgrass sighed.

"I am transferring you from office duty reluctantly,
I must say. Except for some occasional annoyance,
your going off to take a nap (Did he wink? Archilde
wondered) and such notions, you've been a useful
orderly. That's more than I can say for most I've had."

The next words were uttered in the same matter-
of-fact tone, but they shot through Archilde with the
effect of a swallow of whisky (of which he had had
samples before then).

"I am assigning you to Mr. Duffield's office upstairs. He seems to be interested in you. You had better see him now and find out what he wants you to do.
On Monday you will report to him."

No more was said, or, if anything more, Archilde
did not hear. The alcoholic words had set the pictures
of his mind to spinning. He grinned and blushed and
edged away.

So he began an existence which the Government

had not contemplated for its Indian students, and which it would have considered an extravagance had it learned of it. He was listed as a printer's apprentice, but he learned next to nothing about printing. With the other boys he studied music, and on Sunday afternoons drank tea and ate sweet biscuits which Mr. Duffield had sent out from Boston. (He was a native Bostonian and had never got away from it.) It was a strange romantic custom to adopt, this drinking tea of a Sunday afternoon, and there were other strange but wonderful things in the top-floor world.

Archilde had almost two years of that. Duffield demanded loyalty and effort, and if he didn't get enough of either he let a boy go quickly. He might have become friendly with the boy, and even after turning him loose would have him around at tea time on Sunday, but he would not have him as a student. He was kind but never indulgent, and he rarely sounded the praise of anyone. A pat on the shoulder was the highest reward most of the boys got, and they worked to get that.

On leaving school his students scattered like white ash of a camp fire caught up by a sudden wind. Only a few of the several dozen he had taught continued in the direction he had given them. Among those few were some older boys who had played as a quartette at the Sunday teas. They organized an Indian String Quartette which won something of a reputation in Pacific Coast cities. Archilde knew them later, and though there was no doubt of their success, something had gone wrong with them and even they had lost the track. He heard nothing of any of the others.

Once Archilde got started telling about his music teacher he seemed ready to go on forever. Father Grepilloux understood him.

"Tell me, Archilde, wasn't he the first grown person to make a friend of you?"

It was true. After a moment of thinking Archilde realized that it was so. Mr. Duffield had never abused him, had taken no advantage of him; instead, he had treated him with adult consideration free of treacle.

"So I thought. You learned something which you ought to remember if you teach boys some time, or have boys of your own. Give friendliness. It's the best teacher—

"Well, well. About your music. You've gone much farther than I had supposed. Even so, I think Father Cristadore can help you. You have to decide. Do you want to study music?"

"Yes, sure, Father! Only—"

"Only you were planning to go away to study? Is that it?"

"Yes, I was. I worked through harvest but I've been thinking I'd go now. You see, there isn't the kind of life I want here—"

In the end they came to an understanding. Father Grepilloux would not try to persuade him to stay against his wishes, if at any time he decided to go, and in return Archilde agreed to remain for a few months, perhaps until spring, until after Easter.

"If you give us a chance, Archilde, perhaps we can help you more than you realize now." The "we" was left ambiguous but Archilde did not notice it.

In Father Grepilloux's mind, the story of Archilde Leon was placing itself against the story of Big Paul. One's mortal vision was limited, one could guess wrong, but here seemed to be the promise of victory after a long wait. Big Paul should also have had his victory, and might have had it if he had come later. Instead, he had been sacrificed to that chaos and lawlessness which had followed the breakdown of the old ways of life. The interval of waiting had been long, but perhaps it was ended. This boy might be the promise of the new day—

The priest had listened carefully, with these thoughts running through his mind. He said nothing about it, of course.

As for Archilde, he went home and took his clothes out of the waiting suitcase. When, he wondered, would he pack his suitcase for the last time?

Chapter Ten

FATHER CRISTADORE was a pleasant man who smiled a lot, and somehow he did not seem religious. He did not have a religious face, which should be rather long and rather thin and rather sad. Father Cristadore had a perfectly round face and his cheeks were two round red apples. He did not mind laughing if something amused him. He had quick movements and an *outward* way of doing things. His cassock seemed to be in the way of his free stride.

Archilde wanted to ask him why he was a priest, but he was afraid it was one of those questions that wouldn't get a satisfactory answer. There were questions like that, he had discovered. So he contented himself with watching Father Cristadore.

Twice a week they played together in church, the priest at the piano; and on other days Archilde practiced alone in the room they had given him. He enjoyed playing in the choir loft, with the sweep of the high, unpillared nave before him. The violin sounded richer when its tone was free to expand.

"In the violin tone is everything, and you make the tone with the bow. Evidently you know something about that. Yes, you have the idea. In time you may do it very well. Just keep your mind on the bow, on the wrist. Remember! The wrist is always up. . . ."

That was the priest's full range of instruction. He had learned those fundamentals at some time, and though he knew little more about the violin, he was full of music.

"Well, let's do it just once more," he would urge when they had already gone beyond the hour of practice. And when Archilde paused for a moment's rest the priest kept his fingers going, sometimes turning into other music. He had too little opportunity to devote to music. When he could no longer postpone the duties awaiting him he would close the piano with a sigh.

"We had a good practice. Next time I'll show you a better way to finger one of those passages." When the next session came Archilde would remind him of the promised instruction, but the priest would have forgotten.

"Keep your mind on the bow. That is important. Fingering is only a matter of convenience." And he would smile.

It wasn't really studying music; there were no problems set, no special exercises, but the priest had a good ear for pitch. He counted meticulously. Archilde enjoyed himself.

These visits to the church awakened old images that lay at the beginning of life. They were disturbing, half-fearful. It required effort to face them and be self-possessed.

The church! In the beginning, everything. One re-

membered early mass in winter; arising from bed,
washing in freezing water, then marching, half asleep,
in a column of silent boys, the snow whipping into
one's face, stinging one's eyes; arriving in the frigid
church where the air, like one's body, seemed too
stiff to move; the march to the altar in the dim lamplight, finger-tips together, eyes downcast. That had
been all there was to life. One lived in the perpetual
tyranny of the life-everlasting.

The connections between images were gone and
Archilde could not account for the persistence of certain mind-pictures. If he still visualized an old cosmo-
graph showing the righteous ascending into heaven
to join the Father Almighty, while the damned fell
into the flames of hell, he also recalled scenes of un-
orthodoxy, what might have been labeled the First
False Steps. It was curious and unaccountable, how
an incident, of no importance in itself, lodged unnoticed in the mind, took root, sent out branches; and
in proper season the sweet or bitter taste of its fruit
flavored everything.

When he recalled, for instance, the Punch and Judy
shows which old Father Etienne (now dead) performed
for the boys, it was to remember the resentment which
he had learned to feel. In everything else he had been
docile toward his pious teachers, but in that they had
over-reached themselves.

He could not remember the story of the puppet
show clearly, but it was ominous in its morality. It
had to do with a Sinner who went on sinning and

sinning and never repenting, until finally he was hit on the head by Satan and dragged off to Hell. It was wonderful to watch the dolls, dressed like real people, as they bowed to each other and walked about; but the final scene between Satan and the Sinner always had been upsetting. The Sinner was a happy person, part of his sinning was his happy disposition, his singing and carousing with Merry Companions, and when Satan hit him on the head, to everyone's amusement, Archilde felt wronged; it was not amusing.

A seed as minute as that had been capable of splitting the rock of devotion. It set one to worrying over meanings. One looked askance at the unsuspecting Father Etienne when he was not indulging in his puppetry; one wondered if he were cruel, if he would hit a real sinner on the head. One went to sleep thinking about it and dreamt of sacrilegious puppets as large as men walking around and hitting priests on the head.

There had been another occasion, he now recalled, which had given rise to disturbing thoughts and dreams.

He remembered the day clearly, for apparently it had had a profound effect on him. The students were playing in the school yard late one afternoon, just before the supper hour. The sky was clear except for a single cloud, resembling at first a puff of smoke, which had drifted directly above the yard. Its contour changed, becoming elongated and flattened, and finally, by curious coincidence, it assumed the form of a cross—in the reflection of the setting sun, a flaming cross.

The prefect was the first to observe the curiosity and it put him into a sort of ecstasy. He ran about the yard, shouting and clapping his hands, and collecting the boys in a group in the center of the yard.

"The Sign! The Sign!" he shouted. His face was flushed and his eyes gave off flashing lights—Archilde did not forget them.

"The Sign! Kneel and pray!"

The boys knelt and prayed, some of them frightened and on the point of crying. They knew what the Sign signified—it was to announce the Second Coming of Christ, when the world was to perish in flames!

As Archilde followed the prayers, he watched the cloud, moving slightly so as to place himself behind a larger boy. Before he knew it, his entire attention was on the apparition. The others knelt with bowed heads, ready to be struck down.

He saw the horizontal bar of the cross melt into the blue and for a moment longer an irregular streak of crimson was all that remained. Then the entire structure became woolly, leaving here and there bits of mist touched by the red hues of the evening sun. That was all.

It was not the disappearance of the threatening symbol which freed him from the priest's dark mood, but something else. At the very instant that the cross seemed to burn most brightly, a bird flew across it. Actually the bird was much lower, but it appeared

almost to touch the cloud. It flew past and returned
several times before finally disappearing—and what
seized Archilde's imagination was the bird's uncon-
cernedness. It recognized no "Sign." His spirit lightened. He felt himself fly with the bird. When he
looked at the priest again he saw in him only darkness
and heaviness of spirit. He would never feel at ease
around the prefect after that; and he would never fear
him. There would be something of scorn in his
thoughts.

So, after years, he had returned to the beginning
of life, and first of all it was a shock to discover that
as he walked through familiar dark halls with their
niches of colored statuettes and their odor of resinous
incense he felt quivers of fear. It was as nothing compared to what he had felt as a boy of six or seven, but
it was a shock just the same to one becoming a man.
And when he left the dark halls and entered the empty
and silent church his heart quickened even more
disturbingly. The first time or two he stayed no
longer than was necessary and did not breathe easily
until he was on his way homeward.

But this did not continue. After all, he was growing
into manhood. A boy's fears had nothing to do with
him. And he was curious.

He was accustomed to the church as a kind of thea-
ter of movement and ceremony, but now that he saw
it as an empty room he felt that he must know more
about it. It was like having been frightened by a
strange object at night and then going forth by day-

light to examine the meaningless bogy, not yet convinced that it was unreal.

While the altar light burned there was a Presence there. He had been taught to believe that. But was it true? The thing about curiosity was that it couldn't be ignored or forgotten. It repeated, time after time, was some Being hovering there? He would have to find out.

He stayed behind when Father Cristadore got up to leave the choir loft, and for an excuse would go to one of the benches and begin to pray. When the heavy door thundered into place behind the departing priest, he would remain kneeling. The first time he did not stir from that position until, thoroughly chilled, he got up to go home. A reaction set in then and real determination was born of it. He won control of himself.

On the next occasion he dared to examine the temperal paintings on the walls—St. Michael with his spear at the demon's throat and hell-fire gleaming; the Nativity; the Flight into Egypt, and many others. From a distance these pictures glowed with color, but when he came close and saw how flat the effect was, it disappointed him. He could not understand the trick, for he had expected close inspection to give a richer satisfaction. His curiosity grew riper. His courage grew with it.

There were moments of confusion. The first time he crossed the center aisle without genuflecting toward the altar, he turned cold, when he realized what he had done. Had he been seen? Was there anyone there to resent his action? The mood passed in a moment and he went on.

He was spurred on by his desire to know. Questions had to be answered. He went beyond the altar railing. He examined the high-backed throne of carved wood and red plush on which the visiting bishop sat during confirmation services. He walked up to the altar itself. He mounted the three carpeted steps and stood where the priests stood during Mass, and he was quaking. Now he would learn whether the place had an unseen protector!

Nothing happened. The adventure fell flat.

What he saw next destroyed one of the last links connecting him with his boyhood, his beginnings. He had gone to look at the rear of the altar, and there he was held spellbound. Unpainted timbers, dust, an accumulation of old candle snuffers, flower vases, rags—he had actually been afraid of those things! He stood motionless while he tried to reconcile his memory of the rich ceremony which went on before the altar with the shabbiness which he now saw. In the effort the simple faith of childhood died quietly.

He had to see the sacristy then. Nothing awed him any longer. He wanted to look closely at a small oil painting which had hung there when he used to serve at Mass. It had been too high for a small boy to see it clearly and had teased his imagination.

The subject was Christ driving out the money changers, a small picture, full of faces and half-revealed figures. He tried to examine it in its hanging position but the light was poor and details were obscured by a coating of dust. He grasped the picture, intending to carry it to a window, when something fearful happened. A bat fell from behind the frame. It came alive and began to fly madly around his head. Its wing touched him on one of its passages.

There was no more to it than that, but it swept him back into childhood—when the bat was a symbol of the devil, one of the many forms in which he might appear. He almost dropped the picture. For the moment he could not reason at all. He hurried into the church, paused to genuflect at the altar, and was out in the daylight of late afternoon before he grew calm again. Then he felt foolish.

It was inexplicable, but the dread which had been instilled into the mind of the child never quite disappeared from the mind of the grown man. One had only to go into the daylight to realize how preposterous such things were.

Chapter Eleven

MAX did not know what to make of Archilde. He stared off across the field, forgetting half the time to watch the men he had at work.

What he had hoped for had come about, or seemed on the point of coming about, and he could not make up his mind whether to believe it or not. He went to Father Grepilloux and the puzzle was so plainly written on his face that the priest was bound to express sly amusement.

"What is this, Leon? You get what you pray for—and you can't decide to accept it!"

Max frowned. "It's not so simple. Do people change overnight? Have you ever known boy, man or woman to get up one morning and from then on be a new person?"

"But who has done that?"

"Well, isn't it that way with Archilde? Suddenly he is interested in music, he works for me, he is willing to study. How is it? He wasn't that way before."

"Don't be too sure! Perhaps we didn't know him."

But even when the Spaniard had been told many things about his son he still had his misgivings. He made it clear that he didn't intend to be taken in by appearances.

"Do you know what," the priest remarked after some thought, "I have been thinking that this Archilde is the answer we were looking for one day. You remember I told you the story of Big Paul, and we were asking ourselves how it had happened that certain bad ones had come among us and spoiled the fruit. We could not see how it would end. Our vision was short, as it always is. It was inevitable that a new age would come. It is beginning now. And your boy is standing there where the road divides. He belongs to a new time. He may not stay in this valley, and it makes no difference whether he does or not; it is what he makes of himself that will count. It will be felt by all."

Max could hardly believe it. He said nothing at once, only stared. Finally he murmured: "You think so? You think he has—ability?"

"There's no question of it. He has a musical gift, and he also draws well for an untrained hand. We can't teach him much here. Father Cristadore will give him what he can, but we have no one who can draw. Father Michaud, who painted those wonderful frescoes in the church, should be with us, then your boy could have had a fine start. We'll do what we can, but in another year you must send him away. You have the means, send him to Europe, send him to Rome and Paris. That would make you happy, I'm sure."

It is asking too much when a man is required to close the book of the past, to forget that it had ever been. Max floundered. He could not have said what he was feeling. It was both joy and fear—fear that what he was trying to understand was an illusion.

Father Grepilloux interpreted his frowning silence in those terms. He expostulated mildly: "If you continue asking yourself questions, you'll never have the answer you wish. Doubt breeds doubt and the mind can't prevail against it. The only way is to give your faith to the boy."

Max had not realized it before, but now he saw that Father Grepilloux was weary. And then it came over him suddenly that the priest was an aged man, well into his eighties, and should not have another man's troubles imposed upon him. It was such a shock to think that he had not realized this sooner that he was speechless for a moment.

Then when he begged forgiveness the priest was distressed. They both felt in the wrong and both apologized, and Max went away calling himself a fool.

"Yes," he said to himself, "Father Grepilloux is a very old man—and is he right about Archilde?"

When he arrived at the ranch he went at once to his room and wrote to the Indian agent, Horace Parker, and to his lawyer. He explained that he wished to rewrite his will. When he had taken that step he imagined that he already felt easier in spirit.

It was the beginning of September. Archilde was spending most of his time at the St. Xavier Mission, and now it came time for Agnes' little boys to return to school at the Mission. All summer long they had done nothing but ride the calves in the pasture, hunt and fish, and listen to their grandmother's stories. Now, all that free life had to end.

To get them to school, they had first to be captured. There were no preparations, no buying of clothes, and no talk about what was coming. If they had suspected anything they would have disappeared like scared rabbits and there would be no finding them again. The many tepees of their grandmother's family were widely scattered, and any one of them would provide shelter; or they might hide in the mountains like horse thieves.

Max took them riding in his blue automobile occasionally, and now he made a point, a week before school time, to drive them to St. Xavier and far beyond, even as far as the Big River. And so when it was time for school he played them a trick.

At breakfast he said nothing. He walked into the yard, and still he said nothing. He opened the door of the shed and backed the blue automobile into the yard. The boys were watching him from the kitchen door. Then he shouted.

"You, Mike and Narce, want a ride?"

They almost tore the screen door loose in getting out.

"Sure! Take us to the Big River again!"

"Naw, take us to the Lake!"

Max drove rapidly into St. Xavier and dashed through the narrow lane leading to the Mission. The boys looked at each other. Then he turned a corner short and stopped within the cobbled yard.

They didn't wait to open the car door but scrambled over the side and dashed about looking for the gate, but it had been closed behind them. They were like animals brought to the zoo.

Max did not enjoy playing that trick, but words would have done no good.

"Archilde is around here, somewhere. I'll tell him to come see you." It was the only thing he could think of that might cheer them.

"Big liar!" Mike growled. He was trying not to cry, and just when it looked as if he would, he turned upon Narcisse, who was bigger by a head, and began to fight him. They were tangled in a knot in a minute and the prefect came running to separate them.

After supper that night Max went into the kitchen to talk to Agnes. He had a mild affection for her, though he rarely stopped to exchange a word. She kept his house in order, not too carefully, and never asked for anything. Apart from her marriage, she had never done anything either stupid or clever. Max had cursed her for marrying a full-blood, but after her husband was killed he ceased speaking harshly to her. Now he began to appreciate her stolid loyalty and his attitude gradually softened toward her.

He told her that he had got the boys to school and then he saw that she had been weeping over them. It brought him up short. She did not complain; she said nothing at all; but her silence was accusing. It could not be answered. Lamely, he tried another approach.

"You must go see them, let them know we don't forget. Tell me when you go and I'll drive you in my car."

At that Agnes stirred. "I'll go in the buggy." Her voice could hardly be heard.

"Sure, go in the buggy, then." This much he had learned of his strange family, that it did no good to coax them against their feelings. "But bring them something to eat, or a jackknife, maybe. It's a hard thing for them to be there, but if it's to do them good, then we should keep them happy."

He walked out into the darkness. A rising wind tossed pine tops in slow sweeps across the sky. He passed through the barnyard and found a fence post to lean against. And there he asked himself, what good would come of tricking those boys and dragging them in ways they didn't want to go?

He could not explain it, but he had taken to wondering about his grandsons. He felt that somewhere within their mysterious natures was an inner core of responsiveness, and if possible it should be reached. Nothing was accomplished with the whip, he had seen that; but friendliness, now, seemed to work miracles. Too bad he had had to wait until he was an old man to learn that.

Chapter Twelve

As THE autumn advanced Archilde felt himself grow
close to his mother. There had been times in recent
years when he had felt ashamed of her, when he could
not bear to be near her. The worst of that phase had
passed several years before, in his last year of high
school, and more recently he had not taken it so seriously; he tolerated her and laughed at some of the
cruder of her ideas about the world. The feast she had
given in his honor, which he had attended reluctantly,
really started him on a new train of thought regard-
ing not only his mother but all the old people. He had
really understood their struggle as it was told that
night; he was moved by it. Perhaps the old people had
nothing, and perhaps they were despised, but it did
not seem deserved. He found himself thinking about
them rather often, he kept wondering about their
lives.

He went to his mother's cabin almost every day
when he came home from the Mission and they would
sit together while he smoked a cigarette. Sometimes
the only words they uttered were "Hello," "It was
warm today," and "Well, I play the fiddle every day
now." They got along very well.

He got along better with Max too. They weren't

stiff and suspicious before each other, as they had been in past years. And this brought a question to Archilde's mind which would never have occurred to him if he and his father had gone on in the old way.

He would sit down with his mother now, and while he smoked he would look at her and wonder why she lived in the cabin by herself and would not move into the big house. He would not ask her that question, nor would he ask it of Max; but he asked it of himself and tried to answer it by looking at his mother. What had happened between them that should keep them so far apart? The old lady, he knew, had a good heart. Of Max he was not so sure, but he had begun to think that what Agnes had once said of him was true—that he bit only those who bit him. Then how could it be? That the old lady had harmed Max? That wasn't likely. More likely he had done her some wrong, since she had no protection. Even so, he could not believe that Max meant it or even knew of it. There must be a mistake. He could go no further in his understanding. Every day when he sat down with his mother he thought these questions and looked for the answer.

His mother wanted to go hunting. She had said so at the end of summer, after harvesting, and she did not cease referring to it. Sometimes her references were quite veiled and indirect.

"My friends are old," she would say. "They sit at home and if I ask them to go some place they speak of their pains. Maybe in another year—who knows." And from that he understood her desire to go into the mountains again and smell fresh venison cooking. But he wouldn't offer to go with her.

"Before long snow will fall and that will be another year gone. When an old woman has only a few years left each one counts. It is too bad when an old woman is useless and they won't give her a thought."

Finally he relented and said he would take her hunting. He knew he should not do it. He had a feeling about it which he could not explain. But that wasn't enough to withstand his mother's desire.

When Max heard of it he stared in amazement. What? The old lady go hunting? At her age? Archilde explained his mother's feelings as best he could, and tried to explain why he did not wish to refuse her. Max frowned. The idea seemed unreasonable, even foolish, but he did not know how much Archilde was of his own mind. He saw to it that they were well equipped. It was the beginning of October and snow would fall before they got out of the mountains.

As Archilde left Max standing in the yard and rode away with the old lady, both were thinking: "Here is a piece of foolishness! This should not be." But the horses went forward, and presently Archilde put his reluctance behind him.

He swayed with the lazy movements of his horse, looking up ocasionally to observe the trail as it twisted between boulders or skirted a ridge. Undergrowth of mountain maple and wild cherry brushed his side. This was how it would have seemed years ago, crossing the mountains to hunt buffalo. Nothing would have been much different. He would have kept his eyes open; there might be game and there might be Blackfeet. He would have felt the same sway of his horse; the sun would have given no less warmth; there would have been the same aspect of tree and rock and mountain. But it was different. The mountains were empty of life, that was the difference. This ride with his mother was no more than a pleasure trip; that was the difference. If they returned without fresh meat, no one would worry; at home there were canned peas, potatoes in the cellar, and meat could be had at the butcher's; that was the difference.

He could not tell what his mother was thinking. She said nothing. As she rode along she seemed to look nowhere. How could she enjoy the trip, perhaps her last, if she looked at nothing? Then he remembered that her eyes were weak and that she could not hear well—perhaps she just smelled it all!

Game was scarce. After two days of riding they had not seen so much as a deer track. The mountains indeed were empty. If any creatures existed there they had gone into the blackest bowels of the mountain. The open valleys beyond were too full of sound and rushing life for such things as fed on solitude. Archilde and his mother had to ride on and on, trying to go backward in time rather than onward in mountain fastness.

Then unexpected game broke cover—unexpected and not quite pleasant. Archilde riding along in advance, looked up suddenly when he saw a horse and rider standing in the trail. For a moment he did not recognize the intruder. Finally he knew him without doubt, and felt chilled.

It was Sheriff Quigley, the man whose name Archilde had invoked the night he tried to scare Louis into better sense. It was a name that could frighten most Indians, for the Sheriff had a reputation. It seemed that every time an Indian left the Reservation he almost certainly ran into the Sheriff and had to give an account of himself. Usually, if he saw the Sheriff first, he didn't stop for an explanation but simply whirled about and left a trail of dust behind.

He sat his horse, an imperturbable rock of flesh, his flop-brimmed hat concealing the upper part of his face, his unbuttoned vest sagging with the weight of his badge of office. He was a sheriff out of the Old West. He knew the type—he had read of those hard-riding, quick-shooting dispensers of peace, he had heard stories about them—and he was intent on being all of them in himself. He had made the part his own. So he sat, waiting.

As he came up to the Sheriff, Archilde halted for the customary time-passing when people meet in the mountains.

"We're looking for game. See anything?" Archilde felt himself being scrutinized by eyes that possibly suspected him of the whole calendar of crimes.

The Sheriff only grunted, as if game-hunting were beneath the notice of anyone who enjoyed *his* kind of hunting.

"I'm looking for a horse thief. Don't suppose you saw one?"

This was said with a hard, humorless grin. The Sheriff enjoyed mentioning things that, like death, made people uncomfortably aware of life's threats.

Archilde guessed at once that the Sheriff was looking for Louis, who must be somewhere in these mountains, and he wanted to get away before he was asked to identify himself. He was not at all sure that he wasn't known and recognized. He hardly dared look up. As it happened, he and the old lady were allowed to proceed without being questioned and only after he had passed a mile or more beyond did he begin to breathe regularly. A sinister man, that Sheriff Quigley. Archilde hoped he would never have to submit to his official ministering.

A day later they made camp in an open park between high mountains. Archilde had found deer tracks in a nearby swamp, and while he set out to look over the ground the old lady went to a nearby creek to catch fish for their evening meal. When he returned she had the meal ready.

"They come in the early morning, no doubt. In the afternoon they're on the ridges," he said of the deer.

The old lady scarcely heard.

The fish tasted fatter up here in the mountains, she was thinking. She smacked her sunken lips. It was good to be out of her cramped cabin.

Just before dark the horses jerked their heads erect and gazed down the trail over which they had come. A mare whinnied and was answered in the distance. A rider was approaching. It was Louis, evidently unaware that Dave Quigley was in those same mountains.

"I saw you come up this way yesterday," he told them. He pulled the saddle off his horse and made himself at home.

The old lady grumbled and set about cooking a large fish she had saved for breakfast. "When his belly is empty he comes!"

Archilde told him of meeting the Sheriff but Louis made out to be unconcerned. He went on eating. "What's he got on me? Nothing. I turned those horses loose, long ago. I been staying up here because I like it."

Archilde studied his boastful brother and wondered what the truth of the matter was. It was probably true that he had turned the horses loose— possibly because he was afraid to go through with it. Horse stealing was no longer an easy exploit, as anybody who knew what was going on in the world was sure to realize. Even Louis, child that he was, probably had got the sense of it at last. Of course he had to keep up his front.

"The flies chased 'em and I couldn't hold 'em here after my partner quit. If you'd helped me, like I told you, we could of had some easy money by now."

He was a child talking.

"Eat your fish!" The old lady disliked his brag-ging. "In the morning go with Archilde and help get some deer. He knows where they come to drink."

"I'll go alone. Louis is no hunter. His feet get tangled in the brush and he falls down."

Louis glared.

The tepee was a small one and there would have been no room in it for Louis, even if he had been willing to share it. And he wasn't. He didn't care to sleep like a squaw, he declared. He rolled up in a blanket by the fire.

The sky was overladen with stars. If you looked closely there were stars in the grass as well—dew turned to ice on the tips of grass blades. Archilde did not sleep at once. He heard the horses breathing and moaning in their sleep. They had lain down in a close group. Owls called to each other. This was as it would have been. Certainly the night had not changed with the years. . . . Then there was a shift of images in his mind. He saw the gleaming lights of a city, any city, with people moving, in the street, in large rooms— light and sound and smell of a different world. As soon as he thought of that he cared not what the mountains were like, either now or long ago. It came over him in a surge. This, his home, was a strange country.

The light was just breaking over the mountain tops as he selected a hiding place. A damp fern slapped his face and he shivered. From his position he had a full view of the watering hole, a wide, sandy opening in the brush-choked stream.

The trees against the gray sky seemed to be marching up and down the ridge before him. A flicker of sunlight picked out a high rock, and in an instant everything came to life. Birds fluttered their wings and made a few trial calls. Then a full song burst forth. The first squirrel began to chatter in the high branches of a yellow pine.

At the same moment a full grown buck appeared at the head of the trail and took in the scene. His nose was in the air, his nostrils dilated. Other heads appeared behind him. None would advance until the leader felt at ease.

Archilde had his rifle trained on the buck's wide chest. Peering over the sights, he saw a patch of white.

An inexplicable thing happened to him. He could not shoot. He looked in wonder at the thin-legged, nervous creatures. They had filed down the trail and stood knee deep in water. When they lifted their heads from drinking their black muzzles dripped.

Hunting stories had always excited him, giving him a feeling that he would like to be envied for his good shooting and his hunting sense. But it was clear that he had not understood himself, he had not understood about killing. The excitement was in matching one's wits against animal cunning. The excitement was in-increased when a man kept himself from starving by his hunting skill. But lying in wait and killing, when no one's living depended on it, there was no excitement in that. Now he understood it.

He remembered then that he would have to give his mother a plausible story. It wouldn't do to say that he had been mistaken about the deer coming there to drink. He didn't want to lose credit for being that much of a hunter. It would be bad enough to say that he had missed. Oh, well—

He pointed the gun against the mountainside and pulled the trigger. When he opened his eyes the deer were gone and he could still hear the shot echoing against the mountain. The water was muddy and the bank of the creek was wet where the deer had splashed ashore. His mind was at rest about the fact of his failure as a hunter.

On the way to camp he met his mother. She was coming quickly, a short knife in her hand. "Did you pick a fat one?" she asked at once.

He could not explain it, but he felt like a fool. He frowned and walked on.

In camp, he drank his cup of coffee slowly. His mother gave him bread smeared with bacon grease. She was still bewildered, as he could tell.

"Something scared them just as they came to the water. I waited too long, and when I shot there was nothing but air." The explanation sounded weak.

"A young man waits for a better shot and hits nothing. An old man makes the best of it and gets his meat." It was her way of teaching a lesson by talking in generalities.

"When the smoke clears away the women are still talking." He knew how to respond in her style. He felt satisfied again. It was even amusing to recall how suddenly those creatures had vanished.

At that moment a rifle cracked and the sound seemed to fly through the air above their heads.

"I guess Louis's shooting squirrels." Archilde poured another cup of coffee and drank it standing up.

"He'll not miss his shot," the old lady grumbled reproachfully. It pained her that her best son had come empty-handed.

Archilde did not respond. He surveyed the mountainside and the sky. Clouds were coming up quickly and the brilliance of the heavens at sunrise was already dulled. The wind was turning sharper and Archilde inclined his head and breathed deeply.

"I smell snow," he said.

"Have you been asleep? It was in the wind last night. It will come before night." He was amazed by the sharpness of her perceptions—she who was near blind and near deaf. He with all his senses was dull by comparison.

Louis came out of the brush at that moment. He carried a small deer across his shoulders.

"Here, old woman, is meat. Where's your deer?" he bellowed at his brother.

Archilde smiled. "Couldn't you find a smaller one? That won't make a mouthful for a man like you, and you'll never stretch its hide to make moccasins for such feet."

Louis was enraged. "I suppose you shot a fifteen-year old buck like a God-damned white man. That's tender meat, that, a yearling doe. Well, show me yours!"

"What do you care what he shot!" the old lady grumbled. "You pick a quarrel with everybody."

Archilde thought of having some fun with his slow-thinking brother. "If you want to see my deer, it's up the creek by those willows, hanging to cool." He pointed to a willow grove about half a mile away.

Louis fell into the trap. He turned and was on the point of starting off to see for himself when there was an interruption, not only to that little game, but to the entire scheme of life for those three.

A stranger had ridden into camp. He had come up the trail, unobserved, and appeared before them with ghostlike unaccountableness. Archilde thought immediately of the ubiquitous Dave Quigley. If he were anywhere within thirty miles, you could not be sure of being free of him. It was not the Sheriff, but it was another arm of the law—a game warden. The woods seemed to be full of guardians of the peace.

"I heard some shootin' and thought I'd see who was up this way. I see you got something there." He was a slow-speaking, gray-eyed, unexpectedly pleasant sort of man—on the surface at least. Archilde felt at ease, though he could see that Louis and the old lady were nervous. The Law was a threatening symbol. He would have to speak for them.

"We just shot a small deer," he explained.

"I shot it!" Louis' hot head came to the fore.

"Oh, you did?" The game warden had dismounted. He gave Louis a sharp, examining look as he went toward the deer. "You've got a doe here. You know there's a law against killing female deer, don't you?" The voice was still mild and slow.

Louis' eyes began to shift quickly from one object to another. He was looking for the nearest point of brush.

Archilde spoke for his brother. "We're Indians, and we're free of game laws."

"I guess I'd know you was Indians." The voice turned sharper. "But far's I know there's no exemption on female deer."

Archilde pretended to be sure of his ground, though he really knew nothing about it. At some time or the other he had heard the game laws discussed. "Indians are free from all game laws by special treaty."

"Well, that's a point I'll let the judge settle. I'll take you out and you can talk to him about it." It was clear by now that there was no leniency in the voice.

"How many more did you get?" was the next question.

"This is all."

"He lies!" Louis again interrupted. "There's one up the creek."

"Oh, there is! Suppose you go after it," he directed Archilde. "No monkey business! Go and bring it in."

Archilde protested that there was nothing there. The situation had grown baffling.

"I'm telling the truth. I was joking my brother a while ago and told him I'd shot a deer and left it up there by those willows. He was going to see for himself when you came."

"Oh, hell! Don't fool with me! Another doe, I suppose. Go and bring it in!"

"Well, see for yourself, then! We'll wait here."

The warden was losing his temper. They were not only lying to him but getting impudent. He swung into the saddle.

"You're under arrest, all of you! Get busy and break camp! Tell the squaw to clean out that deer and be careful how she cuts it open. Tell her!"

Louis and the old lady were talking heatedly in Salish which the warden didn't understand. He didn't know that Louis was frightened and wanted to dash for the woods, and that the old lady was calling him a fool. "Wipe your nose and get ready," she was saying. To the game officer it sounded menacing and he watched them closely.

Louis was almost black with his rage. He thought Archilde was lying about the deer he had killed in order to avoid blame. But he was ready to submit. It was clear to him even in his hot temper that it was useless to fight or try to run. The nearest brush was at some distance, and the warden was mounted and armed. He growled and looked fierce as he started to put his things together.

His rifle was leaning against a tree and it was the first thing he went for. He wasn't looking at the warden as he reached for it, but he was still talking in that rough voice of his. His fingers had scarcely closed on the rifle when there was a shattering explosion. Then the officer's voice:

"Damn you! Stand still, all of you! One more move like that and there'll be none left!" His horse reared and pranced about but he kept it under control and kept his gun leveled.

Louis had sunk to the ground, blood flowing from his mouth. The old lady screamed and threw her shawl over her head. Archilde was stupefied. He heard himself muttering,

"You fool! You've killed him!"

"Oh, I did! Well, what would he have done to me? I got him first, and damned lucky! And now you be God-damned careful what you do!"

"You're wrong! It's a mistake—" Explaining was useless. It only added to the stupid confusion.

The warden had dismounted. Plainly he was nervous. He carried his gun in his hand but he was not thinking of using it again. He went to examine Louis. He bent lower to listen for breathing.

There was no accounting for what happened next. Archilde saw only the final action, not what led up to it. He was near the warden, watching him stoop to examine Louis. Then he saw the officer bend at the knees. His face was twisted with pain. The old lady had hit him in the head with a hatchet.

The way he remembered the scene afterward, Louis was lying face upward with blood on his shirt front

He had been shot in the back of the head. The warden had plunged his face into the dirt and lay still. The old lady had covered her head again and was wailing for the dead. That was how he remembered it, and he could not explain how his mother had been able to move without being seen or heard. That was inexplicable.

Chapter Thirteen

"WE got to dig a hole!" Those were his first words, after a period of dazed silence.

"Not for Louis!" His mother stirred, looked up.

"Yes, for both! We can be hung for him just as well."

The old lady's thoughts flew this way and that. She could not let this thing be done. Never in her lifetime had people been buried in the old way. The Fathers had made a special ground and the dead who were not brought there were unhappy. Their souls were tortured. She could not let this happen to Louis. He was her son and some day she could hope to see him again, but only if she brought him to the ground prepared by the Fathers.

"Not for Louis!" Her voice turned to pleading.

Archilde had grown agitated. He was afraid now. He could see Dave Quigley riding in on them at any moment. Surely he was somewhere within the sound of gunfire! He looked for the hatchet which a moment before he had thrown away, and even tried to dig a hole by kicking the ground with his shoe. In the end he found the hatchet and succeeded in digging a shallow trench. Then the old lady crept over the ground and patted his leg. Her sorrowful voice reached his heart. He swore.

"It's three days to go! We can't carry him!"

"Tie him on my horse. I'll walk." No doubt she would have carried him if that had been the only way. He could not prevail against her superstitious dread, and there was a moment in which he felt painful hatred for her childish mentality. Why should she care where her horse-thief son was buried! But it was not a matter that could be reasoned. She was afraid and that was all. Her words, her soft voice left him helpless.

With the dry tepee poles he made a travois on which he tied his brother's corpse. He had wrapped him in blankets. The warden's stiffening body was buried in the trench, which he then concealed under a clever contrivement of old branches and stones.

It was just short of noon when they started off, and out of the thick sky snow began to fall. In a moment a twilight had fallen upon the world. Dave Quigley had not appeared—for that he was ready to fashion a God of the moment and thank him.

They rode through the mountains, the snow enfolding them, softening the strokes of their horses' hooves until they moved with the silence of ghosts. Darkness swallowed them and they wandered in the black belly of the night.

The old lady labored in the depths of a mountain of thought. Her life came before her eyes to perplex and sadden her. A son is part of your body and when a son dies you have to ask yourself: How is it that I am still here? Why do they take only part of me? Of Louis, she remembered that when he was still small he was the swiftest runner of all his fellows. And then when he grew taller and began to ride a horse he was like a bird. In those days he never went far. If she should call he would be there. She knew his eyes. Then he went to school to the Fathers, and there was a change. She could not understand why it was. He rode wild horses. He rode at night singing songs. She never saw his eyes again. He called her "Old Woman." It was: "Old Woman, give me to eat," or "Old Woman, a man stole my horse. Give me a horse." And she would learn that he had gambled his horse away. He drew a knife on a man, ripped him open, and for that he was almost sent to prison. Then he stole horses. Now he was dead. She knew the Fathers had not done it, but it started after he went to school. She could not understand it.

Her thoughts went further. She still remembered how the Fathers had said, in those first years, that the people would know great happiness; they had only to have water put on their heads. That had been done and more too. They told their sins and went to Mass; when the Bishop came they brought presents; on feast days they cleansed themselves and sang the praises of Christ the Savior—all that, and still the world grew no better. The sons stole horses and drew knives and the old people could see no hope.

So she rode with her thoughts.

Archilde, riding in the lead, felt his horse bunch

its feet and slide down the steep trail and watched the mound of snow between the horse's ears. The slipping sound of the poles behind his horse was like a great snake gliding along behind him, whispering as it came —whispering: "Sheriff Quigley! Sheriff Quigley!"

The snake would not let him forget what had happened. It whispered: "The road stood waiting. You had only to go. But you let them talk you into staying. Perhaps it is just what you deserve. If you had gone away you might not have lasted long, since you have such a soft head. Well, you can sit in jail now and think about it. It's the end of you."

The snake whispered such words all night long.

At midnight they stopped and made coffee. The old lady said nothing, though she brought wood and tended the fire. He fed the horses from a small bag of oats he had brought. When they had rested they rode on again. Toward morning he began to doze in the saddle, but sleeping or waking his thoughts were the same. He looked for Dave Quigley to be waiting on the trail somewhere ahead. The Sheriff had become a symbol of his dead hope. Life would go so far— and there would be the Sheriff waiting to end it.

They stopped again in the course of the day. The snow had turned to a fine powder but it fell without pause. Under the trees where they rested there was not a single sound. He fed the last of the oats but the horses were almost too weary to eat. They stood with dropping heads. After a scant meal and a rest of two hours the journey was resumed.

The daylight faded imperceptibly into night and they were still riding. The horses were playing out rapidly. Archilde had changed the travois to his mother's horse and back to his own several times. When they forded a stream he carried the frozen body across his saddle and shuddered.

At midnight they emerged from the mountains and were met by a piercing wind blowing from the prairie. The snow had ceased but the wind carried it along in stinging gusts. Archilde took to walking beside his floundering horse. He shouted back to the old lady but received no answer. She sat atop her horse like a bundle of rags.

They reached home after everyone had been in bed for hours. Max was the first to awaken when the dogs set up a terrific howling. He put on a heavy coat and came out, lantern in hand.

Archilde was so stiff with frost that he had difficulty in getting off his horse. He could not speak. The old lady fell in a heap in the snow.

Max held his lantern over the travois and tried to discover what was under the frozen canvas.

"Meat?" he asked in a genial tone. Then he held the light to Archilde's face and was shocked by the haggard look.

Achilde could not answer and to get out of the glare of the lantern went to his knees and attempted to undo the frozen mass. His fingers would not move, so he merely pointed.

"That's Louis. We found him yesterday, day before I guess. Somebody—shot—him." It was all he could think of saying.

Max's heart sank. Something was wrong. His eyes turned from his son's face.

An hour later everyone was in bed. The wind increased its fury and piled snow on the window ledges only to blow it off again as it changed to a different quarter. It whistled in the chimney and against the sheds, then descended to a low moan as it invaded the pine tops. The heavy fall that had settled on the branches and on roof tops was sent streaming through the air.

Chapter Fourteen

THEY were burying Father Grepilloux. In the crowded church Mass was being celebrated.

Max knew little of what was said and done. Dull of feeling and confused of thought, he stared blankly. Truly, the world had melted like a snowflake in his hand. His friend was dead—and his son was in jail.

The priest was honored and beloved. The tall candles around his coffin burned steadily in the chill air. The choir filled the church with its melancholy music, while the Indians in the rear of the church kept up an undertone of wailing which occasionally rose in shrill crescendo, drowning out the formal funeral music. The primitive expression was more heart-rending. It chilled one's blood.

Max was trying to form a picture in his mind of the dead priest and found that he could not do it, in spite of the fact that he had been at the bedside only a few days before. It was this failure which had thrown him into such confusion. He gazed at the fresco of the Last Judgment above the altar, but it was a meaningless blur. In his last days Grepilloux was thin, his clothes hung loosely, and his hair was white and soft; Max could see the hair, but the eyes, the mouth, the expression—all that was blank. He felt crushed by this failure of his memory.

Vaguely his mind drifted backward through the years. There things were a little surer, he could call up pictures, always of the same man, a man unhurried, soft in his speech, wearing a black cassock shiny and rather green with age. These pictures were also of a man who chopped trees and carried stones, a man who worked like a peasant to make a garden in the wilderness. And he heard him protest: "My part in that was small. I but witnessed the building of the Temple of God. . . . Only one thing they didn't understand, and that was sin. We taught them, and that was the beginning of their earthly happiness."

He knew with what devotion the priest had given himself to the career of a missionary. Back in Poitiers he had already finished the regular philosophical course when the idea came to him. He was then eighteen. He would lose no chance of making himself useful. He studied medicine, then engineering. Before he was ready, he had become a trained botanist, he had worked in a machine shop, and had even placed himself under an artist to learn draftsmanship and wood carving. None of these accomplishments went unused. In the early years of settlement he was often the only man with medical knowledge within a month's journey, and he had doctored Indians and whites, infidels and faithful alike. He had dammed streams and built grist and saw mills, in which he even planned and set up the machinery; and everywhere were bridges and buildings on which his hands had labored. His notebooks were full of geological observation. As for his art training, that too had been put to use on occasion; when no one else felt equal to the task, he had painted murals and carved wooden crucifixes for the wilderness chapels which he planted everywhere. His craftsmanship was not the least of his talents. He had the capacity of several men for work, and he had kept up that pace for most of his life. Men who followed him could only marvel.

His affection for all Indians was deep and in practical matters he understood them. He saw how admirably adjusted they were to the conditions under which they lived and he learned their ways of wilderness travel and existence. He was at once superior to them and able to place himself on their level when occasion required it. He despised and inveighed against those who despoiled the Indians. If the reservation system must remain, he wanted the agents removed or strictly supervised, and he wanted to see tribal laws and customs restored and respected. Above all, he wanted to see white men kept off the reservation and only allowed to trade at supervised posts. He had great faith in the army men who had served in the frontier posts through the years of the Indian wars. With few exceptions, the commanding officers he had known had been on the side of the Indians, even when they took the field against them. One officer had once told him that in almost forty years of campaigning he had never known the Indians to be in the wrong in any controversy with the government or the white settlers. He trusted the army and would have been willing to see permanent posts established in the vicinity of every reservation, not to interfere in Indian affairs but to protect the Indians against their own agents and the white settlers.

His greatest sorrow was the decay of the Missions, when Congress, because of the pressure of certain religious spokesmen, refused to allow funds already owing certain tribes to be used, at the request of the tribes, for the support of Mission schools. The burden had become too great. In the early years priests and nuns had got their funds by going out on annual begging tours of mining camps and settlements. Latterly that and other sources of revenue failed, and when Congress refused support the Mission schools languished. He never quite resigned himself to the sight of unused buildings falling into disrepair.

That was the missionary priest, as his own book revealed him—a man of prodigious labors, a priest of gifted insight and broad sympathy, and a pathfinder. Max Leon could think of him in all these ways. And now that the priest lay dead, he could ask himself what it signified. Blasphemous thought, but Max could not rid his mind of it. What good had been accomplished? What evil?

Throughout the sixty-mile valley, banks, stores and farms flourished. The railroad pushed through in time, and every day its trains rushed along, carrying the produce of many laborers. Children studied in schools. Old men passed their last days, met death, and were laid to rest in the same peace and security as attended any Old World community. Grepilloux had shown the way over the mountains and the world had followed at his heels. Life and industry filled the valley from one end to the other.

But was that enough? The question came unbidden and Max worried with it against his will. Practical man though he was, he asked himself whether people and farms and railroads answered the question. As for the Indians who had been taught to understand sin, certainly they offered no satisfaction. Instead one had to ask of them—were they saved or were they destroyed? Bringing the outside world to them was not exactly like bringing heaven to them. These questions appalled him; and that they should fill his head now, with the priest lying in his coffin, was near-sacrilege, at least it was disloyalty to a good man. He shook them off by telling himself that Grepilloux needed no justification. In performing the labor to which he had been called he had fulfilled himself. That was all a man ever did.

The singing ceased. A melancholy more pronounced than ever entered the church as the people sat back and waited for the visiting bishop to give the signal for the start of the procession. Was the good priest, of whom everyone cherished some venerable memory, was he really to leave his mortal friends? There was a hush of wonder. Some doubtless expected the coffin lid to be cast aside and a white figure to arise. To them it was more of a wonder that he should remain mortal.

When Max took his place with the pallbearers he began to flush and tremble. When he took up the coffin it was as if he alone bore the weight.

Outside the snow blew in flurries and the wind drove frost into the flesh. The coffin was slipped into the rear of the horse-drawn coach. Someone came out with Max's fur coat. He would have forgotten it entirely. The procession went forward to the cemetery.

Everyone for miles around had driven in for the funeral, fighting through heavy drifts and braving the stinging frost. It was not every day they came to bury a Grepilloux in this wilderness. The procession was so long that when its head reached the cemetery gate the last marchers had not yet left the church, and that was half a mile away. Village dogs came out to bark at the strange sight, but the people moved so deliberately and with such indifference to the howling that the dogs grew silent and sat down to watch. Finally they went away one by one to find the warm corners they had left, all except one demented creature, who pointed his nose to the sky and howled. The marchers shivered with superstitious fear and crossed themselves, wondering who would be next to die.

Max was still trying to visualize the priest's face and his continuing failure deepened the despair he felt.

He had won respect for himself at last, and for

something more than his money. As he bore the coffin of his only friend he walked with a Judge before and a State Senator behind. Today he had risen among the accepted citizens.

The snow stopped just as the open grave was reached. Pieces of canvas covered the opening and the pile of earth that had been thrown out. The snow was soiled where gravel had spilled over it.

A funeral address was pronounced, of which Max caught only these words: "We had a saint with us, but he is gone from our house."

Max had been uncovered for so long that numbness had been creeping upon his brain, but those words stirred him up. What made them stand out was the fact that they recalled how the priest looked just before he died. He remembered at last! His hair had a silken gloss and the skin had taken on a transparency which gave the illusion of a light burning within.

But more than recalling the priest, the words came as an answer to the rude questions which had troubled his mind. If Grepilloux were a saint, then it was God's good that had been served and you could not go behind that.

As the last prayers were said, whimpering and low cries broke out and long wailing sounds came from the group of Indians. Everybody seemed overwhelmed by the spectacle of the grave. The nuns in their black gowns, standing with bowed heads, seemed waiting to be struck down.

Eastward, the mountains appeared out of departing storm clouds, and as sunlight struck them they shone with blinding splendor. They rose to astonishing heights.

In a moment the coffin had sunk from sight. Someone threw on the first dirt, a solid mass which sounded like a stone hitting the box. Those near enough to hear shivered, thinking of the coldness of the ground.

Those were the only impressions Max had of the funeral. Much more had been said and done there, but it had been lost on him. He had said his farewell and now he turned to walk away.

Chapter Fifteen

As HE was leaving the cemetery gate George Moser, the storekeeper, rushed up and took his arm.

"My God, man! Where's your hat? They'll be laying you away!"

Max turned and stared.

"Turn your collar up! You're the big man around here now and you oughtn't to be reckless. Didn't we see you up in front with the bishop and those fellows? Come in the store and thaw out. I'll send someone for your car."

Max was the big man all right. When Moser paraded him through the store every man there seemed to be calling out his name.

There was a hot fire in the stove and Max was given whisky. He had had nothing to eat that day and in a moment his head was spinning. He didn't seem to know what he was doing or where he was, and certainly he heard not a word of the storekeeper's stream of talk.

"I never saw such a funeral in my life! Everybody was there. And there was Max right up in front, almost beside the bishop! I don't suppose you saw me. No, I guess you didn't. I made a motion as you were coming out of church but you weren't looking.

143

"It's a shame these people don't come to town oftener. The store is full now, but they're only absorbing free heat before they start home. But I'm glad to have them. Nothing helps business better than to have lots of people around. We need more gatherings of one kind and another." He followed that train of thought for some time, expanding it.

Max interrupted him suddenly. "Excuse me," he said. "I was thinking how frosty the ground is."

Mr. Moser looked reproved. "I shouldn't talk so much. My wife tells me that. I know you're thinking other things." But the apology could not restrain him. His tongue would not lie quiet.

"Death is a mighty funny thing," he began again. "We all know we got to die, but we never get used to it. You'd think we would. If you asked me bluntly, right at this moment, am I afraid of it, I'd say no. But you can't tell. I suppose I wouldn't be so sure if I was really facing it. But I feel there are lots of things just as bad. If a man's got his health that's about as important as anything."

He developed that idea too, without revealing everything that was on his mind. He didn't for example touch on the imaginary ailments which a man's wife may have and use as an excuse to make his life miserable. But there was much to say about health without including a wife's failings.

Max interrupted again, having heard nothing of what was being said. "Do you believe in saints?" he asked.

"You mean ghosts?"

"No, saints. If a man stepped in the door there with a face so kind you knew at once a better man never lived, and if a kind of warm light seemed to come from him—would you know him for a saint?"

The storekeeper didn't know what to make of the question. It startled him. "I guess there was lots of 'em in olden days."

"Would you like to have one for a friend?" Max would not let him sidestep.

"Well, I don't know. I'm not much that way myself and I might feel out of place."

"You don't understand. A saint doesn't let you feel that way. He even lets you feel more important." There the subject was dropped. Max's mind wandered and presently he was reaching out to pour himself another drink of whisky.

This was an encouraging gesture in the storekeeper's eyes. He too had another drink. "Max," he said, "I've got a fine proposition for you. I'm coming up to see you one of these days."

At that he stopped. Max had shot him a scowl that froze the words on his lips and Mr. Moser heard himself murmuring: "It's nothing of importance. . . ."

Max was now stirring out of his lethargy. He seemed to be aware for the first time of his surroundings. He looked about, frowning. The place was distasteful, the storekeeper was distasteful; for years he had wanted to slit his pink skin with a knife; and yet he made no move to leave. His mind was busy with some problem.

"God pity us! All of us!" The words burst forth suddenly, a little drunkenly perhaps. "Did we think we were building a new world here? What's it worth now? Father Grepilloux worked like a convict sentenced to hard labor, but harder. What good came of it? That's what I can't answer. It's in my head and I can't get away from it.

"You know yourself this country is dead broke. I was lucky. God pity the fellow trying to get a start now. It's rich, virgin country but it's broke. I don't understand it. Well, and what about the Indians? What have they got? We killed off their game so they can't live in the old way. They don't know how to work and maybe never will. They gamble away their horses and their tools. The Government gives them a little money now and then but most of 'em don't know enough to buy food when it comes. Drink, silk shirts, and then you pounce on them for what they been owing you for God knows how long—and they wake up from a big drunk and nothing to eat! Fantastic, eh? But don't it happen every day? No, by God! I don't see what the world can thank us for. Put it to yourself—what did we bring? Railroads, banks, a fine business like yours, which you'd like to get rid of— put it to yourself!

"D'you know what I said to Father Grepilloux? I said I'd leave my ranch to this boy Archilde, on condition he doesn't go to jail before I'm dead. I said that as a joke. The Father was trying to get me to make up with the boy. But look what has happened! A man shouldn't joke about these matters."

Moser was sitting with his feet perched on an open drawer of his desk, his hands clasped over his round little belly. From his face it could be seen how disturbing were his thoughts.

"But the money they owe me, Max—"

At these words Max suddenly went wild. His eyes opened wide.

"For the love of Christ! Your money! Why, you belly-crawling worm! You dung fly! Do you know what I've been talking about? People are starving! They're freezing to death in those shacks by the church. They don't know why; they had nothing to do with it. You and me and Father Grepilloux were the ones brought it on. For what good? What satisfaction have we got? And God damn your nerve! I don't mean what money did we get out of it! I hope you rot without collecting one stinking dime!"

At that he stopped suddenly. A murderous impulse had come over him. He wanted to strangle the storekeeper. He made for the door and found his car waiting. Then he drove swiftly out of town, a sharp wind tugging at the weather curtains of his car. Powdered snow blew across the road. When he reached home he was chilled and tired. His bones ached as if he had been laboring strenuously.

"Stiff joints—weak kidneys—so. A man gets old," he muttered.

For a long time after, as he lay in bed, he could not

rid his mind of the ideas with which he had struggled through the day. He had images of Father Grepilloux working like a peasant, of the Indians perishing of hunger and disease, of the outside world pouring into this sheltered valley, a paradise in its original state— and what had been the purpose? To develop boys who committed murder? Merciful God! There must be other reasons!

That, he knew, was the thought which had been torturing him all day, causing him to call into question the usefulness of his friend's life, and to attack that little worm, the storekeeper.

Chapter Sixteen

ARCHILDE had not been held in jail, exactly. If he had insisted, or if anyone had insisted in his behalf, he might have gone home. But he was too confused to know what to do, and Max was plunged into such despair by the accumulation of events as to be left without a will. As a result matters were left in the hands of the Indian agent, Horace Parker.

It was Mr. Parker's idea that Archilde should stay at the Agency for a time, as a matter of convenience. An official inquiry was to sit and a grand jury examination was threatening. The agent had thought it would be convenient if, on his part, it could be shown that he was making every effort to coöperate with the authorities. That was why Archilde had come to be held at the Agency, not in jail exactly, though as a matter of convenience he was locked up every night. Mr. Parker apologized for this but thought that in the end it would prove to be for the best, for all concerned.

Those were hard days for Archilde, though he said nothing. Like Max, he would not let another see his inward feeling. A tight mouth, hard eyes—no one should know.

Pride and spirit—these were his; they kept his back

straight, kept his face forward. These were traits he
had developed as a boy, and they remained. His
teachers liked his appearance and they got in the way
of addressing him in tones of confidence, sometimes of
friendliness, always with an air of acknowledging his
difference. Such things do not go unnoticed. A boy is
quick to sense the value others set on him.

During those weeks at the Agency, walking about
the compound in the daytime or sleeping in jail at
night, he knew by turns fear and shame—fear for what
might happen, and shame for the lies he was swearing
to. But he said nothing that would reveal his feelings.
He let the agent talk and only answered what was
required.

Pride and spirit—these had marked him for a special
existence. He knew this, because he had read it in the
eyes and the speech of others. But something had gone
wrong, uselessly, without reason. The end had come
almost before a beginning had been made. He would
wind up like every other reservation boy—in prison,
or hiding in the mountains.

Forgetting the change that had come about in his
religious life, he fell into a habit of prayer: "Hail
Mary, Mother of God, let me be strong. If I have
sinned I beseech your mercy. Oh, keep me strong!
I don't want to hide in the mountains. I don't want to
rot in jail. Oh Mother! Keep me strong!"

This was Archilde's strange frightened mood after
a month of waiting at the Agency, not in jail, but
conveniently detained. The inquiry was over now

and nothing more was to be done at present, so it seemed that Archilde was to be allowed to go home.

The yard before the Agency was occupied by ancient wagons and crowbait horses. In summer time the horses stood patiently through the day, fighting flies and making piles of dung; in winter the same gaping-ribbed animals were there, their long tails blowing in the wind; and their masters were inside waiting "to see the agent." Usually they got no more than a glimpse of him as he went about his business. There was no use seeing the same people about the same complaints day after day. He had work to do.

Mr. Parker, the agent, was a tall, active man whose hair was just beginning to gray. He liked his job and he liked his Indian wards. He saw their helplessness and realized, without getting excited about it, that he was of little use to them. He did what he could but at every turn he was hampered by a system which penalized initiative and by the Indians' own poor understanding of what was expected of them. Taking over an Indian Agency was always like moving into a ready-furnished house in which the pieces not only did not match but were falling apart and you had no authority to throw out anything or make better use of what was provided; there were doors that led nowhere and some that would let you tumble into a dark cellar; the place was overrun by domestic animals which had to be fed and nursed, and you had no time for it if you were expected to keep the house from falling in on you; not a few of the pets had died before your time and others threatened to die, and altogether there was a bad odor around; the neighbors were always spying upon you because, you at last realized, you were really in a house of prostitution and they were expecting you to add to its ill fame—in a word it was a nightmare which no one could endure without cultivating a certain amount of callousness. Above all, if an agent wished to remain in the Service, he had to keep his record clear. If in doing this somebody was put to an inconvenience or even made to suffer, well—that was when it was handy to have developed a callous layer. Of course, if you were naturally fair, you tried to make it up in some way, off the record. In any case, whether you made amends or not, you had to be in the right position at all times. It was the only way to survive.

Mr. Parker understood this working philosophy of the Service. He had come through a score of years with few complaints. In the present instance, the agent had protected himself by holding on to the boy. He might also have held the mother and been within his rights. Instead, he let her go unmolested and so made up for the inconvenience which he caused the boy. Anyhow, an old squaw could always be found if she were wanted. These things had to be looked at in several ways at once.

Upon seeing Archilde in the anteroom of his office, Mr. Parker's face brightened.

"So here you are! Come in!" Before closing the door he announced that he would see no one else

until afternoon; unless their business was urgent they
had better wait for another day; moreover, it would
be better if they drove home, put their horses in the
barn and looked after their affairs.

These were useless directions, as no one knew better than he. Few had barns, fewer had any affairs at
home. Indeed, few had enough food at home to feed
their bellies. When their own store gave out they
went visiting, and when their relatives had nothing
left, they all came to see the agent—and he asked them
to call next day.

Archilde, entering the room in unguarded cheer-
fulness, received a shock. For there sat Dave Quigley!
He occupied a chair in the corner, with a window at
his back, making it difficult to see him or to face him.
He smiled at Archilde's visible start.

"Weren't looking for me, eh, young fellow?"

He could not respond. The agent had told him the
previous evening that he was letting him go, that
there would be no more questioning, and with that
knowledge he had gone to bed. He had lain awake for
hours, smiling and stretching his limbs and letting a
sense of freedom flow through his body. Then he
slept. And when he awoke at dawn his first thought
was that a special day had arrived. So he had come to
Mr. Parker's office in a mood of having made peace
with the world; he had forgiven it for those nights and
days in the mountains, and for the Agency weeks—
and all the time Dave Quigley sat waiting! "Weren't
looking for me, eh?" Obscene jest! Archilde felt him-

self turn pale and cold, felt his heart die; and then he turned in his misery to Mr. Parker. What had he to say?

The Agent sensed the moment's unhappiness and was himself ill at ease. He adopted a kindly tone. "Mr. Quigley just happened along today, Archilde, and asked to see you. I told him you were going home because the formal inquest had finished with you. He asked if he might talk to you and I assumed you wouldn't mind. Were there any questions you wanted to ask, Sheriff?"

The Sheriff, it turned out, could be faced. Whatever suspicion or conviction lay in the back of his head, he kept it out of his words. He had not come to accuse, though in all likelihood he was there to lay a trap, if he could.

"I want you to tell me, Archilde, where you were camped when you found your brother shot. I'm going up that way soon as the weather softens and I want to look around, see if I can strike the trail of my old friend, Dan Smith. Dan, you know, is the game warden who ain't been heard from since last fall. Funny thing —I met Dan just before I met you that day. He was going across the next range into the deer country. I don't see how you could have missed him."

Archilde did not look up at once and he could feel the weight of the Sheriff's eyes upon him. How much of suspicion lay behind the words? What plan was he following? No matter. He could only repeat what he had already said scores of times, giving an answer which led his questioners far from the scene of murder. He knew the mountains of that particular region and could choose trails at will, even marking them off on a detailed survey map. He indicated a spot full ten miles wide of the mark, up a different stream and in a different maze of canyons and ridges.

The Sheriff, listening to the explanation, gave no indication of his thought, but when Archilde finished he observed quietly: "The trail you say you took was the trail I took after leaving you. We must of been camped right near each other. Funny, isn't it?"

He had leaned forward as he spoke and his eyes searched Archilde's face. He half smiled, as if he sensed that he was making the trail hot and enjoyed it.

"You didn't see our tracks?" Archilde was tense inside, but not from fear. He was feeling his way.

"That's the funny part of it. I didn't see a single track ahead of me."

"Well, how did you go—along the creek bottom, where the trail goes?"

Quigley reflected, gazing abstractedly at Archilde.

"Yes, I sort of stuck to the trail. Generally do."

"That's why then," Archilde spoke without excitement, yet with a feeling that he was out in the open again. "You see, we climbed the ridge on the right. It's not steep, you remember. Then we followed it. The deer are up high in the fall."

Quigley smiled faintly, rose to his feet. "I guess that's all I got to ask you. I'll go up that way soon's the thaw comes and look around."

Mr. Parker looked as relieved as did Archilde. They had all risen by now and the Agent was taking Quigley to the door. "Glad you stopped in. Let me know what you find up there."

The Sheriff was not smiling as he turned back. "I can tell you now what I'll find—it'll be Dan Smith's grave. And it won't be on top of a ridge. That's all I want to find."

He walked off without looking back, perhaps knowing without having to see for himself how his words would strike Archilde cold. It was no threat. It was a prediction of what he was quite capable of achieving. There could be no question about it. Dave Quigley would hunt until he found what he was looking for— and then what? Archilde had turned and was looking out of the window when Mr. Parker came up to him.

At his shoulder the Agent said: "You gave a good account of yourself, boy. I'll stick by you. I don't know what happened up there—it's the queerest business I ever heard of. You find your brother dead—a man disappears into thin air. Queer business. But I believe in you. Now go home."

Archilde could not look up. Moistness dimmed his sight and made him shy. He went out.

Presently he was thinking of Max at home.

Chapter Seventeen

AFTER everyone had gone to bed Archilde and his
father sat together before the stove. They sat there
a few feet apart and said almost nothing. The longer
the silence lasted the harder it was to break it.

Max was nervous and uneasy. At the supper table
he had been inclined to scold Agnes about everything
—the meat was tough, the potatoes were raw, everything was wrong. And now that he faced the boy alone
he had foolishly lost his voice. He knew what he had
to find out. If the boy had murdered a man he must
know it, and then make up his mind what he would
do. He had prepared himself, but now that the time
had come he couldn't ask the simple question. He
thought only of inconsequential matters.

"I suppose you had a cold trip coming from the
Agency?" That was one of the useless things he asked.

"Yes, that's so."

"How are the roads? I haven't been out."

"Lots of snow."

"You're not looking very good."

"I feel fine."

"I've had the grippe for a couple days."

There were periods between these statements. Max's
eyes strayed to the boy. Sometimes their eyes met and

the silence became more awkward. Then he looked
up suddenly and asked. "Well, what are your plans?
Will you go away?"

Archilde was slow to answer. It was a hard question
to answer without a full explanation. "I'd like to go
away," was the way he finally put it.

Then the silence. It wasn't the question Max was
interested in, but even it had required effort.

Thus they continued for almost an hour. It began
to look as if neither would find out anything. They
looked at each other, then looked away. Max tried to
see in the boy's face what he wanted to find there,
what people told him about his son. He was beginning to think he didn't want to know what had happened in the mountains. He couldn't make up his
mind what he would do if he were told the worst, and
it would be better if he did nothing. Perhaps they
would come together again without discussing the
matter.

So they sat, side by side.

Archilde, looking through the window, was surprised to find that it had stopped snowing. The sky
had cleared and a full moon had made a kind of dawn
in the middle of night. Something in him became
clear too. He turned to Max, smiled weakly.

"I'll tell you what happened on the hunting trip,
then you'll understand."

Max looked up quickly, puzzled and partly frightened. He found that Archilde's eyes did not waver
from his own and that prepared him to listen.

"We didn't find Louis already dead. This is what happened. . . ." He omitted no detail and made no attempt to slight his part, even to telling how he dug a shallow grave and buried the man. He paused at the end of the story but didn't wait for his father to speak. He had more to say and meant to finish it in one piece.

What he told about himself was the same story he had told Father Grepilloux. He began with his days at the Indian school and the meeting with Mr. Duffield. It was a long recital, giving the story of his dreams and desires, his notions about life, and how all this seemed to have come to an end.

It was more than Max had hoped for. As he sat looking at the boy he was full of wonder. It would have made no difference now if Archilde had killed a man, he was thinking. What he had feared was not that the boy had killed but that he might be deceptive or cruel or dull of spirit—one of those who begin by killing the good things in themselves. That was what he could not have made terms with. His smile was something that went all through him, like a deep breath after sudden fright.

"Well, Archilde, it's different to what I thought. I hate to think what was in my mind. But what's to be done? That's what we got to think about." His voice sounded strangely subdued to his own ears. His mind dwelt on wonder. "We got to plan something. We won't let it end for you, like you thought. We'll make a new beginning!"

Max had got in the habit in those days of letting his shoulders droop, and he had not laughed much. But now he was changed. He sat looking at his son in a way that was good to see—his eyes flashing, his lips smiling, his body suddenly alive.

"Do you know, Father Grepilloux—God rest his soul!—he wanted me to send you away to study music. I think that's what we should do. Would you like going to the old country, maybe to Rome and Paris—and Spain? I don't know if anybody goes to Spain to study music, but you must go there just the same. That's my country, a wonderful country too. You must see it."

It was Archilde now whose emotions were in his throat and eyes. He took to looking out of the window.

They had been discussing this matter for some time, planning Archilde's trip abroad and how he should find someone to guide him in the foreign world—and it was a pleasure that moved them deeply —when suddenly they thought of the old lady. She came into their minds simultaneously and the talk halted. Archilde was the first to express his thought of her.

"If I go away, maybe they'll come after the old lady some time. Maybe they'll find the warden in the spring."

"No! No! She's so old they'll not trouble her."

Max could not dismiss his wife from the conversation. He saw that the boy's eyes questioned him. But more than that, his relations with her had become a source of regret. The fire of his angry separation from her had burned itself out and he had been ready for some time to make peace, if he had known how to accomplish it. He was not sure that she would agree to forget the past. All this was in his mind; otherwise he might not have been aware of Archilde's questioning gaze, or at any rate would have ignored it. It was awkward to talk about.

"I ought to tell you—I suppose you ask— You see how it is— Oh, hell! I'll just say I was a fool! That's better. I was a fool to think your mother was the cause of my bad luck. But I thought it all right and kicked her out of the house. That was when you was a baby. The older boys were already beginning their hell-raising and I didn't want any more of it. I built myself a house, not this big one; that came later when I got money. I built myself a house and said I'd break the neck of any of the family that tried to come in. I was pretty mad in those days, and your mother was the cause of it. This was how it happened.

"Blasco, my first son, was about twenty then. Well, him and the next boy had been stealing cattle, seems they'd been up to it for quite a while. I had them working for me and they had the makings of good cattlemen. Of course they were wild and were getting in trouble fast as I could get them out of it, and all the time my temper was getting shorter. I wore myself out whipping them but it didn't do a damn bit of good. Then I learned what they were up to. For a long time they'd been picking up cattle, a few head

at a time, and running them in with my herd. When
they got a good bunch they'd cut them out and some
night take them in the mountains, where their friends
would pick them up and drive them to a crooked
buyer on the other side.

"I almost swung for that little trick of theirs. Somebody got wise and picked up the trail leading from
my place right into the mountains, and there was no
damn way of proving the boys were acting without
my orders. I don't know now what saved me, but I
think Father Grepilloux got a hold of one of the fellows working the cattle in the mountains and talked
him into confessing. Anyhow, that's what happened.

"What happened next was this. When they came
for the boys to put them on trial I wasn't home. Guess
I must have been at the courthouse still. Well, the
boys had skipped. They took my best horses and ran
for the mountains. Then the old lady stepped in and
told the sheriff I told the boys to skip. She even said I
gave them the horses and knew where they was hiding.
And then I did have a hell of a time. When they got
her in court she wouldn't talk English, though she had
talked to the sheriff all right. And they got an interpreter but she wouldn't answer the interpreter's questions, just sat there and cussed him and me and everybody. The judge pounded with his hammer and did
some swearing himself but she pretended she didn't
understand. When the interpreter repeated what the
judge said, she told him he ought to be ashamed for
going against his own people.

"It sounds like it didn't amount to much now, but it was serious at the time. They wanted to hang me again. Well, I got free after a while, and that was when I came home and built my house and threatened to break anybody's neck that tried to come in. It was about the time they sent you to the Indian school. I guess they were afraid to let you stay around because you might try to come in the house. Maybe you did come in one day and I pitched you out on your head. I meant what I said all right. The others knew it and stayed at their distance. It was a good many years before I made any change. Then, when Agnes was a widow, I built my big house here and took her in because I was sick and tired of cooking for myself.

"Well, all that is past. For a long time I been telling myself I ought to make it up with the old woman. So I'll do that before you go away and your mind will be free on her account. I'll have her in my house again and the agent will think twice before he tries to take her off for questioning. Anyhow, if she hasn't forgotten her old tricks, he won't get a word out of her."

So Max's story ended in a laugh.

He embraced his son, as his own father had embraced him after a friendly talk, and they went to bed.

Chapter Eighteen

MAX did not realize that night how ill he was. The following day he kept to his bed, complaining of pains and fever. He had been low for several weeks, since Grepilloux's funeral, but he did not like sickness and had never been in bed with any kind of ailment. On this morning it was different. Every bone felt broken and when he got to his feet he fainted dead away. Archilde went for the doctor.

Toward evening of that day Max grew delirious and in lucid intervals his grave face, on which the sweat stood in large oily drops, showed that he was frightened.

"Think I'm pretty sick," he muttered once as Archilde stood near.

When the doctor learned that Max had stood bareheaded all through Father Grepilloux's burial service he shook his head emphatically, which was as much as to say "He should've been dead long before this."

Archilde sat by the bedside all that day and night, giving the medicines as directed and feeling strange and awkward. He had never been in the bedroom, never seen Max undressed, it was all unfamiliar.

It was a dark room, papered with a heavy dark pattern and filled with cumbersome furniture which

Max had bought years before from the stock of a bankrupt rancher. The rancher had brought the furniture with him from the East and stocked his land with thoroughbred stock. The cattle poisoned themselves on loco weed, his wife died in childbirth, and he ended his venture by bringing his baby to the Sisters of Providence one winter night, pushing it inside the door and ringing the bell, then disappearing.

Archilde looked closely at the mahogany furniture, with its carved spirals, and was awed by it. Very likely there was not another suite like it in the country. The pieces were rich in appearance, the wardrobe particularly, with its heavy plate glass mirror, and the chairs were built on large dimensions, with heavy springs which had never worn out. Formerly he would not have shown any interest in his father's possessions, as a point of pride, but now he was curious and felt at ease; not easy enough to pick up and examine the silver paper knife on the desk or to pry into drawers, but he dared to walk about and try his hand on the mahogany finish.

Max was breathing with difficulty when the doctor returned during the night. As he was leaving he took the sick man's hand in his own. They were old friends and companions of a number of hunting trips. Nothing was said, but Max sensed what the doctor was conveying. He smiled at the corner of his mouth.

"It's all right, Doc. You can't scare me. I'll be out of here before you can figure out what I got. Just leave some pills with my boy. Shake hands with Doc

Arnold, Archilde, He's a good fellow, but a poor shot."

Outside Archilde learned that Max would not live. It was pneumonia in an advanced stage. This information was stunning, like a blow at the base of the skull. It was plain enough that Max was low, but that he would die was something Archilde had not thought of. He stared at the doctor, and queer lights seemed to be whirling and darting through his head. How could such a thing be? They had just begun to make plans together, how could that be cut short? They had only now come to an understanding!

But it was to be. Max had only one other interval, one flicker when he recognized Archilde. He whispered:

"Too bad to leave you now. Have to learn many things yourself. Take the money, and keep it. If that goes, you'll have it hard. Study—work—"

That was the end of the flicker. There was no time for anything. The reconciliation with the old lady, the plans for Archilde, the new beginning—everything went with that flicker.

At five o'clock in the afternoon, already turning dark, Doc Arnold returned. He found Archilde sitting as if frozen, holding Max's hand. The doctor looked closer.

"He's been dead a long time. Didn't you know?"

Chapter Nineteen

IT is muddy spring. A horse carries its rider at a heavy-legged gallop, throwing clumps of earth far to rear-ward. The trailing dog keeps to one side, leaping pud-dles, disdainful of the ooze. Horse and dog, when they reach town, will have pellets of mud hanging from tips of hair, and the dog will seek a dry spot where it can lie down and clean its paws.

Eastward, the towering mountains are swirled in mist, and overhead fresh clumps of rapidly moving fluff clouds drift mountainward. There is no rain fall-ing but the wind dampens one's face. On such a day geese lose themselves and cry frantically and the shift-ing clouds echo their cries in strange ways.

It is a subdued day, sluggish, filled with the sound of dripping—a day to raise doubt in the minds of the young of ever seeing clear sky or treading solid earth.

The land, on such a day, is barren. Having been first withered by frost, then crushed by a burden of snow, only the strongest forms are left standing; only the hardy pines bear their natural aspect, and they seem more black than green. Everywhere on the land is the imprint of ruin, dead grass pressed into mud, and in hollow places leaf forms massed in decay. These are shells and husks. The juices that flowed strengtheningly were blackened and destroyed by the first frost of the autumn.

Archilde's mother came out of her cabin to look at the world of spring. She sat on her doorstep with a shawl pulled tightly about her shoulders. Sitting there all in a lump, with her face looking pale and her hair turned almost white, she too seemed to have been frost-killed and crushed by the passing year. The spring of a new life might be coming to Sniél-emen but she did not respond to it and she did not rejoice in it. It would not be her life and she could not understand what it would be like. There were many like her who watched that spring come and could not say what the new life would be. These too were shells and husks of life-forms that had once possessed elastic strength.

The old lady had not gone untaught. She might have learned what was to come. It wasn't as if this spring had crept upon her without warning and created a new world. There was that day long ago when the Sisters of Providence—the Lady Black Robes they were called—came to make a school. Catharine, the daughter of Running Wolf, was then fourteen years old, and at fourteen one learns easily, so they say. Catharine was there to see the Sisters arrive.

In Father Grepilloux's history there was a passage telling with glowing remembrance of the coming of the Sisters, whom he had escorted over the mountains. Starting from the mother house at Montreal, they had sailed to Panama, crossed the Isthmus, then continued coastwise to San Francisco and northward to Vancouver on the Columbia. There were four of the Sisters, two of whom were frail-looking creatures, none of whom had ever been in the wilderness. They had never followed a trail into a nameless forest, never gone bobbing down a wild stream in a tub of a boat, never spent the day on the back of a horse. They came with great bundles and trunks filled with their starched linen, their little packages of flower and vegetable seeds, their needles, thimbles and thread, their garden tools, their schoolbooks, and the rosaries and medals they would give as prizes for learning. The mountain crossing was of course the most difficult of all their journey, but no matter how startling were the obstacles or how wearying, as Father Grepilloux recalled it, they were never dismayed. They went through the nameless forests singing hymns and silencing the wonder-struck squirrels; at night in their own tent they talked gaily of the day's adventure, and one of the priests in the party would say, "The birds are chattering, we shall have good weather."

The Sisters arrived to find their school building just completed but unwashed, unpainted and full of oddities. Almost without stopping to rest—they had not come to the wilderness to rest—they unpacked their brooms and their mop rags and their garden rakes and set to work. And the Indian women were there to watch them.

Catharine Wolf remembered the day. She had watched the strange women sweep a floor with rush

brooms. She had seen them wring a cloth out of water and wash away the black footmarks where the
carpenters had walked after a rain. These were curious activities. It seemed that you could not live in a
house as you lived outdoors or in a tepee. The outdoors cleansed themselves and so did a tepee. You
moved it and the dirt fell out. Besides you did not
mind a little dirt.

Afterward, when she went to the Sisters' school, she
learned more about where to find dirt and how to get
rid of it. That was only the beginning. She already had
a steel needle and knew how to use it, but the Sisters
made it do wonderful things, as she discovered. Still
more amazing were the things they cooked with stove
and oven; even meat became something you had never
tasted before. Then there were such mysteries as butter and cheese making, washing linen and passing a
hot iron over it until the linen became like the iron,
turning hot tallow into sticks that burned and gave
light, and making soap out of fat and wood ashes. And
all that was a small part of what she learned. They
showed her how to dig the ground and plant seeds,
how to tend the growing plants, and how each plant
turned out differently and you had to know what was
coming and what to do with what came. Then she
learned how to cook all those things. Cows, pigs, and
chickens came along and she was shown how to take
care of them, how to make milk come from the cow,
how to fatten the pig, and how to listen for the hen
when she laid her egg. Then it seemed that there were

only certain ways in which she could speak to the Sisters or to her friends, certain ways of eating, certain ways of opening the door when someone rang the bell, and certain ways of sitting down and saying nothing when visitors came. Beyond all this was the mystery of books and of writing to her friends who couldn't read: "This is a fine school. We have good times at school. I wish you would come to this school because we could have good times together. I am as ever, Your friend, Catharine."

Those were some of the things she learned. Then at twenty she was married to Max Leon. The Sisters sewed a handsome cotton robe for her wedding and she continued to learn new ways. He built the cabin in which she still lived. They started there together. He bought a stove to cook on, and he bought her needles, dishes, tubs to wash clothes in, a butter churn, whatever he thought necessary. She looked at the furniture but never used it. The stove had been worn away by rust but not by use, because she went on cooking over a camp fire. With every other new thing it was the same. The Sisters had taught her many arts but they had not quite taught her to be interested in using them. Possibly there was a deeper reason for her neglect, but on the surface that was what she felt. It was nice to do those things just to find out what they were like; but as for doing them every day until she died, that was just a nuisance. The cask butter churn dried up and fell apart, the washtubs had long ago been battered into junk iron by her children, and what clothes she washed were just soaked in the creek and any dirt that could be shaken loose was carried off by the force of the stream, and so it went.

Even without those complications it was difficult to be a white man's wife. In the old way of living one never stayed in one place for very long. One camped wherever there was game and grass and water for the horses. As a matter of fact, there were certain places where one always camped at the same time each season, unless for some reason game failed to appear in the usual way or a fire burned off the pasturage. When the old way came to an end and the Indians had to live on the Reservation, the habit of moving persisted; people went visiting. They would live on their allotment until they got restless; then they would take their tepee poles and travel to some relative's place or to some likely vacant site; later they would try still another place. With a white man you could not do that, she learned. Also a white man went by a clock. Winter or summer he got up by the clock, he worked by the clock, and he wanted to eat by the clock. You just had to be there. The clock was a new thing and, small as it was, it was mighty. It made a man march around. A woman marched too. That was one thing.

She learned also, after her marriage, that a white man does not care to have his relatives or his wife's relatives come to live with him. He will slam his door in their faces. That was contrary to the old way, because it was only right that if you could go and live with your relatives any time you got tired of your place, they in turn could come to you. A white man wanted his house to himself and you were not welcome there unless he asked you to come. That was another thing she learned.

Only a small part of what she learned stayed with her. She was an old woman now, and it seemed that the older she got the further she went on the trail leading backward. Great changes had come into the world of Sniél-emen but she had not been touched deeply. It was true that she lived in a log cabin, but she preferred a skin tepee and could easily have returned to one. She still ate meat almost to the exclusion of everything else; her stomach had not been pampered by exotic foods. The kindly Sisters who had labored so hard to cross the mountains and to teach their arts of living to a generation of girls might have denied it, but the truth was that Catharine, in her old age, could have seen the Sisters return across the mountains and scarcely have known that they had ever been there.

And worse had happened. She did not realize it until she came outdoors to sit in the spring air—then it came over her all at once. Something had happened to her since last fall. She had lost something. She was a pagan again. She who had been called Faithful Catharine and who had feared hell for her sons and for herself— her belief and her fear alike had died in her. It was difficult to face it, but it was true. She was not mistaken.

The Church had come so long ago that she really

knew nothing of how people lived before it came. In past years, when she heard stories about the old beliefs, about prayer-fasting and about the souls of people and animals who died, she would try to imagine what it was like to believe those things and she couldn't quite do it. Yet she had not hated those ideas the way the Fathers did. At High Mass one of the Fathers would sometimes turn his sermon upon "pagan beliefs" and he would get very angry about it. He would say that whoever clung to them would burn in hell forever. When he spoke like that the old lady would pretend that she did not hear, because it made her feel sad to be told that the past was evil. She did not understand it and yet she would rather not have anything said against it.

She had been loyal to the Church. There had been a period of her life, just before her marriage, when she had been intensely devoted to it. She went to early Mass and to Confession every day, she was always on hand when the Sisters went to clean and decorate the Church and altar and she would beg to be given the hardest tasks; and then she would go from cabin to cabin to inquire if anyone were sick. When one of the Sisters would read from the "Lives of the Saints" she would listen in complete absorption. She was that way for about a year, and then she married Max Leon and moved away from St. Xavier. His cabin was about five miles from the Church and since she could not travel that distance each day for early Mass she gave it up. After that she was satisfied if she went once a week and later once a month. But her loyalty had never been shaken. She urged her children to remember their duties and when they strayed from grace she was full of sorrow and dread.

So strongly was she attached to the Church that only recently, when age had come upon her, she could have given up or forgotten most of what she had learned under the Sisters; but she could not have existed without the Church. If that had been taken away she really would have felt struck to earth. She would have wailed as for one dead. And yet, who knew? All that time, perhaps, she was going farther away from it.

When she came back from the mountains, having killed a man, she felt more dead than alive. It did not seem possible that she would be forgiven this sin and be allowed to walk the earth. Sin had become a mighty thing in her mind. Since childhood she had been meticulous about confessing the least, venial transgression; the commission of a mortal sin terrified her. And then this thing happened. She confessed her crime, but before that she had already decided that she would have to go to hell. It was the end of her long efforts to keep her sons and herself living in grace. She accepted it and she did not want to be told that absolution was possible. No, that was asking too much. The Savior and Redeemer was full of goodness, His Mercy was boundless, but this was too much to ask. Sin had become too mighty a thing in her mind, or rather she had built up a sense of proportion about it which could not now be reasoned out of existence. If a trifle made the soul unhappy, how could it be restored to goodness after all goodness had been destroyed? That was the confusion.

That was when it happened. She had started to carry out the schedule of penance imposed upon her, and then she stopped. That was just before Christmas. She had not gone to Mass on Christmas Eve, for the first time since the Fathers came, and she had not been to Mass since. She stayed away from Church completely. She spoke to no one about it, but it was a fact that she was as good as a pagan now.

Today she had come out of her cabin to look at the world of spring, and it was then, as she saw the earth emerge from the doubt of winter, that she felt the full shock of what had happened to her. Of all the strange life that had come to Sniél-emen in her lifetime, she had need only of the Church, and somehow she had cut herself off from that. What was she to do now?

She sat in her doorway all in a lump, looking as crushed and lifeless as last year's prairie grass. It was not quite the same. There was a spark in her which still responded to the wind of her thought, asking, "What is to become of me? What have I done?"

Chapter Twenty

ARCHILDE had not seen much of his mother during the winter. She had kept to her cabin, and the few times he had looked in on her she had been too closely occupied with her thoughts to notice him. He would stay only to assure himself that she was all right, then he would go away.

Now that spring had come he would really have to talk to her. It was one of the things he had to do for Max, who had wished to make peace with the old lady. That was in his mind as he walked across his father's land on one of the first of the spring days. He was looking at the winter wheat which Max had planted and he was deciding that he would have to stay and harvest the crop. He would not plant more but he would harvest what Max had planted. It was a way of fulfilling the trust placed in him. He was just learning what that meant, that trust.

First and most surprising (he had not thought about it), it meant money—more money than he had ever heard mentioned in casual conversation. Max had managed shrewdly and had sold off his Shorthorn herd in a good market. Horace Parker, spent a good deal of time while the estate was being settled telling Archilde (a little pompously) what a capable man Max Leon had been, how he had not allowed himself to relax morally, although many in his position would have, and how he had encouraged the arts of civilization among his Indian friends. At first Archilde had been shy in the Agent's presence for he had never felt sure that he had lied successfully. He did not think the Agent trusted him. But there was no indication otherwise. Mr. Parker did not even mention the happenings of the fall and winter, and gradually Archilde grew at ease. He gave up looking for hidden meanings in the commonplace remarks of the Agent. Then he began to grasp some of the details of the estate settling —and he was amazed; fifty-four thousand in stocks and bonds, ten thousand in insurance, a few thousand in a savings bank, another ten thousand in cash, real estate in St. Xavier and in Swift Current, the county seat, and odd shares of mining stock of doubtful value. It was "shrewd husbandry," as Mr. Parker phrased it.

He could think about all this, on this day in spring, as he walked around the field of winter wheat. He could feel that he had won his father's trust. Turning that idea over and over, it became more than the barren word. It warmed him, even as the sun slanted downward and warmed his bare head.

He spent his days at home. He had not been to the Mission since the day he left to go hunting with his mother. Father Cristadore might be waiting for him to continue his music lessons, but Archilde did not even communicate with him. He was no longer interested in the Mission. After his fit of fear while waiting at the Agency, he had also stopped praying. It made him uncomfortable to recall how he had given in to that mood. The religion of the priests was definitely gone from him. It had died as he passed out of childhood, in spite of momentary lapses into the old fears and patterns of prayerful thought. It would never possess him again.

As for his violin study, he knew that he could resume that easily enough when he went away. Father Cristadore had taught him nothing. Sometime soon he would have to come to a decision about going away, set the time for it and make his plans. Just now there was enough to do to keep him occupied.

He wasn't always alone. For the first two months after Max's death he was visited almost every day by the agent or the lawyer and they brought documents to read and sign and a hundred matters to discuss about Max's estate. The lawyer was a small, red-haired man, as abrupt in his movements as a squirrel. He would sit in a low chair and screw up his eyes at Archilde. After a while Archilde decided that this grimace was intended as a smile. He looked at the lawyer and wondered why he disliked him on sight. He couldn't decide about it. It was just the impression he gave you that if you put him down in the grass he would wriggle away.

Another visitor came to shake hands, to condole with him, and to "have just a chat." That was Mr. George Moser. It was the same story with him. Another harvest had left him no better off. It had been an average year, which meant that some of his debtors had reduced their obligations by as much as ten per cent. Meantime, another seeding time had come and every day men were coming to him for supplies and machinery and promising to do better next fall. He wanted to throw them out of the store but if he did that they would just go to the new Brower Mercantile Company which wasn't up to its neck in high-priced land and could afford to sprinkle money around like water. At least that's what they seemed to be doing. They were taking Moser's old customers as sugar takes flies and it kept him busy writing off bad debts. His wife was having another spell too. Last week she had got so hysterical that she fell down stiff as a board and the doctor was coming to see her every day. He was recommending a change and a period of rest and quiet. There was nothing "humbug" about a prescription like that.

Mr. Moser had quite a story to tell Archilde, not about his wife and his hundred other troubles, but a good story just the same. It seemed that Max had been anxious to purchase the Moser business, the store, grain elevator, warehouse, motor trucks, lumber yard, everything. The business was so profitable that he wasn't really interested in selling, but Max had been so insistent, and so on, and finally a price had been agreed upon, a bargain, $75,000. Now, Mr. Moser had just been thinking it over and he was ready to set the price even lower, if he could get it all cash, $60,000. Think of it! The annual business turnover was one-third of that amount!

This went on for quite a while before Mr. Moser stumbled upon the obvious fact that he was wasting his breath. Archilde looked at him without any show of interest. He hadn't so much as nodded his head. Mr. Moser tried to get angry about it. He puffed out his cheeks, his neck seemed to swell at the collar. He muttered that Indians were "damned glad to borrow money, then they didn't know you." He didn't stop to explain how this could be applied in the present case. He drove away in his automobile. When Archilde saw him a few days later in St. Xavier, Mr. Moser was pleasant, if somewhat distant in manner. There was a far-away look in his eyes.

It was the spring, already after Easter, and the old lady and Archilde sat together in front of her cabin. He was looking at her rather closely, without seeming to. He knew that something was wrong. She had not been to Christmas Mass and, even more startling, she had stayed away from the Easter services. No one ever tried to make the old lady do anything, and they never questioned her, but of course they watched her all the time. Agnes had reported that she had suffered from the cold all winter. In her cabin she kept the two small windows and the door stuffed with rags while the stove glowed red. It was enough to have killed her. But you couldn't tell her, "Old woman, you're a fool!" and open her windows. You had to think of some other way.

She sat very still, her thin lips scarcely moving when

she talked. Her eyes appeared sightless. Looking at her, Archilde felt again that nearness which he felt the night her relatives sat around a fire and told stories out of the past. He saw then that she had a kind of importance which a stranger might never understand but which he, after missing it at first, had finally glimpsed. It was the same today. He could see that she had a way, all unconscious, of making other people seem small and squirmy, like something you might pluck out of your hair (not that he had anything to pluck out of his hair!) She would sit quietly gazing off into space and you felt a longing to see what she saw, but you would not risk her contempt by asking her to confide in you.

"Spring is early," she said.

Archilde was squatted on his heels, smoking a cigarette.

"Yes, there will be heavy hay this year."

"Is the snow deep on the mountains?"

"Yes, on the high ranges."

"I can't see in this strong light. Maybe in two, three days I can see more."

He looked at her watery eyes and doubted if she would ever see much. "Yes, the light is strong." The talk paused. A woodpecker pounded against a dead tree.

"You should move into the big house," he said finally. He had told her that before and had been put off. Her excuse then was that the big house was too cold, the cabin was just right. "Old people should not try new houses," she had explained further. At the time he had not insisted for fear she might catch cold and feel bad about leaving her cabin. But warm weather was coming.

"Agnes will fix a bed by the kitchen stove."

The old lady gave no indication of the drift of her thoughts. He had not yet mentioned Max's name; he was not sure how she felt toward him. He would just have to say something and count on her to forget bad feelings.

"Max felt bad about it because you lived in the cabin. If he had not died so soon he would have talked to you about it. He felt bad about the old days. He told me this before he died, and he gave the house to you. Now you must come and live in it."

He did not look at her as he said this. He gazed at the creek at the bottom of a short hill. He heard her murmur "Ah, Max!"

And that was the reconciliation. A few days later she had her belongings carried into the big house and Agnes, all in smiles, hurried to prepare a bed by the kitchen stove. At first Archilde was surprised by this move. He had forgotten, or perhaps he had not realized even then, how warm-hearted his mother was, how easily she forgave.

He ought not to have forgotten that quality in the old lady. And the fact was that, where he was concerned, he knew what to expect. The memories of childhood in which his mother figured were all pleasant. Even then, it seemed, they said but little to each other, yet nothing went unsaid that needed saying.

In those days they were much together. If she went on horseback to gather chokecherries on Dry Creek, she put him behind her saddle and tied him to her with a shawl. When they climbed the hill for strawberries at the end of June, she did all the picking and allowed him to run about and tramp the berries into the ground. Sometimes she spoke sharply and ordered him out of her way, but usually she went on with her work as if he didn't exist. When he tired he went and lay with his head against her, and after that she wouldn't move. Covering his shoulders with her shawl, she would place her hand before her mouth and sing a wordless song, pitching it in such a voice as to make it sound as if it came from a great distance. He often slept until sunset, and when he awoke she would push him away and grumble at his laziness. He would sit up and begin eating the fruit out of her can, until she thumped his head. But if she had not gathered many berries she would not murmur at his eating what she had. "Eheu! The birds would get them if you didn't," she would say.

Such were his memories of her. It was clear that Max need not have doubted her willingness to forget what was past.

These were some of the matters with which he concerned himself during those winter and spring days. His violin study was interrupted and would not be taken up again until he went away. He did not regret this. He was anxious to arrange everything as Max would have had it. It was not hard to wait.

His nephews would be home soon and he would have to decide what to do with them. They did not like the Mission school and he was ready to take their part. What more than that could he do for them? The Fathers swore damnation on the public schools. What influence had they over the boys?

Chapter Twenty-One

WHEN Mike and Narcisse returned from the Mission school something was wrong.

Mike was quieter. He showed no desire to clip a horse and ride break-neck across the meadow, he had given up shouting and blustering. The change showed itself in another way. Mike was afraid of the dark. He couldn't be dragged from the house once night had fallen. When the family laughed, he hung his head sullenly but said nothing. Narcisse appeared to be normal—that is slow, easy-going, and maybe a little dull-witted; but he was his brother's best friend and would not talk about his secrets.

One night at bedtime, when Mike refused to go outside, Archilde teased him.

"If you don't go outside you'll make a puddle in bed, then we'll have to get a pot for you."

Instead of flaring up Mike hung his head.

That very night, after midnight, Mike woke up screaming. He frightened everyone in the house. It was a piercing cry, and it had a peculiar "lost soul" sound. This description flashed upon Archilde's mind at the instant he awakened. He found himself sitting in the dark, frightened and, to his amazement, crossing himself! He stopped in the middle of the act.

The cry came a second time, muffled, but still fearful. Then he located the sound as coming from his nephews' room.

When he turned back the covers he found Mike with his fists dug into his eyes, his knees drawn up, and his body rigid. It was several minutes before he would relax, and then shame kept him from removing his hands. Narcisse had jumped out of bed and was squatting in a corner, his face hidden.

Agnes came upstairs with a flaring lamp in her hand, her eyes wide, and found Archilde sitting on the edge of the bed with Mike's head in his lap.

Mike had wet the bed. Agnes saw it and looked wonderingly at Archilde. He too had been looking at it and recalling how he had teased the boy. He was sorry.

"The old lady shakes like a wet dog," Agnes whispered. "I sent Annie to her. The devil is after her she thinks. You must talk to her. My talk does her no good."

Archilde brought the boys into his room to share his bed. Then he went to see the old lady. She sat upright in bed, moving her lips. As he talked quietly, explaining that Mike had had a bad dream, he felt her watery eyes searching his face. And he knew that mere words were of no use to her.

In the breast of everyone, as the family went back to bed, strange emotions lingered, strange beings encumbered the night. The lamp in the kitchen, where the old lady slept, was not extinguished.

Mike was no longer teased but was rather looked upon with awe. It was clear that something had gone wrong inside. Agnes looked at her son and shook her head. She could not make it out. Archilde set about to discover what had happened.

He went to every boy who he knew had been at the Mission school and asked: "Why is Mike afraid? Why does he wake up and yell?" Sometimes the answer was no more than a shrug of the shoulders, but at other times he saw eyes shift uneasily and he put other questions, with cautious indirection.

Much of the story he was able to supply from his own experience, once he had been given certain hints. And in time he pieced together what had happened.

Mike had been frightened at school.

It seemed that he had been incorrigible. He had started out by refusing to have his hair cut off, but he was unruly in worse ways. During grace at table, in the class room, or in bed at night, he was always whispering; in marching two-by-two he would trip up his marching partner. Also he had wet the bed three times, although punished and warned each time, and in this too he was thought to be acting defiantly. And to all that he had added a bit of defiance which had made everyone quake.

On a morning after he had again wet the bed and was to have been punished, he bet one of the boys that he was not afraid to chew the host which the priest put on his tongue at Communion. The several boys who knew about the bet saw him turn from the Communion rail and chew, and this, as they knew, was sacrilege. He was reported by someone before they reached the refectory for breakfast. Mike was taken out of line just as it was filing into the dining quarters. No words were said, the prefect simply took him by the collar and marched him away. By that time every boy knew what had happened in church and there was silence all through the meal. They wondered what would happen to Mike and were sobered.

In one corner of the dormitory was a small room of unpleasant reputation. As the door was always locked, no one ever saw the inside except those committed to it, but there was much whispering among the boys. Some said that it contained a crown of thorns—the *real* crown of thorns—and some bones, a skull. Some went so far as to say that whoever was put in the room was forced to wear the crown of thorns and kiss the skull. It was apparent that none of the boys who had ever been placed in the room had remembered, or cared to describe, its furnishings.

Mike was locked up and no one saw him again that day. Since the dormitory was closed in daytime, it was impossible even to whisper through the keyhole. That night, when the boys had prayed and gone to bed, the prefect took unusual care to see that all beds were occupied. He marched up and down the center aisle telling his beads long after the lights had been turned off. In the dark they heard the clicking of his beads and the rustle of his cassock as he passed. It made the hair prickle on their heads.

At midnight everyone was sound asleep. Mike's friends tried to stay awake but weariness closed their eyes at last. Sometime after midnight they were awakened by screaming. The first cry merely awakened them, it was the second that set them trembling. The cry ended suddenly, just as it reached its shrillest point. It was that sudden breaking off, and the silence that followed, that seemed most terrible. They could not imagine what had happened. The cry echoed in their heads and made them feel weak.

The prefect appeared, they could not tell from where, because none dared sit up in bed. He entered the solitary chamber, closing the door firmly behind him, and a moment later they heard him praying. It was half an hour before he reappeared. Mike was with him, supported on the prefect's arm. He was pale and, as everyone could see, as limp as a rag, as if he had been restored from a faint.

The prefect remained at Mike's bed through the remainder of the night, praying over him. Mike's friends thought he stayed so they couldn't talk to him.

The next morning, at breakfast, the prefect made a short announcement. "The Father Superior has ordered that a week of prayer be observed, beginning today. In keeping with this order, it will not be seemly to play any rough or loud games. Accordingly, your recess periods will be given to prayer and at all times you are to deport yourselves with humility." There was no explanation of this action, but the boys needed none.

They needed no explanation either of what had happened to Mike. He had been placed in the infirmary and had talked to no one, but they knew that he had been visited by the Evil One. That was why they had to pray. They discussed this in whispers and looked about uneasily. Their active imaginations could perfectly well visualize good and evil spirits flying through the air; they were prepared to see the earth crack open at any moment and reveal the fires of hell, as the large painting on the church wall showed it. They knew that the devil had appeared to Mike because there was a tradition that such a thing had happened before in that room, to a boy who later was dragged to death by his horse.

"Something will happen to Mike, now, you see," they whispered. "The devil's mark is on him."

Some would not discuss it at all. "God can hear when you whisper. Take care what you say! Something will happen."

Meantime, Mike continued to be afraid of the dark, only he tried to hide it now. He had to be urged to go fishing, but nothing could induce him to ride a horse. He knew the story of the boy who had been dragged to death. Archilde stayed close to the boys. He fashioned spears and sling shots and tried to make fishing and hunting as exciting as it used to be, but Mike would walk through the woods and have no eyes for a squirrel sitting at close range. If the woods were deep and shadowy he would never walk in the lead.

One day when he was alone with Narcisse he tried to get close to the trouble. "Will Mike get better? What d'you think?"

Narcisse shrugged his shoulders.

"Listen. You must tell him—" He didn't know how to reach Mike through words. But he would try it. "Tell him it's all lies, what the priests say. It's all lies about the devil. Tell him to look at the birds. They fly around, and they don't know nothing about the devil. Look at them fly!"

Narcisse watched some birds fly past. Then he contemplated the earth again. He frowned to show that he was thinking. "But the hawks!" His face cleared with the words. "They're afraid of the hawks! Maybe the hawks are devils!"

"Pshaw! The hawks—" Archilde frowned in his turn. "We shoot the hawks, and they die. If they were devils, could we kill them? Not the way the priests talk."

Narcisse was taken with the idea. When birds again flew by he watched them until they were out of sight. "I'll tell that to Mike," he promised.

Archilde did not expect anything to come from his theological argument. Something more than words was needed to lift Mike out of his dark mood, but he didn't know what. He thought hard, in bed at night and while walking through the woods on a spring day, but no ideas came to him.

These efforts to bring peace and order into the lives of his relatives before he left them forever did not please him greatly. Whatever he did, he felt that he remained on the outside of their problems. He had grown away from them, and even when he succeeded in approaching them in sympathy, he remained an outsider—only a little better than a professor come to study their curious ways of life. He saw no way of changing it.

Chapter Twenty-Two

THE end of June marks the final flowering of the seeds of spring, and by the time the fruit ripens on the service-berry bushes there is nothing new or fresh to come. The dust grows heavier in the road and wayside bushes turn gray and unpleasant to touch. The exultation of the first green days is now dissipated, drawn off like morning mist, and living becomes sober—the straight-back pull of horses drawing their load uphill.

Here, in this last week of June, Archilde was riding Max's white mare, who had reconciled herself to him. He was going to visit the blind chief, Modeste, who had sent word that he wanted to talk. Since that evening of feasting almost a year ago, Archilde had not seen the old man, but he was frequently thinking of him and of the story he had told that night. Modeste's story about the old days was the first one, and he had heard many, that Archilde had listened to with his mind. It was the first story about his people that he understood. He could not explain why he had listened and understood, but since it had happened he was continually thinking about the old chief.

He was crossing Buffalo Creek at the ford a mile below his house. The spring rise was just subsiding and the water, as it splashed over round boulders,

filled the air with a solemn roaring. The trail dropped
out of the hot sun and went aslope of the steep bank,
down into shadow and dampness. Her forefeet awash,
the mare paused to drink, looked up once with mouth
closed, then after a second draft came up champing
and dripping. She was ready to proceed. She chose her
footing cautiously.

As he neared the house, dogs rushed upon him from
front and rear, from the barn, and from a distant
meadow where there had been a game of digging out
gophers; some snarling with peevish tempers, approaching threateningly, while others roared with foolish satisfaction at the sound of their throaty voices and
showed their good nature by keeping at a distance.
The mare was of no common breed and she resented
such manners. She flattened her small ears and stepped
along nervously. But when the chance came her heels
flew out, and a shaggy-haired beast that had tried
quietly to hamstring her was sent rolling in a ball of
dust. After that the hubbub subsided. Archilde stroked
her neck.

There is a kind of chaos about an Indian's home-
stead that, however complete and hopeless, is never-
theless not inherent; it does not belong to the man.
In the tepee, everything is in place; but when houses
are built and farming implements acquired, then nothing is surprising; the hayrake stands before the front
door and a mowing machine, with many parts missing,
turns to rust; a wagon not far away is covered with an
assortment of harness and saddles which never find

their way to the barn; as there is no concentrated rubbish heap, tin cans are scattered to the yard at large;
here are the ruins of some shade trees, sold and even
planted by an energetic traveling nurseryman, but
broken away limb by limb to provide whips for a lazy
horse—they had never been watered anyhow, except
by the dogs and a kind sky; a grindstone that has long
ago jumped from its iron trestle lies fractured, one end
of its rusty shaft obtruding, like the upraised arm of a
drowning man; and these are only a few of the evidences of a foreign world.

Modeste's ranch was an accumulation, an amalgamation. His own house (built by his son-in-law, the shiftless Octave La Rose, on money borrowed on God
knows what pretense of security) was a modern affair.
At least it was a frame structure of several rooms,
plastered, and painted brown and yellow, with a brick
chimney. All the rooms were used for sleeping, though
there were no beds, and the cooking was done outside,
in a nearby shed in winter time. As this was the main
establishment, it was occupied by Modeste, unwillingly (the floors broke his old bones), and by the great
Octave and his wife and daughters. In addition to the
new house, there was a log cabin—a relic of the cruder
days, as Indian agents were fond of expressing it—and
this and the hayloft furnished sleeping quarters for the
boys of the La Rose clan. Finally, there were two tepees in use and two stacks of tepee poles over which
canvas could be stretched when any of the relatives
came visiting; the used tepees were occupied by two

married daughters and their families.

The dogs had been dispersed by the time Archilde drew up to dismount, and the young boys who had sprung from the earth to perform the act of dispersing —using sticks as charms and the incantations of French, Salish and English swearing—returned to their hiding places. Archilde dismounted unattended, at some distance from the old man.

Modeste and Octave were seated on an outspread blanket in the narrow band of shade provided by the house. Octave was fat and the sweat stood on his face like drops of oil. His hair was dressed in the Indian fashion, long and braided, a braid hanging down each side of the chest. Whatever else he had, he lacked the Indian manner, for all his living like a tribesman for some twenty years. He called out in the booming voice for which he was famous and invited the guest to a seat. Archilde felt the embarrassment expressed in Modeste's fluttering eyelids, and went forward quietly. His greeting, spoken with reserve, raised a quick smile and a soft word from the old chief.

Octave offered tobacco and cigarette papers which he carried wadded up in his shirt pocket. He talked in two breaths about a hundred things—the flies, the heat, his horses which he intended to run in the Fourth of July races. He was one of those irrepressible chatterers to whom silence is an agony. Archilde nodded and waited. Modeste also waited, his sightless eyes downcast. He was an ancient man, with his white hair yellowed and his skin hanging about his face and neck in dry folds.

Finally, when the fountain gave no indication of running dry, the old man held up the bones which were his hand. Octave sighed to a stop, uncrossed his legs, and stretched out on his back, thus signalizing his withdrawal. Modeste did not speak at once, but his words, when they did come, had a dry, high sound, like the snapping of twigs.

"What I hear is bad. No doubt you think it is bad."

The talk was in his mother's tongue, which he understood easily but spoke uncertainly. It would have been better if Octave had gone away altogether.

"You will tell me, grandfather, what you hear."

The old man gestured with his hand, palm downward, as if to say: "If what I report is untrue, don't have a poor opinion of me. It's not of my inventing."

His words were: "Your sister's boy, that little Mike, they tell me he is sick. He is sick of horses, and of the dark, and of many things. If this is true, it is bad."

"Yes, it is true. He is afraid of these things and it is bad."

(Modeste had used the word "szal," to have sickness; and Archilde used "sngel," to have fear. The word was repeated several times before he realized that, in the old man's mind, if you feared anything you were certainly sick.)

"Ah, ah! Ah, ah! I was told so and I have thought about it. It is a sad thing when a young boy is sick in this way. For if the children have this sickness, what will the old people be like in times to come? That is what I think about."

Archilde did not interrupt to agree, for he knew that the old man was ready to say what was in his mind.

"If an old man comes and spreads his blanket and sits down where he is not wanted, hear him speak anyway. It is easier for a young man to listen than for an old man to go away. There will be a dance of the old times down on Buffalo Creek, below St. Xavier. I will go to this dance. As you know, I have been without eyes for a long time and you know how I go about. My grandchild walks in front, holding a thong, and I follow. Now, it will be a good thing if Mike comes to this dance, to hear of the old times and dance with us who lived in those days. If he wishes, and you let him, he shall take the place of my grandson and lead me by the string."

Archilde could see how it would be. Modeste occupied the situation of honor at all tribal gatherings, and this distinction was heightened by the unique place he occupied in the minds of all men, Indian and white, for his own character. Mike would be stirred by this, his pride would be awakened—if it were still alive. Archilde realized this and was grateful, but in his reply he spoke in the simple terms of the offer.

"Yes, this is a good thing. My sister's boy will be pleased. He will come to you here."

With these words spoken, there was no more to say. Archilde gave his farewell and went to his horse.

As he rode back toward Buffalo Creek, planning the words in which he would inform Mike of the invitation, he heard a horse galloping to overtake him. He shifted in the saddle to look back, and at the same moment one of Octave's daughters, the one called Elise, dashed past, giving her horse the heel just as she came abreast. The forward spurt of her horse was the only urging the white mare required, and Archilde found himself in a race. He accepted the challenge, crying out sharply, and shifting his weight forward. The two horses, the bay in front and the gleaming white a length behind, thundered toward the dark forest emerging from the canyon of Buffalo Creek.

Elise La Rose. Elise La Rose. The name barely recalled images. She had been at the Indian school in Oregon, he seemed to remember, but he had hardly been aware of her. She turned her face to him, her head inclined to the wind, laughing. She rode easily, her skirt gripped under her thighs, and her short hair flying like a black banner.

They breasted just before reaching the canyon's edge and the horses came heavily, though gracefully, to a halt, throwing up sod and scattering gravel with their stiffened legs. Before he had time to speak, her bay horse started down the trail. He had never known a horse that could stay in front of the white mare for as long as this bay had, and the mare threw her head up and down and chafed at the bit in disappointment.

Down in the rocky bottom he trotted up and found her smiling. "That's a good horse you're riding."

She laughed but did not speak at once.

"You are Elise. At first I couldn't remember you.

At school you were a little girl."

"But I've been at school until now. I had to run away to get home again. My old man would a let me rot there." Her face was serious as she spoke, then her smile returned. He liked that smile and he began to look at her oftener, even meeting her eyes.

"They'll send you back then."

She frowned. "Like hell they will! The old man doesn't care, now I'm home. And the Agent will have to catch me." The smile returned.

The horse plunged into the water and Archilde fell back.

On the farther side she trotted forward to an open patch of sunlight, where she waited for him.

"You got a cigarette?" she asked at once. "The old man won't let us smoke, but we do. Eve and Félice and me. We smoked in school, too." He wondered if she were bragging but soon became convinced that she was daring enough to have smoked at school, where if she had been caught no doubt they would have broken her neck.

She drew the smoke in deeply, with a look of enjoyment, and exhaled it lingeringly. His eyes were constantly on her; he had begun to wonder why she had raced after him, what she expected of him, what he was to do next. He learned little through his eyes to satisfy this questioning; they rather added to his confusion and started other queries. How old was she? Was she pretty? What was she like?

For a moment they were silent, then Elise spoke

confidingly. "Eve tried to beat me but she wasn't fast enough and Félice was asleep. They're rough-housers, those two. When they see a fellow he has a tough time getting away. If you come to see me look out for them."

It looked like a scheme and it made him laugh.

"I'll bring my quirt when I come."

"Let me see your handkerchief," she demanded suddenly, pointing to the piece of white silk around his neck. He held it out from his neck for a better view.

"I mean let me see it. Take it off. It looks pretty."

He drew the ends through the ivory ring and handed the square of silk to her.

"Now! You'll have to come for it," she cried, at the same time digging her heels into the bay horse and plunging toward the water.

He whirled to follow, but as he did so he thought of the aged Modeste sitting at home. It would be a strange trick to come thundering back within an hour, at the heels of the old man's grandchild. He looked foolish, and he had his last glimpse of Elise as she mounted the opposite bank, waving her trophy.

Chapter Twenty-Three

IN the old days the Salish people held a great dance in midsummer, just as the sun reached its highest point. They would come together from all parts of the country; all branches of the nation would be there; their tents would be scattered over miles of prairie land. At night their camp fires would be like a host of stars fallen out of heaven. This dance was the expression of their exultation at being alive, it sang of their pride, their conquests, their joys. For them the sun at its height was the most favored time of the year, as they were the most favored children of "Grandfather Sun." In this dance only the toughest and longest enduring took part, because it was a supreme test of strength; they danced until exhaustion struck them down and no one wanted to be the first to drop. It was shameful not to last long enough to express what was felt.

Such a dance could not be tolerated in later years. Its barbarous demands on strength offended those who came to manage the affairs of the Indians in their own homes. There was nothing wrong with the dance in itself but it ought to be kept within reasonable limits. If the Indians wished to express their joy for, say, ten hours a day and then rest, like a factory or office worker, that would be all right. They could go on dancing for as many days as they liked on that arrangement, only they ought not to lose too much time at it. It was probably a fair arrangement because, though the dance was curtailed, so was the exultation it expressed. They decided to dance while they could. Some dances had been stopped completely.

There was the scalp dance of long ago. That of course had to be stopped at once. Maybe it wasn't a beautiful dance but it had its purpose. It took place after a battle, if there were any enemy trophies to celebrate over. It was like a "grand review" without the finer points. The dance wasn't held immediately upon the return of the warriors because those who had returned with scalps had to have a few days to talk about what they had done and point to the scalps they had taken. The scalps were hung up for display like captured flags, then after a few days when they began to "break down" they were thrown into the dust and the dance began. This dance was performed by the women. They simply stamped upon the scalps and uttered insulting language. It was a dance of vengeance and of exultation over the prowess of the men. A dance like that had to be stopped.

Another of the old-time dances which had offended the Indians' guardians was the marriage dance, which in its way was a pleasant performance. The young people used to enjoy it and the old wiseheads would look on and reflect pleasantly on how they had enjoyed it in their time. In this dance the young unmarried women formed a circle about the drummers; they

linked their arms together and sidestepped round and
round, and they kept up a certain song. If a young
man wanted one of those girls he went with one or
two friends, for encouragement perhaps, and broke
through the chain. Within the circle, he waited for his
choice to come opposite him, then he stepped forward
and placed a small stick on her shoulder, and then it
was up to the girl. If she did not want him she made a
face, shrugged her shoulder and let the stick fall off.
At that everybody laughed and the suitor would run
off and perhaps would not be seen for quite a while.
If she accepted him, she bent her head sideways until
her cheek rested on the stick and held it in place. Then
he would take her by the hand and they would go to
his lodge, if he was old enough to have one of his own;
or they simply went to the brush. A dance like that
didn't hurt anybody but they had to give it up.

This dance which was being held on the Fourth of
July was a survival of the old midsummer dance. It
was no longer an endurance test and there was not
much exultation expressed by it, but the Indians enjoyed it because it brought many of them together and
for a while they could forget how bad it was at home.

Before life changed for the Salish people they would
not have begun a ceremony like the midsummer dance
without first having met and cleansed themselves. All
old scores would have been settled, the pipe would
have been smoked between men who had quarreled,
and restitution would have been made of any damages
which had been inflicted upon another. And finally

the lash would have been laid on anyone who was guilty of wrongdoing. (No one could now remember exactly what was punishable with the lash in those days, because after the Fathers came many new "crimes" were added, such as creating a disturbance at church or prayers.) The "whip covered the fault."

Whipping, like the scalp and marriage dance, was now a thing of the past. At first the practice was denounced because it was reported that the Jesuits had introduced it among the innocent Indians. When that story was proved false, the practice was still denounced, and finally abolished, as being too barbarous. The guardians might not always know why they objected to a native custom, but if they objected it didn't make much difference what the reason was.

On the night before the dance was to open, when the tepees had all been pitched in a great circle and the pavilion was built and waiting, a small group of Indians met secretly in a grove of trees away from the encampment. The group sat in a close circle without a fire, the only light coming from a pale moon which was just clearing the tree tops. The Indians' guardians would have been shocked if they had known about that group, because it had met for the purpose of holding court and using the whip.

The blind Modeste, who was the first to speak, was full of doubt. He said: "Years ago they told us that we would get into trouble if we whipped people. Myself, I don't think they should have said that. We know our affairs. But it was said, and since that time we have not used the whip. Yes, I think it is bad. In the old days it was a good thing because it kept the people straight. We knew our guilt and we told it; or, if we tried to forget, somebody would speak up and then it came out. When we were told to give this up, they said they would give us new laws. Well, they gave us those new laws and now nobody is straight. Nobody will confess and nobody will go to the white judge and say 'My nephew has broken the law,' or 'my relative over there on Crow Creek whipped his woman and ought to go to jail.' That's the way it goes now; the old law is not used and nobody cares about the new. I am sorry about this; the young people respect neither old nor new, and the old ones do not enjoy having nothing to say about right and wrong. But I have promised not to use the whip. I will let this woman speak."

He indicated the person sitting at his right. When she lowered her shawl to speak the others could see that it was Catharine, the mother of Archilde, she who since the coming of the Fathers was called "Faithful Catharine."

"In the old days you were whipped and no one spoke of it again. The heart was free. I have asked this to be done to me. I will tell you what it is, but first I will tell you something else."

The old lady paused and for a moment her face was again lost in her shawl. Then she emerged. "You know me from old times. I was the first to be baptized by the Fathers. Since that day I have not changed. I heard about people who stopped going to church and they were telling people they weren't baptized any more. Some shaved their heads where the holy water touched them. I was not one of them, that you know.

"Now I will have to tell you what happened to me and how it is changed."

She then told of the hunting trip; of how, after Louis had been shot, she tried to understand what made things go that way. Why was it that when he came home from school he went "bad"; and when would the old people have that happiness the Fathers had promised them? She had done everything they asked of her, and yet she had it no better than some of those who gave it up. Then she told how she had been to Confession, hoping that it would free her heart. But it had been of no use. Fasting and prayer were no use. Perhaps she would have said nothing about it and after a while it would have been all right again, but she had a dream.

"In this dream, I fell sick, I died and went to heaven in the sky. Since I had lived a holy life I went to heaven. It was like the Fathers told us it would be. I saw some of those Fathers who have been here with us, and their friends and relatives were there and they were happy. Everybody was happy and they said to me, 'You just be happy now.' I said yes I would be happy pretty soon but I would look around. It was all strange. Then I walked a long ways, going here and there, and I could not understand it. I saw none of my friends or relatives there. There were no Indians there at all. I walked some more, but it was no use. These white people had everything they wanted, big houses all painted, fine garments like they wear, rings on their fingers and gold in their teeth, they had it all; but there were no animals to hunt and when I looked in the rivers there were no fish there. It was a good thing there were no Indians there because they would have found nothing to do. Pretty soon the people were saying I did not look happy, so the white God sent for me. He was a kind man. 'Why is it you're not happy?' he asked me. So I told him and he said I could go away and go to the Indian heaven if I wished. Then I went to the Indian place and I could hear them singing. Their campfires burned and I could smell meat roasting. There were no white men there at all. I asked to come in but they told me no. I was baptized and I could not go there. First I would have to return to earth and give up my baptism. When I woke up I just sat and thought about that dream. All that day I could do nothing but think about it. The next night it was the same, that very dream. The second day I talked to no one. The third night came and I was afraid to sleep, but I did, and it was the same. They told me again I would have to give up my baptism. When I woke up I knew I had to do it."

The old lady had completed her retreat from the world which had come to Sniél-emen. Those who listened, and old Modeste especially, since he was her kin, were thunderstruck by what she told them. They "fell dead" of astonishment. Others might lose interest and wander away or mourn because they could not have the old life back, but Catharine had gone on performing her duties and never questioning what she had been taught. The Fathers pointed her out as a model of devotion. "Do as Catharine does and your prayers will be answered," the Fathers said.

The old lady continued. "If any of you think I've done wrong, it will do no good to say so. To me it is clear and I won't go back. Only consider. For years I saw how the world was going. You knew my sons and how I prayed for them and tried to keep them from going to hell. It would have been better if they had been given the whip. Praying was not what was needed for them, and it does me no good. You have made this promise but tonight you ought to forget it. If you get into trouble over it, it will be nothing new. We have had trouble no matter what we do and we ought just to forget about it and live as it seems best."

The voices murmured approval. They were calling upon Modeste to forget his promise about the whip. A thing like this could not be understood by those who made the new laws and it was useless to explain. Better just go ahead like men. They were children in too many things as it was.

Modeste was silent for a long time. Then he announced that he too had been following the path of this woman, his oldest brother's daughter; he also had turned back to that world which was there before the new things came. Then he told a story—nothing was

ever done without telling a story. In that story he told
how his *Somesh* (his guardian spirit) had rescued him
from a snowslide in which he had been caught when
hunting in the mountains. First he had prayed a long
time and it did no good, and then as he was about to
die his *Somesh* came to him in a vision and just after
that somebody saw his gun sticking up through the
snow and they dug him out. That happened some
years ago and since then he too had been going back
to the old things.

So at last, when everyone had told his story and it
was all agreed, those old people turned back on the
path they had come and for a while their hearts were
lightened. The old lady, with the red stripes of the
whip on her back, slept without dreaming.

Chapter Twenty-Four

De-dum, de-dum, de-dum, de-dum, de-dum . . .

The drum had been beating since early morning, faintly, regularly, as if the earth had begun to pulse. It was a sound to quicken the blood. People still at home, going about their daily chores, listened, and then hurried to complete what was still to do that they might be free. The throb of the drum lifted their spirits, urged them forward. It was an intoxicant.

Dust rose from every road leading to St. Xavier and disappeared against the cloudless sky. The sun was at white heat. People were on the move, traveling in spring wagons, in carriages, on horseback, afoot. Every roadside barn and nearly every telephone pole was placarded with the announcement: "FOURTH OF JULY CELEBRATION: BUCKING CONTESTS: HORSE RACES: BASEBALL GAME: BIG INDIAN DANCE: DANCING AT NIGHT WITH RAG-TIME MUSIC: COME ONE! COME ALL! RIDE 'EM COWBOY!"

In St. Xavier groups of men stood before the pool-halls, talking and laughing. Women passed, surrounded by their children; the little girls in starched dresses and ribbons flying, the boys rigged out like baseball players.

In the dusty streets horses reared and plunged at the

sound of exploding firecrackers. The riders cursed, to
the amusement of the onlookers. When one rider was
hurled through a store window the crowd was de-
lighted. On the Fourth of July everybody was a little
bit crazy. They shouted "Let 'er buck!"

The older boys and girls eyed each other's new
clothes and made remarks. They went about in groups,
the girls with arms entwined, giggling, screaming.
When a group of boys went down the street, girls followed—not too near, but not far behind.

Dogs fought in the street, firecrackers exploded,
babies cried, mothers were worried. Nobody above
the age of twenty had a really good time, but they
wouldn't have been found enjoying themselves at
home for anything.

Beneath all other sounds, and giving to movement
as well as to sound an conscious rhythm, was the throb
of the drum. . . .

Dum, de-dum, de-dum, de-dum, de-dum . . .

The dancing ground was a mile below St. Xavier,
in a grove of willows and cottonwoods near Buffalo
Creek. The circle of white tepees, with their smoke-
stained tops, contained more than a hundred camps.
People streamed out of St. Xavier, where many had left
their rigs, going toward the encampment and the
sound of the drum. Dust rose chokingly from the
ground. The air seemed to be turning to fire.

In the early morning Archilde went to Modeste's
lodge, one of the few old-time hide-covered tepees,

and one of the handsomest. Within it, he found the old man sitting with his hands in his lap, in an attitude of contemplation, calling to mind the sweet peace of the past; his lips moved, his eyelids fluttered; in different dress he might have been taken for a priest preparing himself for some ceremony.

Modeste's old woman, a dried-up creature, but possessed of her sight and of surprising energy, was preparing Mike for the dance, and enjoying herself with the detached, suave humor of the aged. She was painting his face, applying red in a band across his cheeks, and then placing six white dots under each eye. In the old days this would have signified that each eye was to have the strength of six; today it signified no more than an old woman's fancy. She chuckled. Bells were attached to his ankles, and she shook each leg in turn to try the effect. Her smile exposed her toothless mouth.

Mike was quiet, but not dull, as he had been too much of late. Archilde watched him closely. His eyes were active, examining the old woman's paint pots and following her agile fingers. At odd times, he looked guardedly at Modeste, revealing a shyness which expressed his awe of the old man and his excitement at the drama he was to have a part in. If Modeste was a priest, Mike was his altar boy, and each was absorbed in the part.

Archilde did not wait for them to quit the lodge. Occasions of that sort, he knew, required a decent privacy. Intruders were not wanted, strange voices were

unkind. The old man with the boy leading him would
move across the prairie in their own dignity, and anyone would show them small respect who sought to
share the honor with them.

He quit the lodge and went to his mother across the
encampment. She too was occupied, making Narcisse
ready. Watching her, Archilde felt suddenly happy.
She was pleased with her duties in the way that only
an old art or an old way of life, long disused, can please
the hand and the heart returning to it. She took up
the folded garments of beaded buckskin and placed
them on her grandchild in a kind of devotional act
that derived satisfaction from minute observances; in
a matter so simple, the least part has its significance or
it is all meaningless. Narcisse submitted to her mood
and to her ministering, even to her hands removing
his underclothing and leaving him momentarily
naked.

Archilde could see that for his mother this was a
real thing, and he had felt the same way a moment before in Modeste's lodge. For these old people it was
real, almost real enough to make it seem like a spirit
come from the grave. Watching his mother's expe-
rienced hands, he could guess how she had lived, what
she had thought about in her childhood. A great deal
had happened since those hands were young, but in
making them work in this way, in the way she had been
taught, it was a little bit as if the intervening happenings had never been. He watched the hands move and
thought these things. For a moment, almost, he was

not an outsider, so close did he feel to those ministering hands.

Upon leaving her lodge he went toward the dancing ground—and at once his feeling changed. There was nothing real in the scene he came upon. The rows of carriages and wagons were bad enough, but that wasn't the worst. The idea was of a spectacle, a kind of low-class circus where people came to buy peanuts and look at freaks.

The dancing ground was a round pavilion, about thirty feet in diameter, with upright posts supporting a roof of fir boughs laid across poles. A tall post was planted in the center of this circular ground, and its upper end, protruding above the roof of boughs, flew the American flag. Benches were placed inside for the dancers.

This pavilion was surrounded by selling booths decorated with bunting, and the crowd was coaxed to buy "ice col' pop" and "strawb'ry ice cream" and to win a "cute Frenchy doll" on the roulette wheel. The crowd was dense and perspiring.

The drum was placed flat on the ground within the pavilion and the drummers sat around it, beating it with short sticks, the ends of which had been covered with red flannel. As they beat time they also sang, without words, a sort of "HI-yih, hi-yih, hi-yih, HI-yih, hi-yih . . ."

The ground within the pavilion had already been beaten bare by the stamping feet. Only a few tufts of the tough prairie grass remained. A fine dust rose, parching the throats of the dancers and causing the women spectators to wave their handkerchiefs before their faces. "Phew! My! My! What dust!" they exclaimed sweetly.

All that was part of the circus atmosphere. The dancers, meanwhile, enacted their parts and showed no concern because of the staring eyes and the distractions beyond the pavilion.

"Ho! Let it be as it was in old times!" The aged Modeste had begun the dance with those words and there were cries of approbation. The dancers went forward like actors in a play and lost themselves in their game. In the pauses between dances bottles of soda water were passed around and old men told stories. These were cheered as if the actions they described had taken place only yesterday.

Archilde had wedged himself into the front line of spectators, but when he got there he was sorry. It was a sad spectacle to watch. It was like looking on while crude jokes were played on an old grandmother, who was too blind to see that the chair had been pulled away just before she went to sit down. He felt the hurt which the old men suffered unknowingly.

They echoed the war cry from time to time and made threatening gestures with a feathered carpenter's hatchet, which was fierce enough to cause a white woman to grow pale and draw back, it was true—but what a small matter that was! The white husband made a joke of it, as well he might.

"Let it be today as it was in old times!"

The throbbing drum, the voices chanting in unison, the bells on the dancers' legs, the stamping feet, each in its way added to the simple rhythm and swelled the volume of sound until it traveled to the surrounding mountains and rolled back upon the prairie. On no other occasion did the Indians make so much noise.

But he had come to see Mike and he would stay until he had satisfied his eyes. He wanted to watch the expression on the boy's face and try to guess how he was taking this medicine for his "sickness."

At first he did not locate him, but after a moment Mike seemed to appear out of a cloud, partly dust and partly moving figures. And then he came forward with a slow, weaving, muscular movement that was inexplicably graceful—a detached element of rhythm, moving unhindered through space. Behind the boy, the dry bones of Modeste advanced with a minimum of variation from normal locomotion. As the pair passed, Archilde stood but two feet away and the vision he had of Mike's face was stirring.

For a moment he felt everything Mike felt—the rhythmic movement, the body's delight in a sinuous thrusting of legs and arms, the wild music of drum and dancing bells, and best of all, the majesty of the dancers. It really seemed, for a moment, as if they were unconquerable and as if they might move the world were they to set their strength to it. They made one think of a wild stallion running free—no one could approach him, no one would ever break his spirit.

That was what he shared with Mike, but it was for

a moment only. Then he heard the spectators laughing. They were making fun of an old man, too weak to move in the circle, who stood in one place and bobbed himself up and down. His face showed his inner contentment and he was oblivious of the laughter at his expense. Someone shouted "Hi, gran'pa! Does your mama know you're out?" Archilde went away, making a passage for himself through the dense crowd.

Just then, walking across the encampment, he came face to face with Dave Quigley—walking, for a change, his thin legs supporting his heavy body precariously on high-heeled boots, his badge of office flapping with his unbuttoned vest. He came forward smiling—and Dave Quigley when he smiled was more to be feared than when his face wore its usual dead expression.

"Thought you'd like to hear what I just discovered —I found Dan Smith's saddle. Yeh. The guy that murdered Dan and turned his horse loose threw the saddle in the creek. Well, I found the saddle lodged against the bank. And this is the funny thing"— He paused and looked squarely at Archilde, still smiling— "it wasn't the creek you tell me you camped on. No. It's another creek about ten miles further along. All I have to do now is search that creek from start to finish till I find Dan's body. That's where it'll be—somewhere along that creek. Of course, if you weren't on that creek where I found the saddle, your story's good."

He did not wait for Archilde to reply but began to walk away before the last words were uttered. He had ceased to smile and as his mouth snapped shut finally he left the impression of knowing more than he revealed. It was a threat, not information, he had left behind.

Archilde was left quaking. He looked stealthily about to see if anyone had overheard the conversation; and even when he found that nobody had been near, he carried away such a sense of guilt that he avoided looking at people passing. He walked rapidly toward the outer line of tepees, his mind a wild scramble of half-formed thoughts. He must catch a train that night! He must sneak away! No, they would suspect him at once! They would telegraph and have him taken off the train! Then hide in the mountains! Like Louis—like an Indian! By God, no!

Suddenly he found himself at his mother's tepee and crept inside, feeling unexpectedly sheltered and safe.

The drum was silenced at sundown and the white people went away. Then the women brought forth the horses and decked them with fancy gear—with saddles of the whitest and softest of buckskin, stirrup leathers reaching to the ground, and painted and fringed caparisons covering the horses from withers to tail. There were horsehair bridles with colored rosettes, martingales spangled with silver, and bells hanging from cinches and saddle backs. When the men had eaten they mounted their horses and began a procession, going round and round the circle of tepees.

The chiefs rode in front, each in turn delivering a
speech to the encampment, and those who rode behind
responded. The bells on the horses rang out, *ca-ring*,
ca-ring, *ca-ring*, measuring the stately pace. Fires
glowed within the tepees and children stood at the en-
tranceways. The dogs sat on their haunches but made
no outcry.

As Archilde sat in his mother's tepee he wondered
at the expression of peace which had settled over her.
From the depths of his own turmoil he looked upon
her with searching eyes. At first he had an impulse to
tell her what had happened, but when he studied her
calm, half-smiling face, he realized that it would not
do. Her hands had taken her far back into the past
that day and he would not drag her forth again.

She stirred the fire and he watched the sparks fly
upward, alive, then dead. They lived just long enough
to know. A man's life was too long by comparison. It
dragged out his misery, or if he had happiness that too
was dragged out until it turned into misery. And he
didn't die until he had tasted all of it. One had just to
go on, taking everything that came, somehow. . . .

Ca-ring, ca-ring, ca-ring . . .

"My people! Listen to my words! When I was
young . . ."

The old lady sighed. She stirred slightly, then returned to her dreaming.

A full yellow moon had risen above the grove of
cottonwoods. The fires within the tepees glowed at the

base of the gloom.

Archilde sat quietly and felt those people move in his blood. There in his mother's tepee he had found unaccountable security. It was all quite near, quite a part of him; it was his necessity, for the first time.

Chapter Twenty-Five

In town later that evening, as he came out of a restaurant, Archilde met Elise La Rose. He would have continued on his way but she took his arm.

"I was looking for you. Take me to the dance."

He was puzzled. "The dance is over."

"Oh, hell! Not the Indian dance. That makes me sick. I mean the regular dance at the Hall."

He had no desire to go there. He had been on his way home. He said so.

"We'll have a good time. And look, I turned down two fellows already. I was waiting for you. So you got to be a sport, now. You ain't got a girl already?"

No, he didn't have a girl. In the pale light her upturned face held his gaze and he could not turn from it. He consented. He had come to town in the blue automobile and now he led her to it. It was not far away. She was dressed in white and made a sparkling figure in the moonlight.

He had not been avoiding Elise, but neither had he gone after his handkerchief. He had not even thought of it. He wasn't afraid of her, he told himself, but now that she had a hold of him he was feeling the way he felt just before climbing into the saddle on a bucking horse. Something was going to happen.

"What made you wait for me?" He wanted to ask why in hell she hadn't left him alone. The car started and she rolled against him. She looked at his unsmiling face and laughed.

"I don't like these scissor-bills around here!" Her explanation got no response from him.

The dance had already begun in Farmers' Hall. Stepping in out of darkness, the glaring lights struck one's eyes. Men were gathered around the doorway and talk and cigarette smoke blew about their heads. The benches around the dancing floor were taken up by the women, those who had come to dance and those who were fat and old, who merely came to look on and wag their tongues.

Archilde did not want to meet people. He still bore the sense of guilt which had come alive that afternoon. He looked carefully for Dave Quigley and finally, when satisfied that the Sheriff was not present, he moved with less constraint. But even without that worry he did not take easily to the dance. Something about it repelled him. He frowned and held himself aloof.

Elise felt it and became irritated. "What's the matter! If you don't like it, I guess there's plenty of fellows around!"

"That fiddler—listen to him!" The idea came to him suddenly—the music rasped his nerves.

It was useless to explain. Elise listened, but it sounded all right. Nobody minded. The people who glided by were undisturbed. He was surprised by what they neither saw nor heard. They had come to talk and push each other around the room, and they required nothing—bare gray walls, glaring lights, rasping music, none of those things hindered. The Indians at least, when they went to dance, were reliving an old way of life and they tried to put themselves in the right mood. They dressed themselves in ways that had special significance, and there were symbols and gestures of various meanings. But for these people there was nothing, as he could see by looking at them.

"Aw, hell! Enjoy yourself." Elise was protesting. "You're a swell dancer. Let yourself go!" She pressed closer until he could feel her thighs moving against his. She leaned backward from the waist and teased him. His arm tightened.

He danced nimbly, whirling through the simple, meaningless steps without effort. By the time they had gone through several dances he began to smile a little and to let himself go, as Elise had urged. Sheriff Quigley was not there—he could let him slip out of mind. The music seemed to grow less harsh.

Before long Elise wanted something to drink. "This dance needs a kick. Let's go find something."

He knew that Max had left a stock of liquor at home, much whisky, some brandy, and a few bottles of wine, but he said nothing about it. Liquor was prohibited on the Reservation and he had no idea where people got the stuff. It was sold freely by certain runners but he had no idea where to find them.

Elise knew all about it. She knew everything about

matters of that sort, just as at school she had known how to fool the matrons, how to get cigarettes, and how to sneak out of the dormitory. To some people nothing is ever hidden and they live by habit in a world beneath the surface of things which most people never suspect even exists. Elise was such a person; she amazed Archilde.

They drove along the stage road leading out of St. Xavier, then turned into a side lane. He recognized an abandoned ranch which he probably drove past several times a week. The log cabin was back some distance from the road and partly hidden by a cottonwood grove. There was no light in the window but several automobiles made shadowy patches off to one side. It was not deserted. He had switched off his lights as they approached.

Elise gave him directions. "Tell Barney—he's the guy you'll meet—tell him you want white mule. The other stuff ain't no good, but the white mule he makes himself. If he asks who sent you, tell him I'm waiting here."

When he returned with the bottle they drove off. Before they reached the main road she had him slow down and showed him an opening in the brush patch which they had been skirting. There was no mistaking her knowledge of the vicinity.

They drank out of the bottle. It was scorching stuff. They smoked and had another drink. Archilde felt himself relax. Dave Quigley was quite gone from his mind. For the first time, too, he quit scheming at the back of his head for an excuse to get away. It was something new for him, this drinking with a girl, and he was unnaturally casual about it. He did not want to act excited and make himself ridiculous.

Elise was watching his face in the pale light. Suddenly she began to laugh. "You're a hell of a funny fellow! Sitting there!" She leaned against him and ran her hand under his jaw.

"What's the matter? Want another drink?" He did not push her away exactly but in reaching for the bottle he did get away.

At that she laughed again. "Sure! Never turn down a drink, that's me." She laughed every time she looked at him. "You better have a couple drinks."

She was showing him other tricks, catching his hand and pressing it against her soft breast, pulling his ear and biting him.

"Don't think I mean anything against you, see? The scissor-bills around this town really make you sick. Some of them have the syph. You have to know who they are and stay clear. You watch out if you go around any girls. Say, I like you!" She pulled his head down to her and kissed him.

Archilde floundered. He wasn't going to be casual much longer. Already his hands were finding her body. "Have a drink!" he cried out and took his hands away. "Let's go back and dance."

Elise laughed. It was a swell game for her.

Elise continued to enjoy herself. She held him at close quarters and yielded to every movement. She watched him, always smiling. A certain fire of recklessness appeared in his eyes. She coaxed it. She heard his faster breathing and felt his arm tighten at her waist. It was all very gay. She laughed a good deal.

They had both taken to laughing. It wasn't that they said anything humorous, for they spoke very little, and neither was a successful story teller. In their mood they needed no more than a wink or a sly pressure of leg against leg to set them shaking with laughter.

It was certainly strong liquor they had taken, but it was as nothing compared to the intoxication they caught from each other. Their laughter grew louder.

People had been staring at them for some time now. The old women on the sidelines scarcely looked at any other couple. Their eyes followed them all the way round the room and they moved their heads from side to side and leaned from their seats as they tried to see around the dancers who got in the way. Those on the floor had also begun to notice them and moved to one side when they passed. Archilde and Elise were so unheeding of everything but the heat which passed between their bodies that they saw no one, and in self-protection the other dancers had to keep out of their way. Some of them giggled, others looked pained.

The whisper went round the room. "It's the Leon boy! Look! He's been drinking and he's after one of those La Rose sluts!"

There were lamentations among the old women

that his father hadn't been buried six months. The money wouldn't last much longer. "He's just getting started on it. Wait till he gets going good." Whenever an Indian had money to spend the talk was always the same—how long would it last?

Finally, some of the older women began to get excited. "Somebody's got to stop it, or I'll take my girls home. The idea!"

It was just about then that Elise had her mouth turned upward to Archilde's ear. She was whispering something. And he bent down quickly and kissed her on the lips.

There was a gasp that could have been heard out in the street. But Archilde didn't hear. Elise had begun to look around and she saw the manager, a heavy-set, middle-aged man, come toward them.

Archilde paid no attention to the tap on his shoulder. Elise said something and gave him a slight shake. He only tightened his clasp.

The thick-set man grabbed him roughly and pulled him half free of Elise. Archilde frowned slightly and what he did next was quite unexpected.

He seemed to keep his eyes on Elise all the time, but his aim was perfect. He freed his arm from her waist and in the same motion swung it to one side and upward. He caught the heavy-set man on the chin and with such stunning effect that he went down without moving an arm.

Then hell broke loose. Men jumped him from all sides. The women left the benches and were running about crazily, looking for their dancing daughters and calling for their men to take them home.

Archilde came to his senses about then and realized that something had happened. His arms were pinned behind and men pressed in upon him. Somebody just in front drew back his fist to hit him in the face, but the blow wasn't delivered. Archilde caught him in the stomach with his foot and sent him hurtling against other men, and several went down in a heap. That lunge almost freed him, but his captors pressed back quickly.

"Don't hit him, boys!" someone commanded. "Wait till we get him outside."

At that Archilde struggled desperately, but they bore him down. He was pressed forward to the door. The scuffle lasted for several minutes before they could get him outside. Clothes were torn, breaths came in gasps. They cursed and tore his fingers from the door.

"Now!" the same voice commanded. He was struck from behind with something harder than a fist, and at the same instant his arms were freed. He shot forward off the step and landed in a loose heap in the dusty road.

It was a minute before Elise, fighting and swearing, her own clothes torn as men had held her from wading into the group around Archilde, could get to him. Then she stood in the road and wished them all in vitriolic hell. She drove Archilde home, but she could never explain how she got him into the car.

Chapter Twenty-Six

THE summer was hot and dry. The wheat ripened before the straw had attained half its normal growth and made harvesting difficult. Since the straw in many fields was too short to be bundled and tied, a header had to be used instead of the ordinary binder. The header was a larger and more expensive machine. There were few of them in the valley and the ranchers had to wait their turn. While they waited some fields became over-ripened and the grain fell to the ground.

It was a summer memorable also for the swarms of grasshoppers that appeared in some sections, where everything green was devoured—the farmer's wives saving their flowers and meager orchards in part by covering them with cheesecloth.

Pastures were burned to a dull brown, hayfields yielded poorly, springs that had always been dependable dried up; not a drop of rain fell after the middle of May. The climax to the summer of misfortunes came, for one rancher at least, in the middle of night toward the end of August, when ten stacks of wheat, waiting to be threshed, caught fire and burned to the last straw. People stood about in nightshirts in the glow that was reflected for miles up and down the valley and murmured:

"My God! What's the country coming to?"

When they returned to bed they did not sleep, for each man lay and counted over his individual misfortunes.

Archilde heard the complaints of the white ranchers as he passed groups of them in conversation on the streets of St. Xavier, but he felt no sympathy. It made one smile to hear them talk about their troubles. If they wanted to see misery and hopelessness let them look around, as he was doing these days (he did not know why, but he couldn't help himself).

If they would walk through Indian town—that part of St. Xavier given over to crumbling log cabins and dogs and Indians, with the high brick church overtowering all—they would see that one summer was like another. In years of abundance no less than in lean years, the Indians sat in their dark doorways with no expectations, looking out upon a world of meaningless coming and going.

With the week of the dance ended, the tepees were taken down and the dancing ground became once more an empty prairie bordered on one side by a grove of willows and cottonwoods. The fir boughs covering the pavilion turned dry and yellow and were swept to the ground by the wind; coarse weeds pushed up through the packed earth where the warriors' feet had danced; paper and refuse were tossed about for many weeks, until in time the earth had cleansed and restored itself. The drum no longer disturbed the surrounding mountains.

In weeks following, the old men tried to go on living on the memories which had come alive then. Modeste went often to Indian town to sit with his friends. He would walk from his house, which was up the creek about five miles, a grandchild leading him. During those days his face seemed more smiling and his step quicker. When he approached a cabin there were cries of welcome and he was given the place at the head of the blanket. Then talk started. The old men lived again; the dead grass of their spirits crackled in the dull wind of their talk.

Archilde saw these groups of ancient men whenever he passed through St. Xavier and their desolation tugged at him. Even when he drove by in the blue automobile and caught no more than a glimpse of them, he felt the pull of their emptiness. He would have stopped if he could have talked and given them something to fill the vacancy which their eyes opened on. But he could tell them nothing and he never stopped.

Yes, if those white ranchers would look around they would see things which would make their small disasters not worth thinking about. Failure of a crop might mean hunger, but next year there would be another crop, maybe a bumper crop. Prices might sag out of sight, but there was always something—potatoes, a pig to kill, something to beg or borrow. Let those fellows look around.

When Archilde drove by the slaughter house, a mile out of St. Xavier, he saw women carrying off pots of blood-smeared entrails, and he felt helpless. Once he stopped at sight of a very old woman who was going home with such a feast. A battered washtub, filled with the greenish-blue guts, on which flies were swarming, was loaded on a child's wagon. The wheels of this cart were of odd sizes and the whole affair swayed on the point of collapsing. The old woman, in her rags and filth, was really revolting, if one did not remember that she could not help her looks or her condition. Presumably she had not chosen such a life.

He stopped the car as he came abreast of her, and then he didn't know what he meant to say. She didn't stop when he called out, so he had to leave his seat and approach her.

"Grandmother, have you no food?" She stopped, apparently from surprise, but said nothing. It was not clear that she had understood, so he repeated his question, trying to make the words sound right.

"Where do you live?" he asked next, but still her face showed no comprehension.

He realized then that she was deaf. Her eyes were inflamed and watery and she was probably almost blind. Failing senses were only part of the desolation into which she had wandered in her old days. She had to live without decency, like an animal, with nothing to live for, except perhaps an old man who was no better off. He stood before her and could do nothing. She could not even understand that he wished to help. The notion was foreign to her, whether she heard or not. He offered money, held it out to her, even pressed it into her hands; but her fingers were nerveless for lack of recognition. She stood motionless for a long time after he had gone, gazing at the money note in her hand. What did it mean? Her old man, no doubt, would shake his head and scold her for being so foggy.

Chapter Twenty-Seven

ARCHILDE was spending much of his time alone. With the passing days the threat of Dave Quigley and what he might be discovering in the mountains bothered him less and less. He had come to a decision in the matter—he would not run away, he would not hide in the mountains. Whatever happened, he was not afraid. Quigley would discover that much. No, he would not run away. He would continue as he had planned in the spring. Max had planted fall wheat which in another week or two would be ready for harvesting; he would take care of that as part of his last duty to Max, then he would pack his clothes. Dave Quigley could not alter it.

For something to do while he waited he would saddle the white mare after breakfast and ride out, skirting St. Xavier, until he came to the open range along the Big River. It was wild and barren, the soil too alkaline for cultivation, and so it was uncrossed by a fence. Locally the district was called the "Badlands." It was treeless, except for stunted juniper, and almost grassless, and there were deep washes cut into the many-colored clay. An occasional spring at the bottom of a coulee watered a patch of green grass and a clump of willows. When a rancher's horses strayed

away he would take a day or two off and ride out
there; and frequently in the fall ranchers with no hay
would turn all their stock loose and forget about them
until spring. Then they would ride out to collect
those that had survived. There were bone piles everywhere and the coyotes out that way were always fat.

It was a good place to ride to if you wanted to be
alone. Nobody ever went out there for pleasure. Archilde would take a package of food for himself and
a sack of oats for the mare and spend a day and a
night. Usually he took a twenty-two high-power
rifle along and watched for coyotes. After sunset he
would lie on the crest of a commanding ridge and
wait for them to come out. The rifle had a good carry
and he could pick them off at a distance.

He rode out there one day, toward the end of summer, when the Fourth of July excitement had subsided and everyone was busy preparing for the harvest. There was never much forage, but this year, owing to the drought, there was less than ever. Where
springs had flowed there was nothing but dried, urine-
stenched mud, with horse and cattle tracks cut deeply.
There were traces of green at such sites but the growth
was cropped to the ground. At this time of year, when
horses were needed, every animal that could pull its
own weight in the tugs had been taken in. Only the
hopelessly old and crippled were left, and they were
a sad lot. The ones Archilde saw rattled their bones
at every dragging step. Many had been willing workers in their day; they still showed collar scars and sad-

dle chafes; but, now that they could not earn their oats, they were turned into this boneyard to make a meal for the coyotes.

Before one spectacle he stopped completely. What he saw was an aged bay mare and her spring colt, the mare moving her muzzle over the bare earth, occasionally nipping at a shriveled spike of grass. She lifted her head part way from the ground and gazed at him. When he rode toward her she let him advance to within a few yards, then she trotted off on her long legs. She was unbelievably thin and gaunt. Every vertebra was visible, even to the point where the rib was attached, and the sharp hip bones had worn the hair away when she lay down. Her colt, who was drawing the life substance out of her, was plump and frisky. It was always outrunning its dam and waiting for her to catch up.

What was most grotesque about the mare was her tail. This was a tangled mass of hair and mud which hung all the way to the ground. It was far too heavy for her to lift, even if it had been flexible. She was helpless against the sting of flies and when she walked it pounded against her legs.

He got off the white mare, who had been trained to stand when her bridle reins were left dragging, and advanced with his hat full of oats. He clucked to the skeleton and shook the oats. He meant to put a rope on her, feed her, and trim her tail. It was the least thing a creature of feeling could do.

The mare would not be caught. She would allow

him to come to within a few yards, nosing him all the
time, then she would whirl awkwardly on her shaking
legs and trot off. She stumbled frequently, tripping on
her outgrowing hoofs, which were like shovels tied
to her feet. Several times he spilled a handful of oats
and walked away. She would watch him, then go to
the oats and quickly lick them up, even biting out
chunks of earth to get every grain and pawing for
more. But when he advanced again, she played her
old trick. This continued for an hour.

He began to lose patience by that time. The hot
sun made him dizzy and he had wandered half a mile
away from the white mare. Her lifted head indicated
her wonder at this unaccountable game. She champed
at the bit when he went back to her. He patted her
neck. "That old fool out there," he explained. "We
got to rope her. If she falls and breaks her neck, that's
too damn bad. Why ain't she got sense!" The saddle
blistered him.

The skeleton was waiting for him, her dejection
assaulting his pity. She saw the swinging rope, stumbled, and scrambled away. The chase began. He could
not understand it, but the fact was that she could run.
Poor as she was and gaunt and rickety, she stayed in
front of the white mare and got down precipitous
slopes with the agility of a trunk falling downstairs.
Her feebleness was a mockery. It put him at a dis-
advantage. He held in the white mare rather than
make the pace too killing, and when the old hideful
of bones dashed heedlessly into neck-breaking ground

he went a longer way round to save his own animal.
It was infuriating, yet he couldn't stop. He kept telling himself that this senseless race might kill off the
old fool, at least it would burn up energy she couldn't
afford to lose, and he was probably driving her away
from water and her usual feeding ground—but he
couldn't stop. He had to show her kindness in spite
of herself. It was more important than ever.

In the end he wore her down. And when finally she
stopped, with quivering legs braced and her eyes glaring, the anger and will to overcome which the chase
had aroused in him collapsed. He was left limp and
ashamed.

But he persisted. He slipped a rope over her neck
and fashioned a hackamore. Then he drew the silk
handkerchief from his neck and rubbed her body. Her
sweat-darkened hide ran streams of water down her
sides. It collected under her belly in large drops and
where it fell on the parched earth it left hardly a
mark. He rubbed her legs vigorously, aware of a feeling of wanting to restore her strength and save her old
muscles from stiffness. Then he went about trimming
her tail with his pocket knife, cutting through tangles
and hacking off mud-hardened chunks. Her head hung
and she never stirred. Her dejection was his reward,
she would not let him forget.

Even then he could not leave her alone. She probably knew better than he how to reach water and
feed, but having driven her to exhaustion his feelings
would not allow him to abandon her. He must see to

it that she got to safety. In the chase they had attained what must have been the wildest part of all that area —not a spear of grass grew, it was all chalk soil, cut into a wilderness of deep ravines and wind-carved formations. He could not leave her there, he must find water.

Then he discovered that she was lame. She held back, refusing to lead, until sheer force overcame her and she tried a step. She almost fell. Should he shoot her, having got her into such a fix? But the leg wasn't broken, and she had a colt; even now it was around trying to get a meal. He rubbed the leg vigorously and by turns coaxed and cursed her. When she moved finally every limping step tortured him. That was it. The tormentor had become the tormented. It made him sweat to look at her. He stopped looking and tried to assure himself by the pull and slack of his rope that she was managing all right.

The sun had set and in the evening light a rider on a strong white horse led an unprotesting skeleton on a rope. It was grotesque.

There was no moon that night but the clustered stars cast a frosty glare over the waste. For the first time since the beginning of the adventure Archilde had begun to feel that his effort had been worthwhile. He had reached the water hole, where there would be rest and food. A night's sleep would soften the memory of the day's madness. He patted the white mare on the neck and she twitched her ears, backward, then forward. Her head was erect at the smell of water.

It was just then, as everything was coming to a happy conclusion and Archilde was feeling cheered, that the perverse creature at the end of his rope suddenly stumbled, pitched forward, and rolled over. She groaned aloud, a final note of reproach for the ears of the man who had taken it upon himself to improve her condition.

Before the night ended he had to shoot her. She could not get to her feet and ungratefully refused both water and oats, so there was no chance of reviving her. He fed and watered his own horse, cooked his meal, then tried to sleep. But the coyotes were after meat. They crept up to the mare and her groans roused him. He shot at the coyotes, without success. Finally, in a rage that was partly resentment at the unfairness of the whole episode and partly interrupted sleep, he went out to her, placed his rifle against her head, and blasted her into eternity.

Then, in a confusion of feeling, he sat down and spent the rest of the night guarding her worthless carcass.

Chapter Twenty-Eight

MIKE and Narcisse were missed one day. It dawned on everyone all at once that they had not been home regularly since the Fourth of July Celebration. Agnes kept no system in her household. Meals were cooked and eaten at all hours of the day and the night; she never knew beforehand how many would be present to partake of the food she offered. It might be only herself and the old lady, or it might be a small village of visiting relatives and friends. Except for Archilde, for whom she had to cook the vegetables and the store foods he brought, her cuisine was of the simplest, meat and sometimes fish; and so it made little difference how many were there to eat. Another chunk of beef more or less in the cooking pot was no inconvenience. Dishes were not a necessity. When there were not enough tin plates to go around one did very well with a piece of meat speared on the point of a knife. Food was the thing.

With the household so accustomed to almost daily changes, a small boy or two went unnoticed. When Archilde inquired for his nephews—he had intended talking to them before he went away—Agnes could only guess that they were around somewhere.

"They go visiting," she said brightly. "They fish a

lot too. Sometimes they bring back a grouse and I cook it for them." She thought highly of her boys.

"Yes, but how long since you've seen them?"

She thought about it and began to frown. She could not remember when she had seen them last. But she supposed they were visiting relatives. Small boys were always welcome. But she could not think what relatives it might be. They had all been there recently and the boys had said nothing about going off with any particular group. The more she thought about it the longer grew her frown.

Archilde shook his head at her. Somebody could steal her boys and she wouldn't know about it.

At that she smiled. "Who would steal Mike and Narce? They're no good to anybody."

She didn't mean it. Whether they were worth anything or not, boys were prized. Take them from her and you could take her life as well. But she was careless of her possessions.

Archilde went out to look for them. He did not think they were visiting because he learned from their sister Annie that they had been carrying pots and blankets out to the woods. Very likely they had a camp somewhere. Perhaps they were tired of everybody at home. He would have a look around and discover if possible what they were up to.

He did not locate them at once. He made a search lasting several days, in which he visited all the familiar hunting and fishing grounds. He went deeper into the woods, higher on the mountain foothills, and finally, as he directed the mare one day through a thick tangle of fallen timber and young growing stuff, he heard a rumbling sound which at first he mistook for the drumming of grouse. On going closer he found something that surprised him.

The boys had peeled a young fir tree at the center of a small clearing, and around it they were dancing. The peeled tree was striped with red paint, giving it some special meaning. One boy danced while the other beat the drum. Archilde whistled. They had a signal for calling each other, and he whistled it.

They looked up, alarmed, on guard.

He went up slowly, leaving the mare behind. After the first embarrassment and distrust passed they began to talk. He learned then that they had been living out there for several weeks. They intended to go on living there. They had a tepee and blankets and cooking pots and they killed their own food. They had a good time. They danced. Nobody could tell them what to do. If anyone should come along and tell them they had to go home—well, just try it!

He watched them. Was it a game, of which they would soon tire? Or was it a way of life which the Fourth of July dance had taught them? Their faces revealed nothing. He tried to get behind their minds.

"What will you do when it gets cold? When the big wind comes?"

"Maybe we'll come to the house." Mike was not abashed. He looked steadily at his uncle and plainly asked what he meant to do about it.

Narcisse spoke then. His voice was proud. Indicating Mike with a nod, he said, "He's not afraid of the dark now."

Mike did not stir. He was still watching his uncle. He wanted to know how matters stood. Finally he expressed what was in his mind.

"We won't go to school. Don't play us a trick and drag us to that place!"

Archilde had to smile. He could remember back to the previous summer, the very day he returned from Portland, when he had talked to Agnes. "Keep your boys in school," he had told her. It made him smile to think of it. He had even less desire to see them sent back to the Fathers than they had to go there.

"If you don't like that school, stay away. I won't send you there."

The boys looked happy. Evidently they had been worried by the approach of autumn and school time. Max had got them by a trick last year and they didn't want it to happen again.

Narcisse had not yet told all about his brother's courage. There was something more.

"He took off his scapular," he announced. "He threw it in the brush."

Mike laughed. "Sure! But Narce, he still wears his!"

"I'll take mine off one of these days."

"Hoh! He's waiting to see what happens to me!"

Archilde laughed at Mike's harsh joke. It made him at once happy and sad, this braggadocio. He stayed with the boys until dark, trying by his words to stiffen their courage and at the same time to suggest that there were other ways of living. He found that they grabbed eagerly at his promises of not interfering with them, but they appeared to ignore him when he spoke of the future. Take care, he tried to tell them. The game was gone from the mountains; even the fish were getting fewer each year; and they could not always stay in the woods and dance. It was a waste of breath. They would not be intimidated.

"What do we care about that?" Mike said finally. "If they just leave us alone that's all we want."

He was always forgetting that his way of seeing things was his own. His people could not understand it, but thought he was chasing after damn fool notions. All ideas were damn fool until they were understood and believed; and it was useless to wish them on to anybody else until the other person had come to them in the same way—by understanding and believing. In his present evolution he could admit this lack of insight in his people without getting angry. Not so very long ago he snorted at their childish attitude toward his going away from the Reservation and the dress and manners he brought back with him. He accepted the strangeness that had grown up between them, yet he persisted in trying to brush it aside. Mike and Narcisse showed him how foolish that was. All they asked was to be let alone, and perhaps this time he would not forget it.

It had never occurred to him that he would find it difficult to break with his family when the time came.

He used to think that he had only to put his clothes in his suitcase, shake hands all around, and be off. But with the moment near he found himself hesitating. What to say? Should he make it final? Or would it be better to sneak off with a hint of coming back someday? It had to be decided. Mike and Narcisse taught him something—it did no good to make a fuss about things; just go ahead and do what you liked, and ask only to be let alone. They had that in common with the mare in the Badlands.

But this going away! It would have been simpler if he had gone on being angry at his people. Instead of learning to live at peace with their limitations he ought to have kept his distance, then he could have enjoyed going away. It had to be decided.

Chapter Twenty-Nine

AFTER the fight at the Fourth of July dance, Elise had taken Archilde home and put him to bed. It was a good thing there was no one at home, because when he woke up next morning Elise was in bed with him. Hell, he hadn't expected her to go home, had he? She couldn't have made it. Anyhow, did he have any complaint?

Every time he thought of it now he had to laugh. She had undressed him, taken everything off but his shoes. She had been too sleepy to undo the laces, so she said. Her own shoes were simpler and she had got everything off herself. Because of the condition they found themselves in when they woke up, it was a good thing nobody was at home.

They had been good friends since then. At least, when they were together they were good friends. But he was shy of her. When she wasn't around he hoped he wouldn't see her again; not that he didn't like her, but she was dangerous. She was the kind of person who was always getting into scrapes, she liked it. And she would get him into scrapes if he went with her. She meant no harm, of course. She liked action, excitement, recklessness, and the trouble resulted naturally. Whenever he saw her coming, or when she sent word that she was coming, he felt the way he had on Fourth of July night, when they set out together. He had a feeling of climbing on the back of a bucking horse.

But it was always the same. As soon as they had been together for a few minutes he began to like her and was glad they had got together. The first thing about her was her good nature. He had never known anyone easier to get along with, not just because she was ready for anything, but because she had a quick mind and was never bored. If they went somewhere on a picnic and a heavy rain came up, she could make it seem as pleasant to have the picnic right there in the car as it would have been on the grass. It amused her.

She was generous, also. She would say "I got something for you," and out would pop a pin for his tie. She had just seen it at the store and bought it. If he bought her anything, even a simple thing like a box of candy, it pleased her tremendously. "You swell bastard!" She swore when she was affectionate. "You don't have to get me things!" That was the truest thing about her generosity. She belittled her own free-giving but praised him for his, as if his were the greater.

Her nature was such that once she had taken you for a friend you could never get angry with her. She was too good-hearted, and you had too good a time with her.

But in calm moments, by himself, he saw that he should leave her alone. Every time he appeared with her in St. Xavier he saw people watching them. They would never forget the fight and he was being talked about and watched. He was going to the dogs and they wanted to see the process. He had heard that bets were being laid on how long it would be before he was broke.

It angered him to be watched and to have bets laid on him. It was the very thing that could have made him become reckless and do the hell-raising they were predicting of him. It would come over him at moments that if he wanted to he could set out and make them all hold their breaths. But he wasn't inclined to hell-raising. That was what angered him. These people knew nothing about him, so their talk came out of spite and dirty thinking.

They were together a good deal, in spite of his attempts to keep away. She would send one of her nephews some evening. The shy little fellow would slip up to him and whisper that Elise was waiting for him at the creek crossing, then he would scamper for the brush like a rabbit. There was nothing to do but drive down there. At other times she came herself, riding the bay horse. They would ride up into the mountains.

On this late summer day, after that affair in the Badlands, they had spent the morning fishing and had cooked a midday meal of fish crossed with bacon. In the afternoon they smoked and lay in the warm sun. She was affectionate, but not in a soft way. She had a boy's strength and used it. Before she would yield to him he had to subdue her. They scuffled and tore up the earth. Then when he had won, her body softened and she heaped love on him. The change always caught him by surprise.

They had been lying quietly for some time now. They smoked and watched the white scum which had spread across the sky.

He had picked that day to tell her about his going away. He had not yet told his mother. Since Elise had to know too, it seemed simpler to begin with her. It wasn't really simple. She was one of those easy-going people who never cared what they did, just so they didn't work hard or never had to live by rules. Perhaps rules were even worse than work. Almost anything amused such people, as it did Elise, and they could get along with anybody, except a fellow who liked to work or who lived in an orderly manner. For such a fellow they had only contempt. They made faces at him, held their noses when he went by.

Archilde knew Elise, he thought, and it was going to be hard on her to be told that he was like those fellows who made a bad smell with their work and their regular habits. She probably would laugh at him and refuse to take him seriously. What, him? Wanting to stop chasing around? Wanting to wear a white collar every day? He could picture her eyes twinkling. She would roll over on her back and have a good laugh.

It was late in the afternoon before he got to the subject. They had been lying there for a long time, smoking cigarettes and watching the sky.

"I guess you won't believe me," he muttered, with his eyes looking upward. He told her about his ambitions, trying to make it appear like something else, like pure foolishness. He told her as much as he dared, always backing away from it by a second statement. Yes, he wanted to play the fiddle, but there wasn't much to it. Then he tried to head her off, to escape her teasing.

"You think I'm trying to cut a figure, get stuck-up. I guess you think I ought to stay where I belong. Maybe so, but it won't hurt to try. I don't count on getting far, I just want to give it a try."

Then she took him by surprise. She had been lying on her belly, watching him as he talked, and instead of rolling over on her back as a sign of dismissing what he had been saying, she sat up. She failed to grin, which would have been like saying; "That's all right! You're a good fellow just the same!"

"Hell!" She could express a good deal in a short word like that. "I been wanting to tell you, but you could of said it wasn't my business. Well, people around here was saying you'd blow yourself before long. I knew you wouldn't, but I thought I ought to tell you. Maybe you knew it yourself, what they was saying?"

He did.

"Well, so now you've made up your mind—that's fine! That's good! Cripes! I can't make it sound like I should, but you know me—I feel lots more'n I say!"

He stared at her until finally he had to drop his

eyes. He was thinking back on how he had treated her, how he had tried not to be seen with her, how he had fixed her in his mind as a person of no great sense —and he was ashamed. It seemed certain that she must know what was in his mind. He tried to explain himself.

"I'm sorry, Elise. I didn't know what you were like. It wasn't that I didn't like you. You can see I didn't let people stop me going round with you—"

And then it was more surprising. She didn't know what he meant. If she had observed him trying to avoid her, she hadn't resented it. Perhaps she had expected him to be ashamed of her company. What she said took him in a different direction.

"You treated me better than any fellow I ever knew. I guess you don't know what a swell kid you are. You got nothing to explain."

When he kissed her, as they got up to leave, he felt that he had just come to know a wonderful person. He said nothing about that, he couldn't just then, but it was a strong, shaking thing to feel.

In the evening Elise and Archilde galloped down the mountain road, the horses scattering stones and snorting with pleasure. The sun had lost itself behind the high grassy hills in the west and a yellow first-quarter moon was discovered already near the top of the sky.

They pounded to a halt at a forking in the road, one way leading to Leon's ranch, the other to the cluster of buildings across the creek where old Modeste lived with the La Rose tribe. The bay horse whirled and started off. There was a last word from Elise, one of her teasing, fun-making remarks.

He listened until the diminishing sounds of the running horse were lost in the faint thunder of the creek, and during that time her warmth surrounded him.

In that moment of waiting and listening, the road lay clearly ahead. Talking to Elise and hearing her faltering encouragement had somehow simplified the task he had now to perform. It was like standing on a hillside and looking into a valley where everything was revealed. He could tell himself, as he stood there, not only listening but seeing, that of all joys, there was none like that of capturing the future in a vision and holding it lovingly to the eye. There was deep pleasure in that.

The sound had been lost entirely, now, and he turned the white mare with a pressure of the rein against her neck. She picked her feet up lightly, trotted forward.

Chapter Thirty

In five minutes he emerged into the clearing above the house, and there he paused. Two things surprised him into raising his head and getting his bearings. In the first place, it was still light. That was a shock to his senses, after the gloom of the woods. And next he heard someone wailing. He held his breath and listened. The lamp had not yet been lighted and the house lay as a dark shadow before him.

After a moment he went forward, toward the sound of grief. The sound was so unmistakable that even the white mare showed nerves, tossed her head, and looked wide-eyed.

Mike and Narcisse were at the kitchen door, afraid to enter the house but too disturbed to go away. He found himself wondering how they happened to be there. At Archilde's approach they stepped aside and by averting their faces indicated that they did not want to be questioned.

He was now aware of two voices—a loud one, which was Agnes', and the softer cry of Annie. He stared at the kitchen door, then turned to the boys.

"What's the matter?"

The boys shifted from foot to foot and said nothing. They would not look up.

"You, Mike, what is it?"

There was a pause before Mike replied, his eyes to the ground: "It's the old lady. I guess she's sick. Maybe dead."

His voice got weak and almost quit him before the last word was spoken.

It was dark inside, the westward window admitting but a feeble light from the darkening sky. The cross bar of the window showed black against the opening. His mind called up a sudden image of Modeste telling his story of how the Salish people set out to find the "new thing"—one stick laid across another; a great power was to come to them when they had that. Here it was, staring meaninglessly at him.

He stood with his back to the door and for some time did not move. He tried not to visualize the scene before him. What Mike and Narcisse had undoubtedly felt, he felt. He did not want to open his eyes to this strange event; he did not want to talk about it; he wanted to stand without thinking or feeling before it. He shifted from foot to foot.

Agnes lowered her voice when he stepped inside and Annie stopped entirely. Perhaps if the voices had not changed, if his presence had not been noticed, he would have acted like his young nephews, and after a minute of standing at the door would have joined them outside. The changed voices insinuated something. It was as if he had been awaited, as if he were expected to show the others what was to be done.

He could not hold back after that. They depended

on him.

"You have no light. You need a lamp."

As he went to fetch the lamp from the adjoining room his moving body was like a strong candle burning in the dark. He knew what to do, how to make use of his wits; that was a wonderful thing.

The two at the door and the two who were inside watched him. Little Annie went sliding away from the old lady's bed, her face upturned to him. Agnes did not move from her position on the floor, at the foot of the bed, but she had stopped wailing. Now she lowered her shawl and watched, saying nothing. What comfort would he bring? He had made it light in the room, what more could he do?

He knelt at his mother's head, thinking as he did so of the night in her tepee on Fourth of July night. The sparks flew up, expired, and he had wished that a person might find oblivion as easily. It was a different matter now. People grew into each other, became intertwined, and life was no mere matter of existence, no mere flash of time. It was time that made the difference. The time that was consumed in moving one's feet along the earth, in learning the smell of coming snow, in enduring hunger and fear and the loss of pride; all that made a difference. And a still greater difference was this entangling of lives. People grew together like creeping vines. The root of beginning was hard to find in the many that had come together and spread their foliage in one mass.

His head hung as he thought those things. The picture he had made of death, of his mother being torn away from the things to which her life had attached itself, infected him with pain. He bent nearer. If by some chance she could sense the depth of his sorrow and regret, it might ease the tearing of her soul. His eyes searched the sagging face.

To his amazement, he saw her eyelids flutter apart. A thin gleam of her faded eyes appeared. She was not dead! He moved his face nearer and murmured: "I'm here now!" There was no response in her face. Her eyes were fixed, not a muscle moved.

Then a still greater surprise—she recognized him; she spoke, without moving her lips. She spoke in English, which she had not used for years. "Those words are like water," she once said. "They slip through your teeth and there's nothing to bite on."

Now she was saying an English word—or were there two words? First he heard "Priest!" and he was ready to jump to his feet. Of course! The priest must come! Then he was frozen. She was saying "No priest!" She was saying it in English! She must be out of her head. The words came distinctly after several efforts, but he could not believe them. Everybody knew how faithful his mother had been. Surely she would not change at this last hour, he reasoned.

She did not speak again and he was left to make his own decision. He lost no time.

He whirled upon Agnes. "Alive! Just look!" He thought of what should be done. "Make a fire in the stove! Put something warm on her—on her feet maybe.

I'll go for the priest—the doctor—"

Nothing had been done for the old lady. They had accepted her doom at once and had sat down to wail. But there was no time to charge them with foolishness.

Agnes had let her shawl fall away and she was looking wonderingly at Archilde. Had he done something, perhaps, to make her open her eyes after she had lain like one dead for hours? She could think of nothing but this marvel. Her eyes grew wide.

"Make a fire quick! She's cold—only feel her hands! I'm going."

Agnes did not move at once. She sat dumbfounded. Not until the sound of the automobile died away did she become aware of Archilde's absence.

"What has he done?" she murmured suddenly. At the same time she bent forward toward the old lady and examined her staring eyes.

Another minute passed before she remembered what she had been told to do and then, in her stupor, she turned to ask Annie to see about the fire. But Annie had already gone outside to break up some dried branches in the light of the thin moon.

It was a mysterious thing, this dying and coming to life! There must be a special power in that Archilde!

Chapter Thirty-One

WHEN Archilde returned with Father Jerome, one of the younger priests at the Mission, he found Agnes up and around. Her actions told him that something had happened in his absence. He could not get near his mother because the priest had already knelt down at her side. But watching from above, he could see that she was not aware. She breathed heavily, as if in deep slumber. He turned to Agnes and again got the impression that something had happened. There was a startled look in her eyes.

He said: "Agnes, come and find me another blanket. I think the old lady is cold." He led the way out of the room.

It was as he thought. She began to talk as soon as they reached her room, which was on the ground floor. "Mama talked to me!" she cried excitedly. When he asked what the old lady had said Agnes looked puzzled. "First she called Modeste. She wants him I guess."

Archilde thumped his head with his fist. Of course she would want Modeste! She would want all her relatives. He had been thinking and acting as if his mother's death was his exclusive affair, but others were also bound to her. He would go for Modeste at once.

"Then she said something I don't know what to think," Agnes continued. "She wants no priest. I can't understand it."

Archilde whirled upon her. "She said that? Tell me, did she say it in English?"

His question puzzled Agnes. "She never talks English now. She said it in Indian. That's what she talks."

There was no longer any doubt of his mother's knowing what she was saying. But what did it mean? He dared not risk the plain meaning of her words. Perhaps Modeste would know the answer. He must go for him.

Archilde did not get away at once. He was delayed by the arrival of Doctor Arnold, who had driven up in his own car. To him Archilde had to give the particulars, after first inquiring of Agnes, of the stroke his mother had suffered. Agnes was too shy to speak directly to the doctor. And still he did not get away. Father Jerome had followed him into the front room, desiring a few words.

Father Jerome was a new kind of priest in Sniél-emen. He had come recently, when enthusiasm had cooled and funds had run low. Being a missionary to the Indians had taken on the aspect of a necessary but somewhat unpleasant drudgery. In the days of Father Grepilloux's pioneering, doors were never locked, doorbells were never rung. The Indians were treated like children and the Mission was their father's house; there was intimacy and trust and even affection. But the Mission had become a charitable institution; it expected a decent humility in its wards. This was not announced or otherwise expressed but the effect was evident. Father Jerome, like other recent arrivals, was apt to be impatient with those who responded slowly or not at all. It rather got on his nerves that the Indian congregation which sat always at the back of the church still followed its old custom of breaking out into its own prayers and its own songs at odd moments of the Mass. The songs had a pagan wildness. He would rather they had been better disciplined. That was private opinion, similar to that expressed once by a visiting bishop, who thought that a pack of "harmonious wolves" must have been turned loose in the congregation. Realities of this sort, which had amused Father Grepilloux or moved him to soft reproach, in time became irritating. The naïve quality had disappeared.

Father Jerome was not really prejudiced; it could hardly be said that he looked down upon the Indians. It was rather that his task seemed thankless and he was not enthusiastic about it. There was no excitement of doing something new. He was dull; he neither scolded nor exhorted; he dogmatized.

To Archilde he said, speaking coldly, and with some scorn:

"I don't understand you. I believe you ought to explain yourself." His eyes were unpleasantly staring. "Your mother came to me last winter for guidance concerning a crime she had committed in the mountains, in your presence. Understand that I am not violating the Seal of Confession. These facts were told me in confidence and my opinion was sought as to what should be done. First of all I told your mother to send you to me; I would see to it that you performed your duty as regards your Church and your legal overseers. She was to return for further instructions. That was half a year ago and not only have you not been to see me but your mother never returned. I believe you are responsible for this action and you ought to explain it. But I have something more to say.

"You have been going your own way for some time now. I hope you are not one of these boys who at the first touch of the world become corrupt. Moral cowards they are and, not content to see themselves damned, they must drag others with them. I hope you are not becoming one of these."

One should not feel compelled to answer such a thrust, and yet that was just what one did feel. And the worst of it was that one fumbled in answering.

"I had nothing to do with my mother's affairs. She told me nothing about this—"

What made him feel inadequate was that instead of boldly objecting to the interference, he made an elaborate attempt to explain himself, as the priest demanded. The explanation was received coldly, as was to be expected.

"You say these things glibly and you haven't faced the real question." This was in reply to Archilde's attempt to make clear his growing agnosticism. "You can speak to me of that afterward. Just now you have to think of your mother. This man she killed in the mountains, you must realize that the law officers should be informed. You are civilized people now. Perhaps your mother acted justifiably, and all the more reason for making it known. Bring them here before she dies and possibly she will be able to give her own statement. Afterward, come to me to confession."

By this time Archilde was too angry to speak his mind. He did not know how to extricate himself.

"I did not speak of this because my mother is too old to have to go to court, maybe to jail."

That was all he said. His voice was so low that he was asked to repeat the words, and that increased his bitterness.

"Well, do as I say, for the good of your soul." Having given that direction, Father Jerome withdrew, beginning a whispered prayer just as he reached the outer door.

Archilde stood where he had been left. A mountain, a whole world, had collapsed upon him.

An hour later, at midnight, he was sitting with Modeste, learning for the first time of his mother's renunciation of her life of faith. This information came so startlingly that for a while he was not sure of anything. If he could be so ignorant of the inner life of one so near him, how could he trust his perceptions in anything? He was dumbfounded.

He had come just as the La Rose clan was settling down for the night. Modeste sat on his bed on the floor, dressed in long drawers and cotton outer shirt. He was smoking a last cigarette when Archilde arrived. Upon hearing of the old lady's condition, he put his hand over his mouth, as a woman does, and exclaimed sorrowfully.

There was no rousing the son-in-law, big Octave, who died every night after his supper and did not resurrect until the sun burned a hole in his bed. But Modeste soon had other members of the family stirred up and was instructing them to ride everywhere to Catharine's relatives and friends and give the news.

While these arrangements were being made Modeste sat smoking and telling Archilde about the old lady.

"She has been a good woman," he said simply. "She did not do this thing quickly, like a man might. She thought a long time and then there was that dream. She dreamt it three times, each time alike, and that made her decide. Once she changed she would not go back. We will go to her."

By the time they were ready to leave everybody was up, all but Octave, and coming to ask questions. To young and old, the old lady was a real person. They let their voices fall in speaking of her, and Archilde looked at them curiously. He was continually surprised by evidence of the regard in which his mother was held. She was important to these people, she belonged to them almost more than she belonged to him. Only recently had he begun to claim her, and as yet he knew very little about her.

Elise stood among the others, and when his eyes fell upon her he stopped. The events of the last few hours unraveled themselves and he felt himself caught up once more in the excitement of their parting on the mountain road. She too, he saw, was thinking of those moments. They looked at each other, half smiling, saying nothing.

Then once more he was in the forward rush of life. His mother lay dying. And he was on his way to tell Mr. Parker what had really taken place in the mountains. When he explained this to Elise, she protested.

"That's foolish, going to him. That fellow will get you put in jail. Stay away from him."

Elise could always smell danger and she had no impulses for heroic action. It was all very well to resent a priest's interference, but getting yourself put in jail just to spite him was, in her mind, not sensible. Better let the priest have his say and forget him; the priest wouldn't spread the story and so long as no one else knew. . . .

Archilde wouldn't hear of it. He had made up his mind to put himself beyond the reproach of the priest, or of anybody else, and no argument could move him. And besides, he added, there was Dave Quigley looking for his friend's grave—no telling when he would make the discovery and come out of the mountains to set up a howl. Why not confess before he found anything?

Elise grew frightened when she saw that Dave Quigley would have a hand in it.

"For Christ's sake, kid! Don't do that! Hold your tongue and let things ride."

"Nope. I'll see the Agent first thing in the morning. Now, I'm going back home."

Elise stopped arguing. "I'm going with you."

He turned upon her, ready to object, but she grabbed his arm and started off. He laughed.

Chapter Thirty-Two

NEXT morning, on returning from the Agency, he found the houseyard full of his mother's relatives and friends. Their wagons and light rigs were lined up against the fence and unhitched horses were tied to wagon wheels or else went hopping about in hobbles. A glance showed him that there was nothing to eat for men or horses; there had been no food to bring along.

The sight of these people stirred him, just as Modeste's relatives asking about the old lady had stirred him. They were a silent lot. For the most part they sat in small groups, the men wearing stiff-brimmed hats, some with shell earrings, others with their braided hair wrapped in fur; the women had their shawls pulled up to the chin. As he walked through the yard he stopped before a group of men: "If you got no feed for the horses, there's oats and hay in the barn. Take what you like." Then he sought out the woman, Mrs. Beaverfoot, his aunt, and to her he said: "You got to see to it that the people have something to eat. Agnes is no use just now. If there's no meat send someone to St. Xavier to the butcher."

Never had he felt so near to these people as now, when he could do something for them. It was a small thing but it was the first.

With Archilde came Mr. Parker, who followed him

across the yard and into the house. The morning's conversation had been surprisingly easy. The Agent had assured Archilde that he understood why he had been deceived last winter; he held no resentment; he would do what he could to help. Of course, there would be consequences to face.

The Agent was frank about it. His continuance as an official of the Service depended on his keeping the record straight. Whatever he might think privately had nothing to do with the matter.

"Let me warn you," he said in a friendly voice, "it may be rather difficult. There's no reason why it should be. If you're telling me the truth this time, and I think you are" (there was a quick smile, in recollection of how completely he had misjudged the boy's truthfulness on that other occasion), "there's no reason why a simple hearing shouldn't clear you. Unfortunately, the law can make these affairs complicated and—disagreeable. I don't mean to alarm you, but be prepared for trouble."

He had come to see for himself whether or not there was any chance of getting a statement from the old lady. If he failed in that, he made it clear, he would have to inform the authorities at once. By that he did not mean the same day. He would allow Archilde to remain with his mother until the end. Somehow he made this out to be a serious risk, but one he took gladly.

These details had become blurred in Archilde's mind by the time he arrived home. Only Elise remained clear to his inner consciousness. She had gone with him to the Agency and had stayed close to him since then. She followed him across the yard, stopping when he stopped, listening to him when he talked, always watching him. She said very little, but he was constantly aware of her and inwardly glad. Somehow, he had come to realize that she would never leave him unless he sent her away.

But he did not think much about her or about himself as he walked through the houseyard and stopped to talk to his mother's people. He was trying to see in their faces whether or not they knew the history of her later days and what they thought of her recantation. Would they too return to their paganism? And would it be a good thing if they did? In the hurry of the moment he did not find an answer. Perhaps there was no answer. Perhaps it no longer mattered what happened to them. By that time he had reached the kitchen, Elise at his heels.

The doctor was saying: "I just gave another stimulant. She ought to come round pretty soon—if she's going to."

Archilde did not know what the man was talking about. He heard the words, but—here was this old woman! They had removed the kerchief from her head and left her looking naked; he had rarely seen her without a head covering. Her white hair hung in strands and her brown skin had paled to ash gray. The bones of the cheeks and brow ridges pressed sharply against the skin. When he looked at her now

he could complete the thought he had of her yesterday evening—death was something besides a tearing
away; death for his mother, at this moment, just as she
had turned her back on all those teachers who had
come over the mountains—it was the triumph of one
against many; it was the resurrection of the spirit.
Looking at her and thinking these things, he felt
proud of her. And that pride marked the distance he
had traveled since a year ago, when he returned for
what he had intended as a last visit.

Mike and Narcisse were in trouble. They were
afraid to stay around, now that Father Jerome was
here, and they were afraid to run away to their tepee
in the woods. Mike voiced the immediate trouble.

"He says we got to go to school."

That was only part of it. The boys had a deeper uneasiness and he knew it. Mike looked pale. It was not
simply that he wanted to be told that he wouldn't have
to go to school in spite of the priest. Archilde had to
speak to him, but he could not speak boastfully; he
had to say something that would be familiar and reasonable. How could he do it?

"Myself, I have never seen a devil." He spoke without addressing them directly. "I've been told he would
get me if I didn't watch out, but where does he keep
himself? He never comes for me. I can't tell you if
this is a lie or not. I just know that for a long time
I've told myself that I can get along without that fellow and nothing has happened. I get along very well."

He did not expect much to come of his talking. He

remembered how a bat flying around his head in the sacristy of the church had set images of the devil dancing in his brain. And he could see in Mike's eyes some dread which reason would not touch. How could he really help Mike and Narcisse. What besides talk? Somehow or other he would get them away from the Fathers—but what would he do then? He might turn them loose in the mountains, like birds let out of a cage, or like a pair of buffaloes turned out of the Government reserve; he had no doubt that they would survive. But there ought to be something better. These thoughts went on in spite of himself, in some remote corner of his mind.

The old lady's condition was changing, there was no longer any doubt of it. Her breathing grew heavier until, in the silent house, it came with a roar upon ears made sensitive by close attention. She was going deeper into the night. The word was passed from group to group in the yard and there were stirrings. Some voices began to wail softly.

As the afternoon wore on the gray sky darkened. A colder wind blew, carrying dampness.

Doctor Arnold, Max's old hunting companion, was ready to give up. "We've done all there's to do," he told Archilde. Evidently she had already suffered a second stroke, both sides of the brain seemed to be affected. He rolled down his sleeves, packed his black bag. No, he could not say how much longer it would be,

Father Jerome somehow knew that the crisis had come, though he had not been in the room. He appeared in the doorway just as Dr. Arnold was withdrawing to smoke and wait. He was ready to administer Extreme Unction, the anointing with oil.

Archilde, until then, had functioned without pausing to reflect on what he might be feeling. He had gone about talking and doing what had to be done. For the last ten minutes he had been standing in the kitchen observing the Doctor. Finally he realized that it was the end. The Doctor was rolling down his sleeves. That was how finality was expressed, in such an inconsequential action as that. He said nothing, asked no question. He turned his face to the wall and wept.

Then Father Jerome was whispering and rustling around the old lady. It was the last indignity.

"Father Jerome—excuse me." His eyes were still running tears as he turned upon the priest. "I suppose you don't know—the truth is my mother gave up —you ought to let her die her own way—"

It was useless. He should have known. The priest considered it blasphemy. Wrath gathered on his face. "God have mercy on your soul!"

Archilde desisted. It was not that he feared speaking his own mind, but he saw the uselessness of it. The priest would have his way—and let him! It was empty. It meant nothing. Only his wilfulness kept him from understanding that the power of the two sticks, the *Somesh* which Father Grepilloux had carried over the mountains, was dissolved.

"Through his holy unction may the Lord pardon thee whatever sins or faults thou hast committed—"

It was unnecessary. *The whip had covered the fault.*

It was not quite all over. When Archilde stepped outside to ask Modeste and some of the older people to go in to his mother, he encountered Mr. Parker.

"The Doctor tells me—I see it is useless. Well, I'll go along." The Agent was anxious to make clear his sympathy. At the same time he had to remember his duty. He had to speak of it.

"Come to me in a few days, when it's over. You can count on my help, as you know. It will be just a matter of form, nothing to fear. I'll go along. I leave you on your honor."

Archilde could not quite comprehend the drift of the Agent's words. Vaguely he remembered what had been said that morning. It wasn't over yet. Nothing could touch his mother now, but as for himself—he too belonged to the story of Sniél-emen.

Elise was waiting for him, ready to lead him away. He did not know where they were going, or why. It didn't matter. She would stay with him; he had been feeling that all day, and so it was natural that she should stand, waiting. He saw that she had saddled the white mare and her own bay horse. They mounted and rode away. And when they entered the timber, Mike and Narcisse were there on horseback, waiting. He did not question what they were doing. Elise was looking at him, smiling vaguely, and that was enough. He was tired.

Chapter Thirty-Three

MR. PARKER was troubled. For three days he had been waiting for Archilde to appear—three days, that is, from the time his mother had been laid away in the consecrated ground of the Mission churchyard. The boy had not been seen and Mr. Parker had come to the point where he could not think of anything else, though he assured himself that he wasn't worried.

"He is taking his mother's death hard. He's a boy of feeling. Give him time."

He walked from his house to his office across the Agency compound, and in his office walked from desk to window, muttering to himself: "He's not one of these—ordinary fellows. Give him a chance." Standing and looking through the window at the dust swirls which were lifted out of the powder-dry clay roadbed, he was conscious of the prick of uneasiness. He shifted his stance. At his desk again he tried to pick up the thread of routine work.

The chief clerk, a pock-marked half-breed who had a habit of smiling to himself, as if in enjoyment of his complacency, came in to plague the Agent. "In the case of Mrs. Max Leon—"

Mr. Parker turned upon him with surprising sharpness.

"What about Mrs. Max Leon? She's dead."

The chief clerk almost giggled. "I was just about to say—shouldn't her son Archilde be called in about her estate?"

"How do I know where he is or what he's up to!" The Agent stopped short, realizing that he was not answering the clerk's question. He made himself very busy with the papers on his desk. "Don't bother me with that now. Remind me again."

Still the clerk hung there, grimacing complacently.

"About Max Leon's grandsons, Mike and Narcisse, you know—you ordered them sent to the Government school—"

"Yes, I did!" Mr. Parker could not understand why he was being plagued with these questions about the Leon family at this particular time.

"They can't be found—" The clerk grinned still more widely.

"Why can't they be found? Where did they go?"

"Nobody knows. That's just it. I don't know where La Ronde is either. I was going to send him to bring them in but nobody knows where La Ronde is."

The Agent knew that Joe La Ronde, the head and body of the Indian police force, had gone on a trip. He knew who had sent him—but he said nothing. He only stared at his chief clerk and seemed to ask what was keeping him. After a considerable silence the clerk got the meaning and began to back out.

"If you want to get those boys in here you'll have to send the police for them," the clerk advised his chief.

"I'll take care of it myself," Mr. Parker said finally, by way of getting rid of him.

Mr. Parker was alone again, turning from his desk to gaze through the window. Dust swirled outside. It was summer's end and the enduring furnace breath of the sun had baked the earth hard. The atmosphere with the changing tide of season grew restless, and wind currents sprang up, sweeping the powdered earth with them. On a day like that one remembered the pleasant green spring and resented its passing. It made a man realize that he was at odds with nature.

Thinking about it—he was unable to settle down to thinking about anything else—Mr. Parker realized that he would have to send out an alarm for Archilde. It couldn't be blinked. If Joe La Ronde came back empty-handed as he probably would, this next step was inescapable. It was an official matter and, in official matters, Mr. Parker was scrupulously careful.

He would have to bring in Sheriff Quigley, and that, perhaps, was the most unsettling thought of all. This question of Archilde's trustworthiness was a worrisome matter, but it wasn't the main source of irritation.

Sheriff Quigley was a difficult man to deal with, Mr. Parker had learned from long experience. He was too downright. He rode around the country with his badge of office flapping on his unbuttoned vest—and one would think that he had invented the idea of law and order and the job of sheriffing. Give him but the least suspicion to work upon, and he would never rest until he had accused everyone within reach of his bald-faced horse and one by one eliminated them from possible complicity. He was one of the last survivals of the "Old West," one who carried with him out of the past a grudge against all Indians—the result of having been robbed and chased into the brush when he first came into the country in the eighties.

He could not get over the fact that the Government had taken the Indians under protection. Whenever he had to bring in an Indian prisoner he acted as if a state of war existed between the two races. He gave no quarter and took no chances. But that was not all. What Mr. Parker most disliked about the Sheriff when called in for help, was his habit of assuming that the entire Indian Agency had been turned over to him. He piled his booted and manured feet up on the Agent's desk, issued orders to the clerks, and wanted to tell the Government just what to do. The insinuation was that if he were holding down the Agency things would be run differently, much differently.

Mr. Parker would be happier if he could get along without the Sheriff—and that was why he waited so impatiently for the return of Joe La Ronde, his Agency police force. Joe had been sent out at once with instructions to find Archilde, say nothing to anyone, and bring him in. Three days had gone by and as yet Joe had not returned and had not sent word.

As the day wore on the Agent grew increasingly irritated. He succeeded in getting some work done, all the time resenting the fact that he could not work untroubled. He was not a fretful man. He had been in the Service long enough to know that things did not get done in a day. Ordinarily that knowledge bore him up through weeks and months of inaction. But this was not a matter of waiting upon someone to make a decision for him. The boy might be getting farther away every hour that he waited. No matter how thoroughly he believed in him, he could not take chances in an affair of this sort.

In the late afternoon, just as he was being given up for another day, Joe La Ronde appeared at the Agency. Joe was moon-faced and jolly, and while most Reservation boys would not accept the policeman's job for fear it would make trouble for them with their friends —and besides many were too lazy for it—Joe took it and liked it and nobody ever got angry with him. When he had to arrest one of his friends, he was very sociable about it. He would tell the fellow that he had come to arrest him, then he would propose that they go fishing first. Sometimes he got drunk with his intended prisoner, and it would be the prisoner, some days later, who would bring Joe to the Agency to restore him to duty. And no matter what he did, Joe's job was secure because no one else would have it.

The Agent fairly pounced at him, once Joe had tied up his horse and, after talking to everybody within hailing distance, sauntered into the office.

"Is this the pace you've been going the last couple days?" The Agent was hungry, as well as irritated by his long inaction.

"What, me?" Joe smiled in a friendly, meaning-no-harm way he had. "You ought to see how I been riding that plug of mine. He's all used up. Why, we been over trails that ain't been used since they was made. We've been everywhere."

"And where's Archilde?"

For the first time Joe looked serious. He studied the floor.

"Say, it ain't only Archilde that's missing. It's that girl, Elise La Rose, and the two boys, Mike and Narce. They all lit out just when the old lady died. Some-body saw them go. But they ain't been seen since. I picked up their trail and followed it some ways, then I lost it."

"You mean you can't follow the trail of four horses in the mountains?"

"They didn't stay in the mountains. That's what I can't figure out. They went in one way and came out another and I can't see where they went after that."

"You think they're not in the mountains, then? Where did they come out?" A suspicion came alive in the Agent's mind that Archilde had already quit the country. If he had come out of the mountains it must have been to get to the railroad.

"Well—I dunno." Joe rubbed his head as he thought. "I believe they're in the mountains all right. Their coming out that way was to cover up. What they did, I figure, was to get on a road, maybe late at night, and ride along it a ways, then go into the mountains again further along. Only I ain't found out where that was."

The Agent did not question him further. He had sat down at his desk to think it out, and the more he considered it the more certain he felt that his supposition was right. If Archilde—and whoever was with him—came out of the mountains it was to get to the railroad and catch a train. The suspicion proved one thing at least—he no longer trusted the boy. He expected the worst of him. The only thing left to do was to make up for lost time.

He reached for the telephone to get Sheriff Quigley. But first he sent Joe La Ronde out of the room.

Chapter Thirty-Four

DURING those days in the mountains Elise made camp, looked after the horses, cooked food—did everything in fact. She was a good hand around horses—she knew something about the cattle business too—but cooking was just tiresome.

She knew the ingredients of baking-powder bread, but no two batches ever turned out alike; sometimes it was stiff, sometimes hard as baked clay, sometimes raw, sometimes bitter; rarely could it be eaten without making a face. No one was more disgusted than she by these failures; it angered her that anything she should hate to do should be so difficult and defiant. Other things she could do a little better. Meat she managed to get cooked in some fashion—though never cooked and salted at one time. But, hell!

"You don't mess around horses without getting to smell like a horse—and that's just why I don't like to mess around with cooking; you get to smelling like boiled onions, boiled cabbage." That was her excuse.

"Me, I can do lots of things besides cook. Most girls I ever knew who could cook didn't know a hondo from a hass-ole." She would say something of this sort just after the bacon had caught fire in the pan and in an outburst of wrath she had thrown the meat into the creek.

"God damn cooking, anyhow!"

Most of this was lost on Archilde. He heard nothing, saw nothing, or so it seemed. He had let Elise choose the trails and the stopping places. He ate what was before him. At night he slept, never quite realizing that Elise slept with him, curving her body against his and warming him.

It was with some surprise, after several days, that he became fully aware of his surroundings and, finally, of Elise's intentions. He could not remember having agreed to go to the mountains, or even having been asked what he wanted to do. She had come to him with saddled horses; nothing was said, as he recalled, and presently they were riding in the foothills. He had to think hard to recall even vaguely what had been passing in his mind; running away, escaping to the mountains, he was sure, had nothing to do with it. No—it seemed to be *paganism*, something about *paganism*— that was what had been in his mind. And then Elise had brought the horses, and when they had been riding for some time he looked around and saw Mike and Narcisse. They also were riding horseback. Elise was in the lead, going somewhere.

When he first realized that Elise had carried him off he didn't care. He couldn't think of any reason why he shouldn't be in the mountains with these three. That mood continued as they went deeper and Elise concerned herself with back-tracking and cir- cling to throw off pursuit. By the time she had got the party established in a high, snug canyon and was herself mounting guard on a high ridge, he began to take the situation seriously. What was her purpose?

Mike and Narcisse, like Archilde, had gone along indifferently. The priest and school were being left behind, but they had no feeling of security. It had been different during the summer. They had lived in a world of their own making—only they were foolish enough to count on it enduring. Just one glance of Father Jerome's stern eyes had taught them again how much greater—how everlasting—was the world of priests and schools, the world which engulfed them. When they had sensed that again, nothing interested them. Everything was hopeless. It made no difference whether they stayed at home or went to the mountains. When they were wanted, by priest or agent or devil, they would be sent for, and that was all.

This was the cheerless company Elise had taken into the mountains. She fed and watered the horses, gathered wood and made fire, cooked, in her high, indifferent fashion, and tried to make jokes. And she went right ahead as if there had been no indifference and no blank looks when she thought of something funny.

Then Archilde got to asking questions and, as it were, prodding himself awake. She had to explain how it had all happened.

"And how the hell did you get the idea I wanted to run off up here?"

It amused Elise to see him so alarmed by what he

had done.

"I just thought it would be fun to run out on those guys. And you, you jackass, had a standing promise to turn yourself over to the Agent. I thought you ought to have a chance to cool off before that and maybe you'd feel different about it. If I'd left you there you'd be in the can now."

He tried to frown at her, only partly managing it.

"You made a swell get-away, all right. I guess nobody knows where we are. But they could find us if anyone took a notion of looking. You can't run away nowadays, Elise."

She snorted. "Hell we can't! We did, didn't we?"

"Yeh, but nobody was looking. And how long can we last? What if they don't find us—how will we live? The first time we try to go for supplies, if anybody is interested in us, we'll be nabbed."

"Don't be so sure." They got more earnest as they talked. They were on a high ridge, from which they could look down on miles of descending country, on a blind maze of canyons and rolling hills. Vision ended finally at the hazy-blue outline of a high range over which they had traveled several days before. There was a sharp wind blowing about them and they had lain belly-down on a lichen-scarred rock to get as much out of the wind as possible. As they talked they turned their heads toward each other, and then looked away at the steep slope below them.

Elise had no doubts. "If we wanted to, we could stay right here. We could build a cabin, or there's a cave down here we could fix up. We'd kill some game and dry it. And you bet your boots, I can get out of here any time I want and bring grub back and nobody would be the wiser. If that's what's itching you—"

He stopped her. A new and disturbing thought had just come to him. "Elise—if they want me they can get me. Dave Quigley would be the man to do it. He's been hunting around up there all summer; maybe he's found the fellow. Even if he didn't—if Parker told him to bring me in—he'd be the one to do it. You see, it's the wrong way."

She knew enough about the Sheriff to make no rash promises. Mention of him silenced her for a moment.

"That's why it would have been better for me to have stayed at home and gone to the Agent. It would have been enough to convince them of my innocence. Running away like this makes it look bad."

She moved across to him, threw her arm over his back and laid her head on his shoulder.

"Look at it my way. You had nothing to do with this business. You just happened to be there. That don't oblige you to go out of your way to tell people something they don't have to know. And—wait now. More than that, if you go and tell this story they'll do their god-damnedest—you see—to stick you for it. They'll say why did you tell a lie about it? Why did you keep quiet about it? Oh—piss on 'em! Look—no. now, let me give you my idea. All you have to do is go away. We'll lie low for another week, then we'll sneak out of here and put you on a train. Nobody'll know what became of you, most of 'em won't care—I won't shed a tear, like hell! That'll be the end of it."

He stopped to kiss her, realizing at the back of his head that she had been at his side for days, even in bed with him, and he had not felt her in his blood. Surprising discovery!

"It sounds easy. But that's just what it ain't. The Agent expects me to come in. He knows the story, and so it's official business from now on. If I don't show up, he has to find me. One thing leads to another. If they find that Dan Smith up there, somebody's got to be asked questions, and I'm the guy that knows. So if they can't get me one way, they'll get me another. Not only Dave Quigley, but all the sheriffs in the country can be called in if they want 'em. Fat chance! Besides, we'd always be expecting it. We couldn't live. Can't you get it in your head, you mutt?"

He had reached down and taken her face in his hand, tilting her head back. He saw in her eyes that she would do anything he wanted; she would go anywhere; she would live with him or away from him, as he wished.

"Another thing," he continued in a softer voice, "when I leave here, and I will, you're going with me. That's a go, ain't it?"

He had never seen her go shy until then. She tried to meet his eyes in her bold way, but instead she giggled and got confused.

"You're a punk to say that! And it's a punk idea.

When you start lugging me around your hard times are going to begin. I'm a hard-luck, no-account knot-head. All I like is tail and if I don't get it I go after it. I got no manners, no educating. I'm a wash-out and you want to lug me around. Hell, there's lots of tail and you're a good-looking guy. You don't have to take me along for that."

She could always make him laugh with talk like that. When she ran somebody down, even herself, she did it in a businesslike way. She left nothing but shreds.

"It's all right with me. The two of us are made kind of on the same gear. I like tail too and your kind suits me well enough."

At that point they moved away from the crest of the ridge, where the wind blew so sharply cold, and sought out a sheltered corner and a sparse bed of patchy moss. The howl of the wind over the rim of the mountain died out as they moved back, but in its place was the howl of the world singing in their blood. Their eyes swam, and tightly near as they crept to each other, they were yet as far apart as two worlds bobbing along side by side. They ached to rush through their intervening world shells, but it was always not quite—reach and surge as he would, and press up to him as she would. Always not quite, though the wild plunging of their senses sucked them on.

Then they were quiet again, lying in the lee.

At that moment, if they had been watching from

the crest of the hill, they would have seen a rider emerge from the dark canyon maze and turn his horse toward them. Luckily for them their senses were unalarmed. They could dream for a while yet.

Dave Quigley walked in on the camp at sundown. He had waited in the woods until they had all come together to eat, Archilde, Elise and the two boys. Then he left his horse behind and crept upon them.

He had not drawn his gun and as he advanced he spoke in an even tone of voice, calculated to avoid an alarm. He said simply: "Is that you, Leon? Your Agent has been looking for you."

Utter silence followed his words. He had been seen just before he spoke, as he had intended, and so his words did not burst upon them like a voice out of heaven. Even so, the effect was startling.

Archilde, sitting cross-legged, with a tin cup of hot coffee in his hand, stared at the Sheriff. Quickly into his mind came the thought that he had expected this. On the day of his meeting the Sheriff in the mountains, as he and the old lady rode forth to hunt, he had accepted him as a kind of last foe—the one who would make the final count on him. Nothing had happened at that time, and therefore he had no occasion for distrust; yet Dave Quigley made him feel that something would be wrong some time, and that he would be there to demand settlement. And it was so. Archilde held the coffee cup in mid-air and stared.

Whatever rage or murderous impulse Elise might be harboring, she too was silent. Nothing was betrayed. She regained self-possession almost at once and continued her work around the fire after hardly more than a pause.

"Had your supper, Sheriff?" she asked coolly.

"If you got some coffee left, I'll take a cup. Thanks."

Elise was leisurely about filling his cup and passing canned cream and sugar to him. She put the coffee pot on the fire again and Archilde wondered if she were aware of what she was doing. The pot must be empty. This inconsequential thought bothered him.

Elise seemed to know what she was about. She was not flustered.

"We got some fish here—won't you have some?" She was almost impertinent in her coolness, Archilde noticed.

"Thanks just the same. I had a bite to eat a while ago."

Archilde was struck by the Sheriff's mild manner. It was unlike him, unlike the stories he had heard of him and also unlike his own impressions. He knew Quigley as a man of brusque manner and short speaking, and common report had it that when he made an arrest he paused for no amenities. Where Indians were concerned, he was apt to be particularly sharp. Archilde finished his cup of coffee and stood up.

"I'm ready. I'll have to catch my horse, but that won't take long."

Quigley was short, but friendly. "I already have

your horses down there a ways."

How could that have happened, Archilde wondered. One man round up four horses, and so quietly that no disturbance had been noticed—it was hard to understand.

"You won't want Elise or the boys, so they can come when they get ready." He made a statement of it but he meant it as a question. He wanted to know the Sheriff's intentions.

"Fact is, I'll take all of you. Those are Mike and Narcisse, ain't they? The Agent wants them, too. The girl will be wanted as a material witness, I suppose. So you better all come along. We'll start now and spend the night at the Ranger's cabin below here."

"Then—" Archilde could not pronounce the words. It was as if he were making the decision, as if it depended upon his will, whether he went or not; this saying so meant that he was delivering himself into the hands of powers greater than he. As he hesitated, he looked at Elise.

She must have sensed his feeling that a fateful decision had to be made. She was nervous and her eyes tried to carry some message to him. What it was he could not guess. All at once he felt unsure of her. He could not predict what she might do. She had been much too quiet and too polite. What was she planning? He moved toward her in his uncertainty. His nearer presence, he felt, might help to remind her of their position.

"I guess we're ready to go." These were the words he had found it so difficult to speak. He walked toward Elise as he uttered them and his voice conveyed an appeal to her. "Keep your nerve. Let's see it through," he was trying to tell her.

Elise had taken the coffee pot from the fire. She was shaking it. Then she spoke, her voice unsteady, or perhaps Archilde imagined it. "There's another cup of coffee, Sheriff. It's hot. If you don't want it I'll throw it out." She advanced toward him.

The Sheriff looked at her, then at the empty cup which he still held in his hand. He hesitated. "Well— if you was going to throw it out— Don't you want it?"

"We had a potful already." She continued to advance toward him, walking past Archilde. Her eyes were fastened on the Sheriff's face, compelling him to look at her.

What was she up to? Something. Archilde sensed it. He wanted to stop her. He could have reached out his hand and held her back. He stood motionless, seeming to hold his breath.

Elise had but one more step to take. The Sheriff was reaching out with his cup. Then her hands dropped down—and up! She had kicked back the lid —and the coffee was hurled into the Sheriff's face!

She needed only that moment while he dashed his hands to his face to whirl about and reach the camp goods. Then she had a rifle in her hands and was shooting—from the hip—one—two—three explosions. The

Sheriff never got his gun from the holster. He was down with three shots in his chest, each one jarring him as it hit.

Archilde had sprung upon Elise and knocked the gun down, but the only result was that he prevented her from emptying the magazine.

"Elise! Christ Almighty! See what you've done!" He trembled.

She, though, was unshaken. Calmly she looked down and if Dave Quigley had stirred she would have been on top of him. She talked as calmly as she looked.

"I decided this when we were lying up there on the hill. I said to myself that if Dave Quigley came for you I wouldn't let him take you. I did it and I don't give a damn. Now we'll have to run away, catch a train out of here, before they find him." She halted, then moved toward him.

"Please—Arsheel—don't stare at me like you didn't want me. I did it because it's so good to be with you—the way we were on the hill—"

The simplicity of her reasoning stopped him. Frown as he would, hold himself aloof as he tried, still he could not be angry with her. His arms had to take her.

"Of all the damn fools—Elise—" He was holding her and stroking her, his body still trembling.

"How in hell you figured killing a man would keep us together—you're just a damn fool!" He kissed her and saw her smile.

"Throw up your hands!"

They whirled together, breaking their embrace.

Mr. Parker had advanced upon them gun in hand, and behind him was the moon-faced Joe La Ronde, also with a gun. The Agent was deadly pale and frowning.

In that instant Archilde understood several things. It was the Agent's presence, out of sight but probably looking on, which accounted for Sheriff Quigley's unusual mildness. It explained too how the horses had been rounded up so easily and put in readiness. And if the Agent had not been there the Sheriff probably would not have accepted hospitality and might not have been killed. That too occurred to him as he stood facing the enraged Agent.

"I believed in you, Archilde—and this is what came of it!" Mr. Parker had to get that much out of his system. It had been eating him.

"You had everything, every chance, and this is the best you could do with it! A man gets pretty tired of you and all your kind. That's all I've got to say to you. Joe, put handcuffs on the two of them."

Just then there was a sound of galloping horses. Everyone turned to look down trail—and there they saw Mike and Narcisse mounted and running away. They had slipped away, probably in the excitement of the shooting.

Mr. Parker swore. "Why, those little fools! How far do they expect to get?" To Archilde he said, as La Ronde approached with the handcuffs. "It's too damn bad you people never learn that you can't run away. It's pathetic—"

Archilde, saying nothing, extended his hands to be shackled.

THE END